JOURNEY TO MUNICH

ALSO BY JACQUELINE WINSPEAR

Maisie Dobbs

Birds of a Feather

Pardonable Lies

Messenger of Truth

An Incomplete Revenge

Among the Mad

The Mapping of Love and Death

A Lesson in Secrets

Elegy for Eddie

Leaving Everything Most Loved

The Care and Management of Lies

A Dangerous Place

JOURNEY TO MUNICH

A Novel

JACQUELINE WINSPEAR

HARPER

An Imprint of HarperCollins*Publishers*

HarperCollins books may be purchased for educational, business, or sales promotional use. For information, please e-mail the Special Markets Department at SPsales@harpercollins.com.

FIRST EDITION

Designed by Leah Carlson-Stanisic

Library of Congress Cataloging-in-Publication has been applied for.

ISBN: 978-0-06-222060-8

16 17 18 19 20   ov/rrd   10 9 8 7 6 5 4 3 2 1

In Memory Of

Joyce Margaret Winspear

1927–2015

Even if the whole world was throwing rocks at you, if you had your mother at your back, you'd be okay. Some deep-rooted part of you would know you were loved. That you deserved to be loved.

—Jojo Moyes, *One Plus One*

The wheel is come full circle, I am here.

—William Shakespeare, *King Lear*

JOURNEY TO MUNICH

CHAPTER 1

Holland Park, London, February 1938

The day was bright, the air crisp, with sunshine giving an impression of imminent spring, though as soon as a person ventured out from a warm, cocooned indoors, a nip in the chill outdoors soon found its way to fingertips and toes.

Maisie Dobbs—as she preferred to be known, though she was now the bearer of a title through a marriage cut short—opened her eyes and decided it was mid-morning, given the way the sun was shining through a crack in the curtains. No one had disturbed her, no one had come to her room with breakfast or tea, though she supposed Priscilla would bring a tray soon, afraid to leave her friend alone and awake for too long.

Someone—likely the maid—had been in to light the fire, for the room was warm, and a gentle heat skimmed across her skin. Upon first waking, she thought she was still in Spain. But the deep mattress, soft pillows, and sheets reminded her that this was not her stone cell; she was not in her plain wooden bed with only a blanket to keep her warm, and there was no one to minister to in this grand house in Holland Park, a world away from battle, from soldiers who came to her filth-covered and bloody.

From a simple community she had grown to love, Maisie had come home to England—at first to Kent, to be with her father and stepmother, then to share the lingering grief of bereavement with her in-laws, who had lost their only son. How could she ever explain to them that service—tending the terrible wounds of those who fought for freedom from oppression—had lifted her own deep melancholy? How would they feel if she admitted that in becoming a nurse again, she'd found a reason to go on? Only now could she come home to face the landscape of her former life, and find her way through its changed paths and byways.

It was Priscilla who had found her in Spain, Priscilla who had brought her home to England, and it was to Priscilla she had come following the muted celebrations of Christmas and New Year at Chelstone, the estate where her husband had grown to manhood. It was Priscilla, she knew, who would leave her alone to do what she needed to do in her own good time—unless, of course, Priscilla had other ideas.

"Maisie? Maisie?" The knock at the door was insistent, as if, having waited long enough, her friend would no longer allow the late-sleeping guest any quarter. "Time for tea and today's gossip!"

The door opened, and Priscilla Partridge stepped into the room— now "Tante Maisie's room," according to her three sons, who had spent their early years in France—carrying a tray with tea, toast, and a boiled egg, her hands steadying the silver platter as she closed the door with her foot. "The egg is soft, the toast is hot and crisp, the tea strong, and as you may have guessed—I didn't do a bloody thing! Thanks must go to Cook."

"Sorry—I slept late," said Maisie.

"I'm giving you a bit of a lie-in. Having that checkup yesterday would have taken it out of you. But at least you had a clean bill of health, and all seems to have healed. Tea?"

Maisie sat up. "Lovely." She raked a hand through her short-cropped hair.

"I think you ought to see my hairdresser—though heaven knows, you didn't leave yourself with much for him to work with, did you? Whatever possessed you to cut your own hair, and with a blunt knife by the look of it? I nearly went through that stone floor when I saw you shorn of your locks."

"My hair was getting on my nerves, and keeping it short made sense—something less to organize."

"Right-ho. I'm going to make an appointment for you in any case—one thing less for you to organize. Now then, onto juicier things." Perching on the side of the bed and resting the tray on the eiderdown, Priscilla poured tea. "I have to tell you the latest about the Otterburns."

Maisie took the cup. "Priscilla, I don't want to know anything about the Otterburns."

"Sorry. I don't blame you for feeling as you do about John Otterburn, but—anyway, this is about Elaine. I just heard the news from Patsy Chambers—I thought you would be interested."

"Ugh. When did you begin hobnobbing with Patsy Chambers?"

"She has her uses. But I must tell you—Elaine Otterburn, delivered of her child just a few months ago, has upped and gone off."

Maisie felt her skin prickle. "What do you mean, upped and gone off?"

"Well, everyone knew her marriage to that chinless wonder, the Honorable Charles Whitney, was all done in a bit of a rush—remember me predicting the birth announcement would read 'born prematurely'?

I confess I was a little shocked at my foresight when I saw those actual words in the *Times*. It seemed that one week she was engaged, the next married, and then in short order a mother." Priscilla sighed. "Let me tell you, they gave that girl far too much rope her entire life, and it came home to roost. Apparently she has some friends, all young women of her age, you know, early twenties, who are in Germany—Bavaria—having a whale of a time. Her best friend—I'm amazed she has one—was sent there to be finished and stayed on with some other friends. All I can say is that it wasn't like that in my day."

"You made it something like that, though."

"No, Maisie—what I got up to at Girton should be no indicator of what happened when I was in Switzerland. For a start, I was younger and chaperoned when I was sent off to finishing school, and I certainly wanted to come home at the end of it. These girls are in flats of their own, and it's one party after another." She paused. "Plus, when I returned to England, I did not run away from my responsibilities. Neither did you. We knew what we had to do when the war came, and we did it. And you lied about your age. How old were you?"

"Just shy of eighteen when I enlisted."

"I rest my case." Priscilla picked up her cup, taking a sip of the hot tea.

"But why Germany? Everything I've read, everything Douglas has said about the situation there—it doesn't sound like it's a place to have a wild time." Maisie paused, musing. "Mind you, Elaine Otterburn managed to find a party in the middle of the Canadian nowhere the night before James was killed."

Priscilla set her cup on the tray but continued to clutch it with both hands, as if to warm her fingertips. "But here's what's happened. Elaine's abandoned her husband and child, and now not even the Otterburns have any idea where she's to be found. She's gone to ground."

"I don't believe that. John Otterburn has money. He'll find her. He's probably got men searching everywhere for her."

"Oh, she won't come home in a hurry."

"It's not exactly safe there, is it, Pris?"

Priscilla reached for a slice of buttered toast. "It is if you have a bit of a thing for Herr Hitler and his raving Nazis."

Maisie frowned. "What on earth do you mean?"

"You heard Douglas at supper the other night—he's writing an article on this very thing, though heaven knows who might have the courage to print it." Priscilla licked butter from her fingertips and pushed the plate toward Maisie, who took a slice of toast. "And you've seen it yourself, years ago, before you married James—didn't you have a couple of cases where you witnessed the Nazi lovers in all their glory? There are people in high places who are enamored of Hitler and his cronies—and, much to John Otterburn's embarrassment, his daughter has become one of them. Perhaps she became disenchanted with young motherhood—who knows? And remember, you were overseas and missed all the business with the abdication. You know what they call that Wallis in certain circles? America's gift to the British! That was one way to rid ourselves of a Nazi-sympathizing king! Don't repeat that with my name attached to it, will you, darling?" She laughed, then smiled at Maisie. "How about Bond Street? You're looking a bit ragged around the edges. A few new garments are in order, if you don't mind my saying so."

Maisie shook her head as she finished a last bite of toast. "Oh, no, no, no you don't! I have plenty of clothes—I just need to unpack properly. Brenda's going to help me when I return to the Dower House next week. In any case, I have a few things to do today."

Priscilla stood up and reached for the tray. "Anything interesting?"

"I'm going to look at a couple of flats. The flat in Pimlico is rented, and I don't want to go back there anyway—but I do want my own nest here in London."

"You could stay here for as long as you like—I would love it."

Maisie reached for Priscilla's hand. "And I love being with you, Douglas, and the boys—but I need my own walls around me, Pris." She went on before Priscilla could counter. "If I've time, I may go over to Fitzroy Square, just for a walk-around."

"Slaying a dragon?"

Maisie shrugged. "Perhaps. And I've to see Mr. Klein too. I want to find out if I can stretch to a new motor car."

Priscilla looked up and sighed. "I don't think that will be a problem, Maisie. But do let me come with you to look—you know I love a new motor car!"

Maisie laughed. "Oh, Pris, I think my idea and your idea of what to drive around in are two entirely different things."

After viewing two flats in Chelsea and one in Maida Vale, Maisie decided she had had enough. Taking the Underground to Oxford Circus, she walked along Oxford Street toward the café where she had often stopped for a cup of urn-brewed tea and a plate of buttered toast. Though there had been changes along the way, thankfully the café was still there. She ordered tea and an Eccles cake at the counter and settled into a seat by the window. Her old contact at Scotland Yard, the Murder Squad detective Richard Stratton, had always referred to the place as "more caff than café." She wondered about Stratton, and how he might be faring. He had been promoted to Special Branch, working with Robert MacFarlane, and had over time found his superior to be a difficult man. A widower with a young son, Stratton had—out of the blue, it seemed—decided to return to the profession for which he had trained before he enlisted for service during the war, when he became a military policeman. Much to the surprise of his colleagues, he accepted a position as a teacher of science and mathematics at a boys' school in the West Country, far from London. His son would receive a free private education, he was given a cottage in the grounds, and—more important—he would be home every day with his boy. Maisie added up the years and decided that the son—what was his name? Had she ever known his name?—of course, he must be fourteen years of age by now. Almost a man himself.

The years spent away from England seemed to render everything around Maisie in sharp relief. Memories came and went as she walked toward Fitzroy Square: of people met, of conversations in the street, of events holding little consequence and others that had taken her breath away. She crossed the road when she approached the place where she had witnessed a young man, disturbed by the war that still raged in his mind, kill himself with a hand grenade, filling the air with the terror of a blood-soaked hell that haunted him.

She wasn't sure how long she had been in the square, standing at the edge of Conway Street and looking over toward the former mansion that had housed the first-floor office of Maisie Dobbs, Psychologist and Investigator, but she felt her cheeks growing cold and her eyes watering. She pulled her now somewhat unfashionable cloche hat down farther to keep her ears warm, and snuggled into her winter scarf. It was as she began to walk away that she felt the nape of her neck prickle, as if someone had run a feather across her skin. At once she was afraid to look around. She had a distinct feeling that she was being watched. She stopped and half turned her head—was that a footstep behind her? Or was it a ghost from her past, reaching out to pull her in? She shook her head and began walking across the square toward Fitzroy Street, but still a wave of anxiety washed over her. She admonished herself—it was early days still, and she had been so afraid of returning to England, so fearful of how she might face the places she and James had been together before she left—before she accepted his proposal, and before their marriage, which was a happier union than either imagined it could be. As her eyes filled with tears, she stopped to reach into her brown leather satchel for a handkerchief.

"Will this do, lass?" The Scottish burr was unmistakable. Maisie turned to face Robert MacFarlane, the former Special Branch detective who apparently now operated in the undisclosed realm where Scotland Yard and the Secret Service met.

"I might have known." She took the proffered white cotton handkerchief. "Have I no rest from you, Robbie MacFarlane?"

"You do a pretty good job of escaping my notice, I'll give you that."

"I hope this is an accidental meeting," said Maisie.

MacFarlane inclined his head toward the building that had once housed her office. "Did you know it's for rent again? The last tenants moved out at the end of the year."

Maisie blushed. "I didn't know, but I'm not interested." She sighed. "How are you, Robbie?"

"Cold. You would think I'd be used to this weather, being a hardy Scot, but that little sojourn in Gibraltar made my blood run thin, so I'm a wee bit on the chilly side." He turned and pointed toward a black motor car idling at the end of the street. "If you're not busy—and I don't think you are—a colleague and I would like to have a quick word."

"I'm not interested, Robbie."

"You might be. Could be just what you need. And I think you owe me a favor, after giving me the slip."

"Oh, for goodness' sake, I'm not interested in cloak-and-dagger as-signments anymore. I've had enough."

"You're freezing cold, Maisie. Let me give you a lift somewhere. If I stand here a second longer, I'll turn to stone."

Maisie looked at the black vehicle again. The driver had emerged and opened the back passenger door, ready to receive them.

"Oh, all right—you can take me to Bond Street."

"That's the spirit, lass. And we can have a wee chat while we're about it. After all, your country needs you."

"Who's your friend in the motor car?"

"Well, I think you've met Harry, the driver. And you've met Mr. Huntley too."

"Brian Huntley?"

"Yes, the very man."

MacFarlane nodded to Harry, who stepped back as MacFarlane held the door for Maisie. She took a seat next to the man who waited inside. MacFarlane climbed in, flapped down the extra seat in front of them, and closed the door. He rapped on the glass partition, and the motor car eased away into Warren Street in the direction of Totten-ham Court Road.

The man next to Maisie turned to face her. His dark gray pinstripe suit seemed brand-new, the creases in his trousers sharp. He wore a white shirt, and his tie, bearing the insignia of a Guards regiment, seemed to stand out even in the dim light. He removed his Homburg and smiled.

"You're looking well, your ladyship."

"I do not care to use the title, if you don't mind, Mr. Huntley."

"As you wish. If *you* don't mind, we'll take a little diversion on the way to . . . Bond Street, was it? I am sure Mrs. Partridge will still be shopping. In fact—" He leaned toward the window to consult his watch. "About fifteen minutes ago, she was still in Selfridges."

Maisie sighed and closed her eyes, opening them again a few seconds later. "How long have you been watching me?"

"Oh, come now, Maisie—may I call you Maisie? We know each other quite well by now, don't we?" Huntley didn't wait for an answer. "There's something that you can help us with, Maisie. I understand very well what you have endured in recent years, but you are the very person we need for a particular job." He looked down at his hands and pushed the signet ring on his little finger back and forth toward the knuckle. "Maurice held you in high esteem, Maisie, and he knew our work inside out. He was my mentor as well as yours—and you've done good work for us in the past."

"I don't know that I'm up to my old work."

"I believe you are. And this is an important task for a woman. It involves a little travel, however."

Maisie did not respond. She wiped a gloved hand across the window and looked out at people walking along the pavement, heads bent, scarves pulled up, hats tugged down. At tram stops they stamped their feet, and others ran into shops as if to gain respite from the cold. She turned and looked at MacFarlane, who had said nothing.

She met Huntley's eyes. "Where to?"

"Munich. Of course it is a little cooler there at this time of year."

She was quiet again. Huntley and MacFarlane allowed her the silence.

Perhaps it was time. Perhaps one small job wouldn't cause any harm. What would she do otherwise? Sit in the Dower House nursing her broken heart? Allow the past to simmer up to a rolling boil again? Perhaps it was the right thing to do.

"All right, Mr. Huntley—tell me why my country needs me." She looked at MacFarlane. He was smiling.

CHAPTER 2

M aisie spent a sleepless night in Priscilla's guest room. The deep, soft mattress that usually made her feel as if she were a cygnet nestled under its mother's wing now seemed hard and lumpy, as if horse hair had been stitched into pillow ticking and laid across concrete. She turned one way and the other, unable to find any semblance of the comfort that would lead to sleep.

Without doubt, part of her felt a sense of excitement and worth—though when she considered what was being asked of her, she wondered if she were not biting off more than she wanted to chew. In truth she had become used to being part of the family, staying at Priscilla's home. The boys delighted her, and Priscilla's ebullience energized her. As friends they knew each other's history, knew the twists and turns that had brought them to this place in the world. And they understood each other's fears and frailties; nothing had to be explained. Now, in the space of a day—a day that seemed to be whirring around in her mind as if it were a film running back and forth on itself in an endless loop—another landscape had been spread before her.

And Maisie knew, as thoughts contradicted each other, conspiring to exhaust her into sleep, that with one short assignment she could test the water. She could find out how it felt to be working again.

During the circuitous journey to Bond Street, the two men had revealed the bare bones of the assignment the Secret Service had in mind for Maisie. The more detailed briefing took place the following day. Arriving at an address in Whitehall, she was escorted along a labyrinthine web of corridors until she reached the department presided over by Brian Huntley. She had first met Huntley some years before, when he was a field intelligence agent sent to follow her and bring her to the Paris headquarters of his department. She'd felt shock, and no small amount of betrayal, when she realized that his superior was none other than Maurice Blanche, her longtime mentor. Following Maurice's death, the house in Paris became part of her inheritance, and though it was leased to the British government, an apartment on the upper floors originally kept for Maurice's personal use was now where she stayed in Paris.

In the meantime, here she was, about to meet Priscilla for a shopping expedition, feeling as if she were straddling two different worlds. In a final letter to Maisie, Maurice had written, "You will be called to service as I was prior to and during the last war. I believe you are ready and suited to any challenges that come your way." He had closed his note with the words, "And I predict that they will be the making of you."

As she walked along Bond Street, she sensed tears welling. A few years earlier, as a new bride in Canada, she had thought that motherhood would be the making of her. Now she felt quite alone.

"Ah, Maisie—let's take a more comfortable seat." Huntley extended his hand toward a table set alongside the far wall of the spacious room. The chairs were of solid dark wood, with padded leather seats. An envelope marked with her name indicated her place. She picked up the envelope and moved to another seat, this one facing across the room to the window, which looked out across Whitehall. From this position she could just see the top of the Cenotaph, Sir Edwin Lutyens' memorial to the dead of the Great War.

"Interesting move, Maisie," said MacFarlane. He'd taken a second look at Maisie as she entered, his eyes glancing from the magenta two-piece costume Priscilla had persuaded her into buying to her short hair, which was partially covered by a neat black narrow-brimmed hat in the fashionable Robin Hood style, embellished by a single gray feather.

"I'd like to be reminded of the reason I'm doing this," she replied as she pulled out her chair.

Huntley cleared his throat. "Right. Let's start by going over a few points from our little chat yesterday."

MacFarlane looked at Maisie and raised an eyebrow. The "little chat" had taken them down to Covent Garden, along the Strand, around Buckingham Palace, up toward Piccadilly, along Regent Street, to Oxford Circus, and finally to Bond Street. The most crooked taxicab driver could not have taken a more rambling route. But that was the informal conversation. This was the formal briefing.

Huntley opened his manila folder, removed the green tags securing one document to another, and pushed a photograph of an older man toward Maisie. She estimated him to be in his mid-sixties.

"Leon Donat. Engineer and man of commerce. Age at the time of the photograph—taken by his daughter—sixty-five. He's now almost seventy years of age. Mother was French; father British, by way of Italy. Donat took over his father's machine-tool factory in Birmingham at age twenty-five. No wartime service. On paper he was obviously too

13

old for service in 1914, but he was very useful to us anyway because his factories—he'd expanded the business considerably—were requisitioned for the manufacture of essential parts required for the production of munitions. He expanded into France following the war, as well as Germany, plus he diversified. In France he went into production of foodstuffs from imported raw materials. His wife, incidentally, passed away four years ago. Donat is known for inspiring great respect among his employees, which has led him to achieve quite enviable production records. He provides educational grants for children of staff, and he will never see an employee sick without paying for medical attention. It has paid off. He has channeled a good deal of money toward worthy causes and is a respectable and respected man—a man in the mold of a Victorian paterfamilias. His foray into publishing academic texts in the areas of engineering, mathematics, and physics seems to have been born of a desire to diversify—and of course the business was not profitable, so it became advantageous with regard to taxation."

He paused, passing another sheet of paper to Maisie. "Well, as we know, it seems parties are the places to meet people. Lawrence Pickering was invited to a reception at an engineering conference, where he was asked to speak about the role of academic publishing in the education of young technically minded students, and there he met Leon Donat. Donat, as ever, was on the lookout for investment opportunities, and he realized that Pickering's fledgling company could do with some help. He took an interest, which in turn led to a partnership. Donat was just the person Pickering needed, at just the right time. Initially Donat was the silent partner behind the Pickering Publishing Company, but his involvement increased, though it appears he took care not to tread on young Pickering's toes. Donat did not run his businesses like a dictatorship, but preferred to nurture talent. By way of information, as you know, Lawrence Pickering met Douglas Partridge at a party, and that's how he also met your former secretary, Mrs. Sandra Tapley, who subsequently became an employee of the company."

Huntley paused and flicked over a page. "During the years of your absence, Leon Donat became increasingly involved in the company, enthusiastically supporting Pickering's plans for expansion. From a commercial standpoint he was right to do so; there were ideal opportunities to secure publication and translation rights in Europe, given the number of academic institutions. Donat is fluent in German, so he took over the task of making connections with German publishers—and until a few years ago, there was more publishing in Germany than in any other country in the world."

"And now Donat is in prison in Germany."

"Specifically, just outside Munich." Huntley nodded at MacFarlane, who handed Maisie a bound sheaf of papers.

"This is a full report on the circumstances of his arrest and incarceration at a camp in a place called Dachau. I'd call it Hitler's torture chamber for Communists, free thinkers, journalists, those of Jewish extraction, and anyone else who dares to have an opinion that isn't held by the man they call the Führer." MacFarlane paused. "It was opened for business in 1933 on the site of an old wartime munitions factory, and has built itself a fine reputation for brutality."

Maisie nodded as she opened the report.

"While in Munich," MacFarlane continued, "Leon Donat decided to pay a visit to the son of an old friend, formerly of Berlin, who is now living in Geneva, and with whom he wanted to discuss the representation of his list of books. The son, name of Ulli Bader, is a writer, and the friend had expressed to Donat a fear that the young man would never make a mark—in monetary terms or by reputation—so he put in a good word for his boy. On the face of it, it appeared to be a match—Bader seemed the right candidate to take on locally as a representative. But our little writer just happened to be involved in an underground rag. He also wrote for other magazines and newspapers on the fairly dull topics that young reporters starting out are usually given—obituaries, meetings, falls on the pavement, that sort of thing—and we believe he plowed every penny he earned into this paper. As you will see from our report"—MacFarlane handed Maisie another clutch of papers—"the Nazi Party have clamped down on any newspapers, any artists or writers, or any individual who does not reflect and support their manifesto."

Having turned to the concluding paragraph, Maisie sat forward, her hands clasped on the table. "So, while in Munich, Donat gave his friend's son—a young man who cannot at present be accounted for—a financial contribution to keep this underground journal running, and he did this out of the goodness of his heart after the young man explained his situation. Donat was observed making the payment, and he was arrested at a location believed to be the home of the illegal press, just one day before he was due to board a train for Paris. Now he is in this Dachau place—a British citizen incarcerated against his will. And for how many years?"

"Two." Huntley did not flinch from Maisie's gaze.

"And all Foreign Office attempts to broker his release have failed."

"You would not believe the paperwork, Maisie," said MacFarlane.

"I think I would." She sighed, and resumed reading through Huntley's notes before looking up. "The situation has not been helped by Donat's competitors here at home, who've been rubbing their hands with glee, believing that with him out of the way, they could move in on his business. I can see here that thus far it hasn't happened, given that his staff are working doubly hard in his absence." She placed the papers back on the table. "But according to what you said yesterday, an agreement has been reached with the Nazi authorities."

"Herr Hitler feels like being friends with us, and we're taking advantage of the situation. Though we realize it is the preamble to more aggressive action on his part—buttering us up before the fray with this and other measures—we cannot allow this opportunity to slip through our fingers."

"Gentlemen." Maisie looked from Huntley to MacFarlane. "You gave me a brief summation of the role you envisage for me yesterday, so perhaps you would be so kind as to fill in a few gaps."

Huntley nodded toward the envelope with her name on it. "There, Maisie, are your marching orders. It appears the German authorities have gone soft on us, and instead of a member of our diplomatic staff, Mr. Donat must be released into the care of a family member. We're not sure what has brought on this little element of cozy-cozy, but it stands. We suspect they believe a family member is not available. And to some extent, they would be correct. Donat's wife is dead—as you know—but he has a daughter. A daughter whom he adores, not least because she was strikingly like her mother, and—"

"Was?" Maisie met Huntley's eyes.

"Sadly, she no longer bears a resemblance to her former self. She suffers from consumption contracted overseas, and is ensconced in a fever hospital in Kent. Fortunately, because she rather lived in the shadows—Edwina was not an outgoing person and had not married—it is not widely known. She had been in a convalescent home in Bexhill-on-Sea before being brought to the hospital. I think it is fair to say she is failing—the illness seems to have taken her in a very aggressive manner, and it's likely her days are numbered. She was never a social butterfly, and suffered from melancholia following the death of her fiancé in the war—her lack of exposure, so to speak, serves us well."

Maisie nodded, staring out the window toward the Cenotaph. She

17

turned her attention back to Huntley and MacFarlane. "And now you want me to assume the identity of Miss Donat, so that a family member might receive the prisoner when he is released."

"A new passport bearing the name Edwina Donat has been prepared for you, and the necessary documents are in the envelope. We understand you would not wish to travel via aeroplane, so all transportation will be by train—though if you could change your mind and return by air, we would all breathe a sigh of relief."

"I wouldn't," said Maisie.

"Yes—Robbie predicted your response with some accuracy." Huntley referred to his papers once again. "A representative from the diplomatic service will meet you—he is a member of the consul general's staff. I should add that the consulate is not privy to the exact reason for this prisoner's importance."

"Hmmph!" MacFarlane folded his arms. "Never mind Smallbones—should be Small Brains!"

Maisie looked from MacFarlane to Huntley.

"Our dear friend here," said Huntley, "is referring to our consul general, Robert Townsend Smallbones. Smallbones believes the German people to be very honorable, and has stated that they are kind to animals, children, and the aged and infirm. Thus he concludes that they have no cruelty in their makeup."

"Well, as far as the bloody Führer is concerned, he concludes wrong," added MacFarlane.

"A fairly accurate response, I will concede, though we are fortunate in that you are not the only one holding that opinion; others see good reason to doubt the integrity of the chancellor."

"So there will be no brass to meet me, no one of importance, just a diplomatic services junior? That's good."

"But he's one of ours, Maisie." Huntley handed Maisie another sheet of paper. "Gilbert Leslie. Formerly of Military Intelligence—not at a high level, but he's nobody's fool. On the face of it, he's now pushing paper and dealing with tourists who've lost their passports, or who want to make a complaint against Germany because they have been required to perform a Nazi salute whenever they see a member of Hitler's army. He will not be briefed any more than he needs to be—as far as he knows, you are Edwina Donat."

"All right, let's imagine I am with Mr. Leslie, and we go to take possession of Leon Donat. What if Donat says, 'Who in God's name are you?'"

"Act, Maisie—you must act. This entire operation is dependent upon it. You must approach him with speed and assure him of your identity. Our guess is that, no matter who you appear to be, he will be only too glad to remove himself from the prison in Dachau."

"And then? Assuming I have Donat under my wing."

"Leslie will accompany you directly to the railway station, where you will travel via express to Paris. Once you cross the German border, we will consider you in fairly safe territory."

There was silence in the room until Maisie spoke again.

"Two questions, neither of which you have answered. One: Why me? And two: Who is Donat really?"

"I'll answer the second question first. Leon Donat is exactly the man I have described—a man of commerce, an engineer, a dabbler in the world of publishing. He is a man of great curiosity who uses his money to support the endeavors of others and to promote education—we thought you would like that about him. But Donat is also what we call a boffin."

"A what?"

"Boffin, Maisie," MacFarlane interjected. "Bit of a tinkerer."

"Maisie, he is rather more than that," said Huntley. "Calling him a boffin is a slight in good heart, if you will—an affectionate insult, mainly because people like me do not really understand people like Leon Donat. We know only one thing—they are very valuable because they do not think like others of their ilk. Donat is not just an engineer but an inventor. It's his pastime, and it has served him well—his company has developed many interesting bits and pieces over the years. Such men—and women, let it be said—will become more important to us in the coming months." He sighed, and for the first time Maisie was aware of his hesitation. He looked up at her, then at MacFarlane. "I can tell you no more than this, for this information might lead to your death if you fall into the wrong hands. But we have come to understand that Donat has developed plans for a very specific type of seaworthy landing craft. The trouble is, the plans are all up here." He tapped the side of his head.

"A boat?" asked Maisie.

"No, not a boat. A vessel. A very advanced vessel of its type."

"What would this vessel be used for?" asked Maisie.

"There's only one thing a landing craft might be used for, Maisie—and that is an invasion to meet an enemy," said MacFarlane.

Maisie was silent, looking once again past the men to the Cenotaph beyond, the grand memorial to the war's dead, still surrounded with brown-edged red poppy wreaths from November's Armistice ceremony.

She sighed and turned to Huntley. "And what about my first question? Why me?"

MacFarlane answered, "We considered several possibilities, Maisie, and we kept coming back to you. We need someone with a calm head on her, someone we can work on to make her resemble Edwina Donat. For a start, she has your height."

Maisie nodded slowly. "And I suppose, in your estimation, I have something else going for me. I have nothing to lose."

Silence enveloped the room.

"One more thing, Maisie. You should know that the meeting you attend at Nazi headquarters will be conducted by a member of the SS—the Schutzstaffel. It is a powerful paramilitary organization formed by the Nazi Party, and now under the jurisdiction of a man named Himmler, whom we believe to be a most dangerous individual. The SS encompasses quite a few investigative, military, and administrative departments, including the Gestapo, a secret police force; the Waffen SS, an elite fighting force; and the security service. It also controls the prisons and other disciplinary camps, which seem to be sprouting up like mushrooms."

"So if I put a foot wrong, a trapdoor opens and I'm lost forever—is that it?"

"Not quite, but it's important for you to know the lie of the land." MacFarlane pushed a document toward Maisie. "You've already signed one of these in the past, but just to make sure, we'd like another signed copy for our files."

"Is this the 'Cross my heart and hope to die, I won't tell anyone' promise to king and country? Official secrets and all that?"

"Yes."

"So you think I am still going to say yes, even given the risks you've described?"

MacFarlane grinned. "We know you are."

"How?"

"Because after everything you've been told in this little meeting, if you say no, I'll have to kill you. Now then, lass, sign the bloody form and let's get on with it. You've got some training to do."

"Training?" said Maisie as she picked up the navy-blue fountain pen Huntley had passed to her.

"Give me a few days, and you'll be shooting like a sniper, Maisie. And you'll know how to kill a man—so he doesn't kill you first."

"Did you see any flats you liked, Maisie?" Priscilla handed Maisie a gin and tonic. "Don't worry, I only waved the bottle over your glass so the tonic absorbed a few fumes."

Maisie took the glass. "I think, after this afternoon, I could do with a real one!" She moved the glass as Priscilla reached to take it from her. "No, not really—it's still a bit early for me. Perhaps a little later I'll have a normal gin and tonic, though."

"No luck with the flat-hunting, then?" Priscilla slipped off her shoes and made herself comfortable against the opposite arm of the sofa.

Maisie shook her head. "I'm looking for something light and airy, overlooking a square or with a garden, perhaps, and close to the Underground."

"What about Fitzroy Square? It's still not the best area, but you like it there."

"Fitzroy Square means work."

"Not anymore—you're a woman of leisure now." Priscilla sipped from her glass and regarded Maisie. She began to tap one manicured red nail against the crystal. "Don't tell me you're going back to work in Fitzroy Square. Oh, Maisie, give yourself some breathing room, for heaven's sake."

"Don't worry, Pris, I'm not—as yet—returning to work. Mind you, I am leaving your clutches soon, but probably only for a week or two."

Priscilla leaned toward the low table in front of them, picked up her silver cigarette case, and began to press a cigarette into the long holder she favored. "Where are you off to? Pray tell."

"Paris. It's to do with Maurice's estate—the property there, and—"

"Excellent! I shall come too—we can trip along to see a wonderful dressmaker I know near Montmartre. She can copy that costume—"

"Oh dear, Pris, I'm so sorry . . . but Mr. Klein is accompanying me. I won't have a moment to myself." Maisie felt herself panic—Priscilla was not easily fobbed off. "But how about closer to the end of my visit? We can stay in a hotel—you choose."

Priscilla tapped the glass again and lifted the cigarette holder to her lips. Only after she'd exhaled a single smoke ring into the air did she speak again. "You're up to something, Maisie. I can tell."

"Pris, I promise you I am up to nothing more than looking after Maurice's estate and ensuring that his wishes for his medical clinics for the poor are followed to the letter. I have things to do in Paris, and when they're done, then you can take me to your little dressmaker."

"She's five foot ten."

"Your big dressmaker, then."

Priscilla sighed. "Well, if you say you're not up to something, I'll take your word for it." She rattled the ice cubes in her almost empty glass. "Oh, I nearly forgot to tell you—well, it might have been a deliberate omission. You probably don't want to hear it. Lorraine Otterburn telephoned today, wanting to know if you were in town. She said she and John would love to see you, and could they come here soonest?"

Maisie held out her glass to Priscilla. "You can make me a proper one this time."

Priscilla took the glass. "Well?"

"No, the Otterburns can't come anywhere to see me."

CHAPTER 3

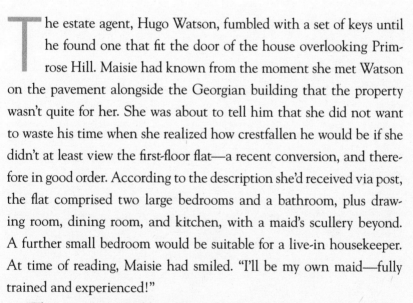

The estate agent, Hugo Watson, fumbled with a set of keys until he found one that fit the door of the house overlooking Primrose Hill. Maisie had known from the moment she met Watson on the pavement alongside the Georgian building that the property wasn't quite for her. She was about to tell him that she did not want to waste his time when she realized how crestfallen he would be if she didn't at least view the first-floor flat—a recent conversion, and therefore in good order. According to the description she'd received via post, the flat comprised two large bedrooms and a bathroom, plus drawing room, dining room, and kitchen, with a maid's scullery beyond. A further small bedroom would be suitable for a live-in housekeeper. At time of reading, Maisie had smiled. "I'll be my own maid—fully trained and experienced!"

"This way, Miss Dobbs." Watson ushered her into the entrance hall, its red tiles polished to a shine, with a matching red runner of carpet leading toward the wide staircase giving access to the upper floors. "Up the stairs we go."

Maisie glanced at Watson and smiled. *Up the stairs we go?* She assumed he must be quite new to the work, and thus was endeavoring to be seen as more adult by speaking to her as if she were a child. She could not wait to leave.

"This is it, Miss Dobbs. I am sure you will agree that it is a beautifully appointed residence. Fresh decoration and a new kitchen—the owner has made a significant investment to attract the right tenant."

"I was really thinking of making a purchase, Mr. Watson."

"Keep an open mind until you've seen this property, Miss Dobbs." Watson inserted a second key, turned the handle, and pushed open the door into a small entrance hall flooded with light. The drawing room windows before her, which looked out onto the street. The smell of fresh paint and new carpet was strong, and for a second Maisie held her hand to her nose.

"Note the small but airy entrance, leading straight into the drawing room. A warm welcome for guests—and the view is a pleasing one."

Maisie felt a chill in the air around her, and wondered why estate agents didn't ensure a property was at least warm when a potential resident entered. She felt unsettled. What might have come to pass in this flat; what past sadnesses lingered in the fabric of the building? The sensation that she and Hugo Watson were not alone rendered the very air around them heavy. Her chest tightened, and she coughed.

She turned to Watson. "Is there someone else here?"

"I—I—beg your pardon?"

"I had a feeling that we were not alone, Mr. Watson. Is someone else in the flat?"

Watson looked at his feet as the sound of a door opening caused Maisie to turn around.

"I'm sorry, Maisie—it was the only way to see you face-to-face." The voice was deep, its mid-Atlantic rhythm giving away the identity of the man who stepped into the drawing room through a doorway to the right. "How sharp of you to know that someone else was here."

Maisie felt color rush to her cheeks, and she struggled to keep her voice calm. "Mr. Otterburn. I might have known you would find a way to see me." She turned to Watson. "And to think I put your manner down to first-day-on-the-job nerves. You'll have to answer for this breach of my privacy, Mr. Watson."

"I—I—but . . ." Watson could not even stutter his words.

Maisie turned to leave. "Oh, just leave me alone—both of you."

"Maisie—stop! I need your help. Lorraine and I—we're desperate." Otterburn's voice was strained.

Maisie turned to face the man she held responsible for her husband's death. The shock of witnessing the small experimental fighter aircraft James was testing fall to earth over farmland in Canada, had led Maisie to lose the child she was expecting; her daughter had been delivered stillborn, and Maisie bore physical scars of the fight to save the babe's life and her own. James should not even have been flying. Otterburn's two children—both adults—were accomplished aviators, and his indulged daughter, Elaine, was rostered to be in the cockpit that day. Instead, she was nursing a hangover, so James had stepped up in her place.

And now John Otterburn had used his contacts to corner Maisie.

Watson slipped out of the flat as she faced her nemesis. She noted the gray pallor, the drawn look to his face, the bluish pockets under his eyes.

"I wish I could have met you in a different place, Maisie. Somewhere we could sit in comfort."

"There is no comfort for me in your presence, Mr. Otterburn." She walked to the window. Outside, trees bare of leaves were picking up a cold wind, blowing back and forth. It seemed to Maisie as if they were fingering the sky, scratching toward bulbous gray clouds to bring rain. She turned back to Otterburn and sighed. "You might as well tell me what this is all about. Then we can be done with it."

"My daughter has vanished. We don't know where she is."

"That's not news. I understand from Mrs. Partridge—who is far more au fait with these matters—that the whole of a certain strata of London society knows about Elaine abandoning her husband and child." Maisie pressed her lips together. She wished she could sound less bitter. It was an unwelcome feeling, as if she could sense her heart becoming harder with every word.

"No, it's not news. But I do need your help."

"Oh, spare me the intrigue. You have people everywhere who can find anyone and—as I know only too well, you can even have them murdered." She could not help but refer to Eddie Petit, whom she'd known since childhood, an innocent man who had become an un-witting victim of Otterburn's undercover machinations to strengthen Britain's security.

"I cannot seem to find my own daughter, and I understand you will soon be in the place where I believe she is now residing."

"As I said, you have people everywhere," countered Maisie.

"She appears to be very good at either avoiding discovery, or when approached, refusing to come home. We understand she is in Germany, most likely Munich. Her child needs her, Maisie."

There was silence in the room. Maisie bit her lip and felt her jaw tighten. She turned away toward the street again, toward a window-pane spattered with raindrops racing down to the sill.

"I suppose I should not be surprised that you have knowledge of my travel outside England."

Otterburn was silent.

Maisie raised a gloved hand and wiped away the condensation where her breath had caught the window. "I don't know what I could do anyway. Elaine has no reason to listen to me, even if I found her. She has her own plans and her own life. If she has abandoned her child, that is her loss." Her voice caught at the last word.

"Please, Maisie. I was never a good father to my daughter—an indulgent father, but never a good father."

"That makes no difference. She's a grown woman."

"I believe you can bring her home to her child. I beg of you, please—"

"Stop!" Maisie rubbed her forehead and once more turned to face John Otterburn. "Stop." She walked toward the door, but halted. Without turning her head, she spoke again. "I have no sympathy for you, your wife, or your dilettante daughter. But I ache for her baby." She felt pressure on her chest. "If I discover her whereabouts—oh, and that is a huge 'if'—then I will endeavor to see her. But only once. No more. And I will not beg. I will not force her. I will make one request, and that's it. I have more important work to do—as you probably know." She took a deep breath, as if to garner strength. "Send any information you have regarding her whereabouts to me, care of Mrs. Partridge. And that will be it."

"Thank you. On behalf of my wife and myself—thank you."

Maisie turned the door handle and left the flat without looking back.

Where should she go now? She had no home in London, no place that was hers. There was no anchor. Her father and stepmother lived in their own bungalow on the edge of the village of Chelstone, and although Priscilla was always saying, "Our home is your home,

Maisie," she felt at sea, adrift. She continued to use her maiden name because it held her tight, whereas her title by marriage, and James' name, Compton, only served to make her widowhood feel even more acute. She was a married woman without a husband. And yet in Spain she had come to terms with her loss. In the daily grinding work of tending the wounded of a terrible civil war, in the simplicity of her life there—a nun's cell, a bed with straw mattress, a small rug, and a window to look at the sky when there was time to gaze—she had rediscovered the raw material of her character.

In November 1937 she had left the convent, now a small field hospital. She had funded an ambulance, and there was no want of medical supplies. She had done all she could for the people of the village, and for the men who fought on behalf of Spain's working citizenry.

Sister Teresa had lifted her hand to Maisie's cheek as the motor car idled with Raoul, Maisie's driver, at the wheel, ready to take her back to Gibraltar, where, together with Priscilla, she would board a ship bound for Southampton.

"We will miss you, Maisie. Come back one day—come back when there is no more bloodshed. It is time for you to go home now. You will be safe, for you are very tightly held."

Where do I belong? As Maisie emerged from the Underground and made her way toward Pimlico, she could not banish the thought. It was as if, having traveled for so long, she had changed shape and no longer fit in anywhere. It occurred to her that perhaps her financial independence hindered her ability to settle. After all, if the options were simple, so was the matter of choice. *A nun's cell, a bed, a mattress of straw, and a window to the sky.* Perhaps that was why it had been easier to remain in a place of danger than to sail for England, where there was so much more to fear. The past, her happiness with James— memories brushed against her skin like gossamer shadows, alive but not alive, ghosts standing sentinel, watching as she went about her daily round.

She sat on the wall outside the flat she owned, now rented by her former assistant, a young woman she had encouraged to move beyond the bounds of domestic service to greater success in her education and work. Sandra was also a widow.

"Miss Dobbs . . . I mean, Mrs. Compton . . . your ladyship . . . oh dear, I'm getting it wrong. Are you all right?" Sandra Tapley approached Maisie. "Have you been waiting here long? Oh my goodness, you look all in—come on, let's get you a cup of tea."

Maisie looked up to see a quite different young woman from the one she'd once employed to help with administration in her business. Sandra seemed to carry herself with more confidence—gone was the slouch of despair that seemed to press down on her as if it were a weight on her back. Maisie wondered if her own posture had changed as grief settled into the fibers of her body.

She stood taller, mindful of her bearing and how she would feel if she allowed her frame to reflect her emotions. "I was out on a few errands, and I thought I would drop by. I'm sorry, Sandra—I should have telephoned."

"Not at all—you never need to telephone, miss. . . . After all, this is your home—"

"The first thing we have to get sorted out is that you can call me 'Maisie.'"

"Well, anyway," said Sandra, fumbling in her handbag for her keys, "let's go in." She led the way along the path to the glass front door of the building. Maisie had bought the flat some years earlier, when its builder hit hard times after the market crash in 1929, and had to sell all his flats at a cut rate. Maisie had squirreled away funds for a down payment, but struggled to obtain a loan. Only later did she learn that her friend Priscilla—a woman of significant independent means—had in secret secured her mortgage by guaranteeing the loan.

The door to the flat swung open, and Sandra stood back. "After you, miss—I mean, Maisie."

Maisie stepped into the flat, noticing the small box room to the right—it had been Sandra's room when she'd lodged with Maisie for a short time some years earlier. They went past Maisie's old bedroom to the left, and into the large drawing room. Maisie had removed her photographs from the wall above the fireplace before she moved out. Along with a painting of a woman looking out to sea, which reminded her so much of herself, they were now stored in the cellar of the Dower House at Chelstone, the home she had inherited from Maurice. In their place, Sandra had hung a painting of a vase of flowers. Otherwise the room seemed familiar. The furniture Maisie had acquired—a couple of pieces bought new, some given, others found in secondhand markets—was still in place, but books were stacked on the dining table and on the floor beneath the window, and the blinds were raised, so now Maisie looked out onto the dusky pallor of evening.

"I think you need a bookcase or two, Sandra."

Sandra pulled off her gloves and unpinned her hat, setting them on top of one pile of books on the table. "I know, but I've had no time to think about it. I'm so sorry about the clutter—I'm afraid I've become a bit less than house-proud. We've been very busy at work, and of course Mr. Pickering is worried about—"

Maisie smiled, putting Sandra at ease. "This is your home, Sandra, for as long as you want to stay here. What you do inside these walls is entirely your business. Now, then—let's have that cuppa. And you can tell me all you know about Leon Donat."

Sandra reddened as she turned away toward the kitchen.

Once they were settled in front of the gas fire, Sandra poured tea, passing a cup and saucer to Maisie, who leaned back in the wing chair and took a sip.

"Oh, I needed that. A good cup of strong tea. My friend Priscilla favors one of those blends that always seem more suited to dabbing behind the ears than wetting the whistle."

Sandra laughed. "My life might have changed, but I know how to make a good strong cuppa." She placed the saucer on the table in front of her but held on to her cup with two hands, bringing it to her lips once again.

Maisie waited for her to speak.

"I suppose I first met Mr. Donat soon after I went to work for Lawr—I mean, Mr. Pickering. He came into the office to see Mr. Pickering, and he made a point of sitting down in front of my desk and talking to me, as if he really wanted to know who I was. He was interested in my studies, and what I had done, and when he asked what I did before I worked for you, I thought, Oh, here we go—he'll have me chucked out now. But I went ahead. I told him, 'I was in domestic service, sir. I was a maid in a big house in Ebury Place.' And he didn't bat an eyelid. Just looked at me and said, 'Very well done, Sandra, my dear. Very well done.' He never called me 'Mrs. Tapley.' And the next thing you know, Mr. Pickering is telling me he's giving me more money because Mr. Donat said I deserved it. How about that?"

"You've worked hard, Sandra—going to the college while you were holding down not one but several jobs. That takes determination and spirit—an asset to any employer." She paused. "So you liked Leon Donat?"

"Very much. And I think Mr. Pickering really appreciated his advice on business matters. At first he told me he was worried about having a partner in the business, but Mr. Donat listened to him, and only ever asked questions—and Lawrence . . . I mean, Mr. Pickering, sorry—he said that the questions made him think a lot about how he did things, especially with distribution. I mean, it's all very well publishing all these books, but you've got to get them in front of people. Mr. Pickering spends a lot of time going to the universities and taking the books to show the lecturers. And we're doing very well, all things considered. It was Mr. Donat who pushed him to look to the foreign markets, especially Germany, where they have a lot of publishing. First of all, Mr. Pickering said we couldn't compete with the German publishers—that's when Mr. Donat said, 'What about translations? Sell the rights, and you don't have to worry about sending over the books and trying to sell books published in English.' And he was right. The first time he went, he did very well for us—treated Mr. Pickering like a son, as if it were a family business, and they both liked that. Then he went back to Germany a second time, to 'bring home some more good news,' he told me. He spoke several languages, by the way, whereas we would have stumbled over the German. And that's when the terrible things happened."

"Tell me about the terrible things, Sandra. What happened? How did you find out?"

"If I remember correctly, Mr. Donat had been away a few days, and was due back. He always went over there by aeroplane and returned by train. But this time he didn't return when he was supposed to. Then we received a message via another publisher who had been over there. He heard Mr. Donat had been arrested and sent to a prison. I can't even remember the charge, or if there was a charge—but when Mr. Pickering went to see a man at the foreign office, he was told the whole story. Apparently, while they were trying to secure his release, there was an indication Mr. Donat had insulted the chancellor over there, and for such disrespect and his involvement in producing antigovernment propaganda, he was imprisoned pending review of his case. That review has gone on for two years now."

Realizing that Sandra knew nothing about the negotiations to secure Donat's release, Maisie moved on to other territory. "Tell me about his daughter."

Sandra blushed again, lifting her teacup. "Would you like some more? Mine's a bit cold now—do you mind?"

"I'm all right for now, Sandra. Please, make yourself a fresh cup."

Maisie waited again, listening to the sounds of Sandra boiling the kettle, then pouring more water into the pot and stirring the once-used tea leaves. She returned to the drawing room, the cup and saucer held with two hands. Maisie noticed she was shaking.

Sandra took her seat once again. "You know, miss, I'd worked in your office long enough to know that when the official people come to ask questions, they're digging around for more than you think at first. I know very well that you sometimes don't know what they're digging for until you've said something and they get this little grin at the side of the mouth, as if they didn't really know what they were looking for either, but when you gave it to them, then they knew."

Maisie relaxed back into the wing chair and nodded for Sandra to continue. As she expected, Sandra too became more at ease. She shook her head.

"I don't know if I said anything wrong that day, when Mr. MacFarlane was there. They asked me all sorts of questions, about how often I'd seen Mr. Donat, and whether I'd ever met his family. I told them I'd met his daughter, Edwina, but only the once." Sandra sighed. "It was a silly bit of conversation, really. They asked me a lot of questions about her, whether she was interested in the business, what she was like. So I told them she was nice enough, a very quiet sort of person. And she was a tallish woman, 'about Miss Dobbs' height,' I said. Apparently her mother dying made her ill, so Mr. Donat sent her overseas for a while to get a bit of sun. But she came back even worse, coughing and having a terrible time with her breathing. She'd never married, either—but that's not so unusual for a woman of her age, what with the war."

Maisie felt her eyes smart. She reached down into her bag for a handkerchief, then brought her attention back to Sandra, who returned her gaze with heightened color.

"And I suppose that's when I saw MacFarlane look at me as if I had given him a grain of something."

"I think he always looks a bit like that, Sandra." Maisie sipped her tea. "What else do you know about Mr. Donat's incarceration?"

"Well, he's been in there a bit over two years, I would say. Mr. Pickering was doing a lot to try to get him out, but then the foreign ministry told him to draw back. Mr. MacFarlane informed him the situation was in capable hands, and that Mr. Donat's release would be secured in good time, though there were channels to go through. It was all very well having channels, Mr. Pickering said, but in the meantime Mr. Donat might die. We've had news from our various business contacts over there, and it is not at all a promising situation."

Maisie allowed a moment of silence as she framed her next question.

"Sandra, I can only say that there is a plan in progress, but I am telling you in confidence. You cannot tell anyone, and not even Lawrence Pickering at this point. That is something I think I can trust you with." Maisie looked at Sandra—at her eyes, so wide and intent, and the way she'd leaned forward. She knew Sandra was aching to ask more questions, but she pressed on with her own. "Is the company all right for money, given Mr. Donat's absence?"

Sandra nodded. "Oh, yes, he left everything very well tended. His bankers make sure his companies have their running costs covered, and of course each of his businesses has a manager in place to oversee everything. He stepped back from running things years ago."

"Except to sell textbooks," said Maisie.

Sandra laughed. "Oh, I think he fancied writing one. When I first met him, he didn't strike me as a businessman, though he's been very successful. No, he's more of your absentminded professor type—he seems to bumble, and then he'll take you by surprise with a really difficult and interesting question. And he has a heart of gold, really he does. Family is important to him—and his businesses are his family too." She paused and sipped her tea again. "I think he liked helping with the publishing side of things. It gave him a chance to talk to these professors about our books, to get into a room with a scientist, a mathematician, or an engineer. He loved discussing new inventions, new discoveries. And believe me, in this job you hear from a lot of slightly barmy but very bright people."

Maisie laughed as she rose to her feet. "Well, I must be off now. Mrs. Partridge will be ringing everyone in her address book trying to find me if I don't return to her house soon."

"Um, Miss Dobbs—Maisie—will you be wanting the flat back again? I mean, I can move out—after all, this is your flat, and I know it was only for a short term, renting to me, and—"

Maisie held up her hand, shaking her head. "No, really, stay here for as long as you wish, Sandra. The flat holds too many memories for me and, well . . . you know."

"I didn't know how to say it to your face, how sorry I am. I couldn't believe it when I heard—I mean, you were so beautiful when you walked down the aisle, and you both looked so happy. We were all just overjoyed to see you content, and the smiles across your faces, you and your husband." Tears welled in Sandra's eyes. "I mean, I know how it is. I saw my Eric die a terrible death, and—"

Maisie put her hand on Sandra's arm. "It's all right. You came through, and look at you now. You will never forget, but you've endured, and you have made so much with your life. I will use you as my example, dear Sandra."

Sandra pulled a handkerchief from her sleeve and pressed it to her eyes. "It's just terrible, the things that happen to people. To you. To Mr. Donat. And look at Billy and how he and Doreen lost their little Lizzie."

Maisie put her arm around the younger woman's shoulder, and they stood for some moments before Maisie declared that she really had to be going.

"Oh, and Sandra," she said as she reached the door. "It's quite all right, you know, that you and Lawrence have become more to each other. You aren't betraying Eric—had you not known such love, you might never have loved again. It was his gift to you. So no need to hide, if you are indeed involved in more than publishing books together."

Walking toward the bus stop, Maisie considered her words, and wondered if she would ever accept the opportunity for love again, and how it might feel. For now, though, she had work to do. Work had brought her through the steepest arc of her grief, and work had saved her in the past, when she was no more than a girl, in France. Perhaps stepping into the shoes of a very sick woman to bring a much-loved man home would help her in more ways than she might imagine. But how would Leon Donat react, when he learned his daughter's health was so compromised?

Maisie pulled her silk scarf up around her neck and made her way to the Embankment, where she knew she would find a taxicab. Time to go back to Priscilla's house in Holland Park, time to walk into the warmth of her friend's embrace and the noisy ebullience of her three boisterous sons. She imagined them sliding down the long banister, yelling, "Tante Maisie, Tante Maisie, look at me!" And she would watch, and laugh, and know that this was as good as home, for now. In just two days she would travel to an as yet unspecified location, where Robert MacFarlane would teach her how to kill a man. Tomorrow, though, she would visit Lorraine Otterburn. A mother whose daughter was so lost, she had abandoned her own child.

CHAPTER 4

"The son who will set me off in the direction of the lunatic asylum is Timothy," said Priscilla. The two women were sitting in the breakfast room the following morning, Priscilla at the head of the table, Maisie to her right. "He's the unpredictable one. I mean, I can depend upon all three to be naughty, to find trouble where there should be none, but Tim can be quiet, and when he is not making a sound, then you know some sort of devilishness is being planned. My mother always said, 'It's the quiet ones you've got to watch.' And I have to confess, he reminds me so much of my brother Peter." She barely paused before continuing. "Thomas is becoming a more sensible person, and—I might add—he shows every sign of being something of a ladies' man, which we will have to see off in short order. I don't mind a healthy interest in girls, but I do not want a Lothario in my midst. I want sensible boys."

Maisie looked at her friend across the table. She wished she could assuage her friend's fears. It seemed to her that every morning, Priscilla raised more and more concerns about her sons. Some were quite insignificant, although without doubt, the loss of all three of her brothers in the war, and the later discovery that one of them, Peter Evernden, had been working as an intelligence agent behind enemy lines, affected her deeply. Maisie smiled and reached for Priscilla's hand. "You would hate having completely sensible boys. Come on, you love it, Pris—you love every bit of it."

"Mark my words. Thomas is maturing into a good young man—albeit one with a glint in his eye—and Tarquin is still a naughty little boy. But Timothy—beware the boy who has secrets, Maisie. Anyway, you're one of the most beloved people in his world, so if necessary I will prevail upon you to help." Priscilla twisted a cigarette into the holder. "Assuming you might stay for a while."

"I think I need my own flat, Pris, and I don't want to go back to Pimlico. Too many memories. I know Lady Rowan would love me to live at Ebury Place, even though she concedes it's too big for one—but again, it has too much of the past leached into the walls for me. In any case, it's rented to a diplomat at the moment, some sort of consular official from a far-flung corner of the Empire, and I know there's that second cousin in the family, Edward, who has his eye on it."

"Of course you couldn't go back there. But I do wish you would stay with us for a while, really I do. I am the lone woman with all these men, and it is quite lovely having you here."

"Well, seeing as I have not found anything that makes me want to take a second look, I will be among you Partridges, and indeed my father and Brenda, for a little while." Maisie sat forward. "Priscilla, I—"

"Oh, dear—when you call me Priscilla, I worry. It means you're about to ask me something, and I should have to be on my toes when I answer."

"Just wondering about Elaine Otterburn. What do you believe made her run? I mean, to abandon her baby. What do you think?"

Priscilla lit the cigarette, snapped the lighter shut, and inhaled deeply. "You mean, apart from being a selfish child in the body of a woman?" She tapped the lighter on the table as she appeared to ponder the question, then removed the cigarette from the holder and pressed it into the ashtray. "You know, I'm beginning to feel very guilty every time I light up a gasper when you're in the room—despite your confession to having been a secret smoker after . . . well, anyway, after what you've been through."

"There's something you're not telling me, isn't there, Priscilla? About Elaine."

"Oh, blast! Look, there really isn't anything to tell. It's just something Lorraine said that made me think, and she would never have said this to you. But as you probably know, Elaine had a terrible crush on James. Terrible. Typical of her age—what was she when we saw her at that party, before you were married? Twenty-one? Twenty-two? I warned you about her then. Anyway, according to Lorraine, the girl got herself into quite a state after you were married, and she found it difficult to be in the same place as you and James. Frankly, she could have done with a mother who brought her up short instead of indulging her. I would have, if she were my daughter. If ever a girl needed a mother with a bit of iron in her spine, it was that one." Priscilla paused, as if weighing whether to go on. She sighed and began speaking once more. "According to Lorraine, on the day James died, Elaine maintained that she could not go to the airfield because seeing you—in full bloom, as it were—together with James was just too much. That's why she didn't fly that day." Priscilla picked up the discarded cigarette, pulled off the crushed end, and relit it without using the holder. "I should have kept my mouth shut. I'm so sorry."

Maisie at first could not speak, then found her voice. "I suppose I knew that, really. I cannot say it makes me feel any more kindly toward her, but . . . but I suppose . . ." She heard her voice catch. "I was going to say, 'I suppose she's young.' But Pris, as you have said in the past, when we were that age we'd already been to war, we'd already seen terrible things, and there's nothing to excuse her abdication of responsibility. I mean, how old is she now, twenty-five? And where is her baby?"

"With Lorraine. And a nanny, of course. He was with the father, but the chinless wonder could not cope, even with the nanny—I mean, really, he only had to swan in once a day to wave a rattle in front of the child's face, but apparently it's all too much for him. Ditto his parents, who do not want an abandoned Otterburn child in their midst, especially as they didn't approve of the match. You see, Elaine's husband, he without a backbone as well as a chin, only wanted the stardust that came with squiring around a very vivacious young woman. And she threw in her lot with him—child on the way and all that. His parents love the fact that there's a veritable mound of Otterburn money, and it flows quite readily, but at the end of the day they consider the Otterburns colonials—and colonials in trade, into the bargain. So any chance to get rid of the baby is to be welcomed, though a bit tricky, as the child is the heir. Mind you—heir to what? The son-in-law's people have nothing but a money-soaking pile somewhere in the shires, where they cannot even afford to heat more than one room at a time. All title and no substance. One would have thought it was a match made in heaven—wealth on one side and a heritage on the other."

Maisie sighed, pushed back her chair, and leaned toward Priscilla, kissing her on the cheek. "I don't think I needed to be party to the family's problems, Priscilla, but it puts it in perspective a bit." She rested her table napkin to the side of her plate and stood up. "Anyway, I'll be out for a few hours this morning—perhaps I can take Timothy to a picture show when there's something good on at the cinema. I know he loves those American cowboy films."

"You spoil them, Maisie. You indulge their independent whims—you'll make terrors of my sons."

"They're already terrors, Pris. That's entirely down to you!"

Maisie left the house twenty minutes later, her stout brown shoes suggesting a woman who would not be climbing aboard a bus or taking the Tube. The Otterburns' London mansion was situated opposite Hyde Park, and she'd already decided a brisk walk in the wintry sunshine would be in order. In truth, Priscilla's news had unsettled her deeply. She still considered Elaine Otterburn to be a self-indulgent young woman, one whose negligent attitude had led to James' death. But on the other hand, Maisie also knew that she could not hold Elaine completely accountable. It was James himself who'd decided to fly that day. It was James who broke his promise not to pilot an aeroplane again, not with a baby on the way. The test flight could have been canceled, could have fallen to someone else, but James wanted to fly. The boy in the man had jumped at the chance to be aloft with the birds on a fine day.

A butler answered the door when Maisie arrived at the Otterburns' home and led her into the drawing room, where she was asked to await Mrs. Otterburn. Both Otterburns hailed from Canada, but whereas John Otterburn seemed to retain elements of a Canadian accent, Lorraine could easily have been pegged as the daughter of Home Counties aristocracy. She entered the room wearing a tweed skirt with kick pleats, a silk blouse, and a long cashmere cardigan. Two strings of pearls adorned her neck, and Maisie noticed diamond rings on both hands.

"Maisie, how lovely to see you. We have all been so worried about you!" Lorraine held out her hands to receive the hand Maisie extended in greeting. "How are you getting on? I am sure those who love you are glad to have you home."

Maisie inclined her head. "Yes, indeed. It was wonderful to see my father and stepmother again."

"Of course, of course. Do sit down, Maisie. Our coffee will be here in just a moment—I like it brewed nice and fresh. We have it sent from Jamaica, you know—Blue Mountain coffee truly is the very best."

"Thank you, Mrs. Otterburn, I—"

"Lorraine, please. We know each other well enough by now, Maisie—you and James were frequent guests, so let's not stand on ceremony. And I know why you are here."

Maisie pulled off her gloves and unpinned her deep purple beret, revealing her cropped hair. Lorraine made no attempt to conceal her shock.

"It was easier to cut my own hair when I was in Spain," said Maisie. "Long hair is a burden if you are a nurse. And I discovered that I quite like being free of the bother of long hair."

Lorraine collected herself. "And what an adventure Spain must have been. Did you know we have friends there? Mind you, they went up into France as soon as the peasants began revolting, to coin a phrase."

Maisie looked at Lorraine Otterburn, at the bejeweled hands, now shaking, the drawn-in cheeks, the fine, almost transparent veins lacing papery skin under her eyes. Her once-blond hair was now gray, drawn back in a chignon accentuating taut skin that, Maisie thought, reflected how her heart must feel.

"Lorraine, Spain is in the midst of a terrible war. It wasn't an adventure, any more than going to Germany will be an adventure. It's what I felt I must do. Now, we both know why I am here. If I'm to locate your daughter, it might help to know more about the circumstances of her flight from England."

At that moment the butler entered, gripping the handles of a tray bearing a pot of fresh coffee, a jug with hot milk, sugar, two cups and saucers, and a plate arrayed with a selection of biscuits.

"Ah, not a moment too soon, Palmer. Just set the tray on the table here—I'll serve. And thank you, that will be all."

Maisie saw the butler raise an eyebrow before he offered a short bow and left the room. Lorraine poured a cup of coffee with hot milk and passed it to Maisie. "I remember you like your coffee quite milky," she said.

Maisie smiled. "I do indeed. I find it comforting, though I also like my coffee strong—my former employer made a very good cup."

"Yes, Dr. Blanche. I've heard of him—a forensic scientist, wasn't he? One of those clever clogs they call in when there's been a murder."

Maisie nodded. "He was an exceptionally gifted man; it was a privilege to work with him." She sipped from the cup and returned it to the saucer, which she held with one hand, resting it on her knee. "So—to Elaine." Maisie took a breath and wondered how forceful she should be. "Perhaps you could tell me why you think it should be I who goes to find her, and why you think I will be successful when the men—and I would imagine women—your husband has in his employ to protect his family have failed. She is a headstrong girl, and she is clearly enjoying herself—why else would she leave a husband and child?"

John Otterburn's wife began to cough. She patted her chest with one hand as she returned her cup and saucer to the table with the other, her eyes watering. "Do excuse me. It seems the coffee was a little hot for me."

"Please take your time, Lorraine."

The woman composed herself, sighing as she appeared to search for an answer to Maisie's question. She straightened her back, a sign to Maisie that she was garnering the strength to give an honest answer, albeit one she did not like at all.

"Maisie, the dark side of my daughter's cheerful and energetic nature was—is—a tendency to believe she can have anything she wants. For some reason, her brother managed to rise above similar traits—his father had a stronger hand with him—but Elaine, I hate to say it, was spoiled from the moment she was born. I have tried to temper my husband's overgenerosity with the child, to no avail."

"She is not a child. She's a woman with family responsibilities," said Maisie.

Lorraine pinched the top of her nose, as if endeavoring to keep tears at bay. Maisie wondered if she had been too harsh, allowing her anger to get the better of her. She took a deep breath. There were, without doubt, family tensions at play, and Maisie knew that Lorraine Otterburn was in all likelihood blaming herself for her daughter's abdication of responsibility.

"You have a lot on your plate, Lorraine. It cannot be easy, caring for your daughter's child, knowing she has all but left you to it."

Lorraine Otterburn looked up at Maisie, her eyes reddened by unshed tears. "Oh, and he's a lovely little man, really—I adore him. The nanny complains I don't leave her enough to do, but how can I? And John goes straight to the nursery as soon as he is home. We three play together—well, as much as you can play with an infant—and now John does not even want to return to Canada, as he knows he should when the weather improves. We can't go, not until Elaine is brought home, and certainly not without our darling boy here."

Maisie smiled and took Lorraine's hand. "Bear with me—I must ask these questions."

"I know, Maisie. But first, I must answer the question I knew you would ask. The truth is, my daughter would listen to you because she wants your forgiveness. That is the bottom line, as my husband would say. She believes it was her fault, the terrible tragedy that befell you. She almost cannot bear to be with herself, so now she is living another life, and I fear that life is destroying her. She believes herself to be of no account, unworthy of her son. Frankly, I couldn't care less about that husband of hers. The family are snobbish scavengers who are only interested in Otterburn money. They think we don't know. Ha!" Lorraine clasped Maisie's hand as a drowning woman might grasp the hand of a rescuer. "Elaine wants to be absolved. There was no reason for her not to fly that day, no reason whatsoever. I knew she was experiencing the unrequited love that girls of that age often indulge in, and instead of telling her to get a grip and stop her daydreaming, I allowed her to remain at home and wallow in self-interest. I bear the blame too."

Maisie drew breath and, almost fearing the sound of her own voice, met the pressure of Lorraine's grasp. This was her moment too, to voice words she had kept inside since the loss of her husband.

"James made the decision to fly, Lorraine. James knew what was at stake, and he broke a promise. That is the truth I live with, that my husband and child died in a moment of hubris, of—what did you call it? Self-interest? Yes. James loved to fly, and there it was, on the day he died, one more opportunity to be borne up into the clouds by a very fast aircraft, a chance to show everyone on the ground that he was still the fearless wartime aviator. More than anything, there was the desire to do his duty to his country, even though at that moment the duty could have been postponed until another day. Now he is gone, it serves neither his memory nor that of the unborn child I cherished—and indeed my life, which has to be lived—to bear ill will toward the husband I loved. That is the truth as I have come to understand it—that everything came to pass as it should, and I must remember and hold in my heart the gifts our courtship and marriage brought me. If I do not move toward light, Lorraine, I will go in the opposite direction, and I cannot do that again." Maisie pulled her hand back and regarded her hostess. "And I almost slipped."

She paused. "Elaine is in the dark place of regret. I will do my best to bring her home, but there are no guarantees. Now then—we have work to do. Another cup of coffee would go down a treat, and I have more questions for you. Her father says she has not been in contact, but I would imagine she has communicated with you, without her father's knowledge. Am I right?"

Lorraine pressed a button behind the sofa, summoning the butler. "Yes, there has been a communiqué—a letter sent via an old school friend. That does not mean I know exactly where she is, but I do know roughly where she has taken on some sort of flat with one or two other girls."

"Good. That's a start. And I think it's time to stop calling her a girl. She is a woman with responsibility to her child, her husband, and her parents. It's time she grew up."

The butler entered, and Lorraine asked him to bring some freshly warmed milk. As he was leaving, she added, "Oh, and please tell Nanny to bring the little man down in about half an hour. I am sure Miss Dobbs would love to meet him."

By the time Maisie left the Otterburn home, she was anxious to visit her father. She made her way to Charing Cross, where she placed a call from a telephone kiosk to Priscilla's home, leaving a message with the housekeeper to the effect that she would not be in town until

Sunday evening, and Mrs. Partridge should not worry—she would be with her father and stepmother. Exiting the kiosk, she joined the queue at the ticket office and paid her fare to Chelstone Station, a branch-line halt requiring a change of trains in Tonbridge. That she had not brought a case with clothing did not concern her. There was still an unpacked trunk at her father's home; it would be taken to the Dower House as soon as she was ready to resume residence. Though her tenants had left, she had not yet felt secure enough to live in the house on her own once more.

A cold rain was falling by the time the train pulled up to the buffers. Doors opened and slammed shut, and a snaking line of passengers made their way toward the exit, some taking their time, making sure they had their belongings, others rushing, knocking shoulders as they passed, tickets held out ready to submit to the collector. Soon the train was taking on passengers for the next journey, and though Maisie was not exposed to the elements as she waited to board, it felt as if the damp air had seeped into her clothing and was forming a film across her skin. She shivered and pulled her collar up around her neck. A guard opened the door for her, and touched his cap as she thanked him. Soon she was in the warmth of a first-class carriage, seated on heavy deep red velvet upholstery, a small cast-iron stove pumping out heat to keep the South Eastern Railway's better-heeled passengers in relative comfort. She pulled a small notebook from her new black document case and began to make notes.

According to Lorraine Otterburn, her daughter had fallen pregnant and given birth to a boy just over two months before she left the country. She had been living with her husband at the family's estate in Northamptonshire. Maisie imagined the spirited Elaine languishing in a cold mansion with many rooms and no heat. Elaine was a colorful person, filled with spirit and energy—she must have felt crushed.

Granted, her father had indulged her, but he had also given her a purpose—she was an accomplished aviatrix, and he had drawn her into his covert work on behalf of the British government. Admittedly, he had his reasons—keeping such work in the family as far as he could meant keeping plans close to home. She wondered to what extent he trusted James, who was not family, though Otterburn had obviously pegged him as loyal to his country, a man who understood aviation and who knew what it was to be at war. Maisie suspected that perhaps Elaine had felt less than able to be a mother, not suited to play country wife to a tweedy peer-of-the-realm landowner. Opening fêtes and judging flower arrangements at the county show would not have gone down well with a woman used to finding parties wherever she was in the world. So she had left her child and her husband and absconded from a place she must have considered a prison.

She must miss her little man, thought Maisie, though she wondered if she were not attributing her own imagined feelings to a woman who was quite different. And why had she not just taken the boy with her to her parents' house? It was clear they adored the child, and without doubt John Otterburn would have thrown a protective fence around his daughter. Then it occurred to her that in London, their paths would cross. Perhaps Elaine would also have found a meeting difficult in the extreme. But was such fear enough to push the younger woman so far away?

The ticket collector interrupted Maisie's thoughts.

"Change at Tonbridge, madam."

Maisie thanked him and settled back into her seat. *Change at Tonbridge.* She smiled to herself, though it was an expression of irony, not one of amusement. So many times in the past, Tonbridge had seemed to mark the place where she had to change who she was, from the London woman to the girl coming home to her father and, earlier, from the nurse who had seen so much to someone who told those who loved her, "Oh, don't worry about me, I'm all right." Now she would be a daughter again—ready to assure her father and stepmother that she was doing very well indeed, was thinking of the future again. She would tell them about the flats she'd seen, and that she fully intended to return to Chelstone at every week's end, and for long periods over the summer.

On Saturday afternoon Maisie and her father pulled themselves away from a warm log fire to walk a favorite route through the village, then out along a country lane and across winter-sodden fields, close to the edge where the mud was shallow. On the other side of a stretch of land in the midst of being tilled, a farmer was encouraging his horses to pull harder against the traces, while the plowboy led the team around a corner to carve another row. They stopped to watch for a while, each with their own thoughts. Then father and daughter strolled on in silence for a few moments.

Finally Maisie spoke. "Dad, I want to explain how sorry I am that I stayed away so long, and why I didn't come home with you after being in hospital in Toronto." Unsure of her words, she looked up again at the horses and the plow and the farmer pressing his body forward, as if to give more power to the task. "I know it's a while ago now, but I still can't really explain what happened to me after James died. I was paralyzed, in a way—there was nowhere I could get comfortable, and I couldn't face coming home. And then I went to Spain, and it seemed the best thing to do—to be of help to people was a way to banish the dreadful memories, and—"

Frankie stopped walking and laid a hand on her arm. "You've no need to start saying sorry to me. You were grieving, Maisie, and there's no prescription for it, nor any right way to go about it. After your mother passed away, I was lost—and I think I forgot that you'd lost something too. And what did I do? I sent you off into service, because I didn't know what to do with myself or you. I'll tell you now, knowing you won't hold it against me, but it was more to do with me being at sea with myself than with thinking it would be good for you, though it's all turned out right for the best, hasn't it? I'm not going to rake over old pasture, but I've come to an age where I've seen people lose the people they love, and I've been through it myself. There's no proper way to go about what comes afterward. You just put one foot in front of the other and you get on with it the best you can. Trouble is, your best ain't always the best for those who want a say in the matter. But you've not done poorly by anyone, Maisie. You had to look after yourself, and now you're home. That's what matters. We're all coming through it in our way. Brenda and I set a lot of stock by James, and of course his mother and father loved him, but we all have our own way of going about these things, and no one can criticize anyone else for how they do it."

"But Brenda said—"

"I was all right, Maisie. Just creaking a bit more about the knees and back, but I was all right. Brenda just wanted you home where she could take care of you, but I said to her, 'She'll come home when she's good and ready—she won't let us down.' And you haven't. You're home."

"Yes, I'm home, Dad." She paused. "But I'll be away for about a week or so starting next Monday. Then I'll be back in England and not going anywhere for a long time."

"Going on a little holiday, love?"

"Not a holiday, though it will be nice, I think—I've got to go to Paris to take care of some matters to do with Maurice's estate. Nothing too taxing." She turned to her father and linked her arm through his.

"And when I get back, I'll be with Priscilla during the weekdays until I find my own flat, and here at week's end. I can't miss Brenda coming up to the Dower House to cook Sunday dinner, can I?"

Frankie nodded in the direction of the plow. "Taking his time getting that done, ain't he?"

"The soil's probably a lot deeper than he thought."

"Should have left it for a finer day."

Maisie stopped, her hand in the crook of her father's arm, and looked across the field toward the farmer, who now seemed to be having words with the plowboy. "Yes, I suppose he should."

And as they walked on in silence, she thought about her return to London on Monday. There she would meet MacFarlane for a journey to another location—he had not revealed the proposed destination—where she would be plunged into intense preparation for what was to come. She knew that by the end of the following week she would be leaving the country with a gun in her hand, and she would know how to use it if it became necessary to protect herself or those in her charge. She would undergo a briefing and be tested time and again, and she would receive clearance to leave for Munich not only with her schoolgirl knowledge of the German language refreshed but with a deeper understanding of Leon Donat. She would know the city inside and out, her every step planned. Except, that is, for her diversion to a place known as Schwabing, which was apparently where many artists, actors, and writers lived. Elaine Otterburn had mentioned the area in a letter to her mother, and Lorraine believed she was living in the midst of the Bohemian enclave.

CHAPTER 5

"So, this is your Enfield Mark II service revolver. And as the bods at the Royal Small Arms Factory might say, it's been improved. You will see it's lighter, only a thirty-eight caliber, but a nippy little piece of tackle." MacFarlane lifted the revolver, sighted a target, and fired, the bullet tearing through the center of the bull's-eye. He held out the weapon to Maisie. "Go on, your turn."

Maisie looked at the revolver and reached for the wooden grip. "Oh, it's heavier than I thought."

MacFarlane laughed. "Lassie, it's a wee feather compared to anything I was brandishing in the war! Now then, this is what they call a short-range weapon, so don't be looking down the street and thinking you can take down a man who's fifty yards away. But she's a nifty little thing—you don't have to put a lot of effort into firing, and it's an easy reload. First of all, though, let's get this bit over and done with, and we'll go through it again. Then you'll be in the hands of Strupper— that's him over there, watching. He's our weapons man. He'll be in charge of making you what they call a crack shot. By the time he's finished with you, you could make a few bob as a sniper."

"Why am I not starting with Mr. Strupper?"

"Because I wanted to see the whites of your eyes when you used a revolver for the first time, Maisie. Now then, off you go—aim and do your best."

Maisie was sure MacFarlane would not have missed the whites of her eyes from quite a distance, though she did her best to keep her arm steady and her attention on the target. She had always considered reason to be the most powerful weapon in any arsenal, along with compassion, empathy, and a desire to see into the heart of another person. And as a nurse she had seen the terrible wounds inflicted by guns of any stripe, so she'd never wanted to handle one. But something had changed in her too. She recognized the need to be armed, should she need to use such a weapon to protect Leon Donat. Bringing him back to England would be akin to carrying a very valuable piece of china in her hands. He had to be delivered to Brian Huntley without damage.

She looked at the target, squinted just a little, and held up the revolver. She felt the weight in her hand as she cast her line of sight along the barrel, leveling it with the bull's-eye. Fearing movement in her hand as she discharged the weapon, she felt herself tighten the muscles in her shoulder. She pulled back on the trigger, fighting the urge to close her eyes. The report ricocheted from ear to ear, filling her mind, and she almost dropped the gun.

"Well, that's a surprise, your ladyship."

"Robbie—I've told you about that. No titles."

"I should call you 'her snipership.' "

Maisie looked in the direction of the target.

"Good shot, Maisie. A perfect bull's-eye. Now let's get the expert in to make sure it wasn't beginner's luck. And this afternoon we'll up the ante."

"What do you mean?"

"How to get rid of the unwanted individual when you don't have a gun."

"And how will I do that?"

"Oh, the pen in your handbag is a start."

Maisie looked at the ground and felt her head swim. At that moment she wished someone else could have taken on the guise of Leon Donat's daughter.

The grand country house where Robert MacFarlane had left Maisie in the hands of a man known only to her as "Mr. Strupper" was, she surmised, somewhere in the Cotswolds. MacFarlane had apologized for the need to blindfold her about an hour into their journey—the "blindfold" having been a pair of darkglasses with opaque lenses—so she could only guess at the location. She would be in situ for one week, and would leave directly from the mansion for Victoria Station, where she would board the express train, bound for Munich via ferry across the English Channel.

It was during the journey that Maisie decided to tell MacFarlane about John Otterburn. She recounted their conversation at the newly decorated flat in Primrose Hill.

MacFarlane pressed his lips together and shook his head. "Lass, there are certain people—your Mr. Otterburn being one of them— who are, as I am sure you know, 'untouchable.' They have too much value because they know too much, can do too much, and have made themselves indispensable. The canny Canadian is involved in ways you would not even be able to imagine when it comes to protecting these British Isles." MacFarlane shook his head and sighed. "When we do business with men such as Mr. Otterburn, we shake hands with the devil we know. And what we know is that he has access to information we would rather he did not have." He looked at Maisie. "So he told you only that he knew you were off to Munich."

"Yes."

"And he didn't have a reason for letting you know."

"No."

"He didn't want you to look up an old friend, did he?"

Maisie shook her head.

"I daresay he's just interested. By all accounts he wasn't fond of Leon Donat. Not at all—Donat was the tortoise to Otterburn's hare when it came to a very big order for machine tools, from a company down Brazil way. About ten years ago, I think it was. Otterburn thought he had it in the bag—all that flash he has, he thought he'd won the day over Donat. But no, they preferred to do business with the man who appeared more solid."

"I see," said Maisie.

"But there's respect there, one for the other—always is among enemies when they're strong. And these men with their businesses have enemies all over the place. Donat has them in Germany, as Huntley told you in the briefing. You see, Maisie, you and I, we're not of this world of commerce, but I can tell you one thing—there are more captains of industry than officers on the battlefield willing to kill a man. And people like Leon Donat—quiet, methodical, thoughtful, yet very, very clever—they will always have as many against them as for them. But as we know, Donat's people were always for him." He blew out his cheeks. "Anyway, at least Otterburn is on our side, Maisie."

Surrounded by mature Leylandi cypresses, and fields and forest beyond, the house had originally been built in the early 1600s, with a later addition in the mid-eighteenth century. At the back, over-looking the manicured lawns, it had the hallmarks of a Tudor palace, with beamed construction and candy-cane chimneys. Maisie thought the front of the mansion would have been at home in Georgian Bath—she imagined Jane Austen taking a turn around the fountain that divided the carriage sweep. But it was now the twentieth century, and it was clear the building no longer accommodated a well-to-do landowner, or a clergyman with an enviable personal income over and above a church stipend. Each day she saw a few men and women coming and going, some toward various outbuildings, others—mostly women—scurrying along corridors clutching folders, or writing notes as they went. No one stopped to converse with her, and if they greeted her, it was in German. Every teacher—from Strupper to the man who told her exactly how she could use her pen as a weapon—now spoke to her in German. She took her meals in her well-appointed rooms, the maid announcing her entrance with "Guten Tag, Fräulein Donat. Ich bin hier mit dem Essen—hoffen wir, dass Sie hungrig sind!" *Good day, Miss Donat. I'm here with your food—I hope you're hungry!* Or per-haps "Guten Abend, Fräulein Donat. Es war so kalt heute, so habe ich einige heiße Suppe für Sie." *Good evening, Miss Donat. It has been so cold today, so I have some hot soup for you.* In general the conversation amounted to a comment on the weather, and a desire to know whether Maisie—or Fräulein Donat, as she was now known—was hungry, be-cause Cook had made something special for her. At first Maisie offered a halting "Thank you" in German, but necessity forced her to dredge her memory's depths for the language she had learned almost twenty years earlier, and even then it was only enough to get her through the basics of polite conversation. In one week she was not expected to demonstrate fluency, but she needed to be able to offer pleasantries—and to grasp the essence of any conversations taking place around her.

On the morning of Maisie's penultimate day at the manor house she found a note pushed under her bedroom door, informing her that she should proceed to the conference room following her lesson with Mr. Strupper, which was planned for the hour just after lunch. There was no indication of whom she would be meeting, or if preparation was required.

With a high-pitched whine still ringing in her ears, Maisie made her way down from the shooting range to the conference room. She had been to the room only once before, on her first day. It was here that she received her schedule for the week and instructions regarding how her immersion in the unknown territory of what she considered to be diplomatic risk-taking would proceed. The walls were lined in dark wood, with some panels bearing a coat of arms and others carved to depict hunting scenes and vine fruit. Rich velvet curtains draped leaded windows, and a heavy iron chandelier hung over the table. As she entered the room, two things struck her: the smell of lavender and beeswax, as if copious amounts of the polish were used every day on the long table and sturdy chairs, and a woman standing by the window, looking out across the gardens. The woman turned as Maisie closed the door behind her.

"Oh, my goodness," said Maisie.

Dr. Francesca Thomas stepped toward Maisie. "Dear me, we're failing you if you've managed to forget to speak in German at the first shock of the day!"

Maisie had met Francesca Thomas several years earlier, during her first assignment for Huntley. MacFarlane was still with Special Branch at the time, but it was to him that she reported on her work at a college in Cambridge, where there was a suspicion that subversive activities against the Crown were taking place. Maisie had taken on an academic appointment in an undercover capacity. In time she realized that Dr. Francesca Thomas was also working in a clandestine role, but for the

Belgian government. Later Maisie learned that Thomas was a woman of great bravery, having been a member of La Dame Blanche—a resistance network of mainly women engaged in intelligence activities, including surveillance and sabotage against their German occupiers. It was Thomas who had warned Maisie that having worked on behalf of the British Secret Service, she would never be free.

Thomas reached out and placed her hands on Maisie's shoulders, as if to inspect her. "You've weathered some storms, Maisie."

"No more than you, Dr. Thomas."

"Francesca, please. And in a break with the formality established since your arrival, you will not be required to converse in German during this meeting."

"Just as I was getting used to it," said Maisie.

Thomas smiled as she pulled out a chair at the head of the table and held out her hand to indicate that Maisie should sit next to her. Opening a file on the table in front of her, she explained her presence at the manor house.

"You are now aware that not only do I work on behalf of my own country, but also Britain—in the interests of Belgium, you understand. Mr. Huntley thought it would be a good idea for me to have some involvement in preparing you for your assignment." Thomas took a deep breath. "I think he believes another woman's perspective might help you feel more at ease."

Maisie had opened her mouth to inform Thomas that she felt quite at ease when the other woman raised her hand.

"And anyone who says she is perfectly all right as she prepares for such an expedition is, my dear, not facing the truth of the matter. There's no need to feel you must put *me* at ease—a healthy dose of doubt may well keep you safe. Now, to work. We're going to look at Leon Donat."

"I've already been briefed on Mr. Donat—I've read his dossier a dozen times. In fact, I can tell you what he might have for dinner on a day like today."

"And that is?"

"Liver and bacon, mashed potato, gravy, and cabbage. Steamed apple pudding for afters, then some cheese and biscuits with a glass of port. He never takes a first course, and goes straight to the main."

"Good work." Thomas pulled out a collection of photographs from an envelope. "This is a little different."

Francesca Thomas laid out five photographs of Leon Donat—some formal, at an event; some informal, probably taken at the family home. One by one, Thomas asked Maisie to study each photograph and point out aspects of Donat's physiognomy she'd noticed, or the way he stood, folded his arms, or clasped the ring on the third finger of his left hand.

"Good. Now then, look at this photograph."

Maisie picked up the print Thomas pushed toward her.

"What do you see?" asked Thomas.

Maisie studied every aspect of the man whose eyes seemed to stare back at her. "Well, I'll be honest," she said. "I'm not sure. Something's different. Yes, the area around the nose, the folds here"—she ran her finger across her own skin, just below the left cheek—"all right, yes, he looks as if he's had a tooth removed. He's swollen."

"Well done. He had been playing with the son of his manager at the factory in Hertfordshire, and had just been hit by a ball on the cheek. It was the factory summer picnic." Thomas paused, and then pushed another photo toward Maisie. "What about this one?"

Maisie reached for the photograph and again focused on the features. "Here too he looks different. Perhaps a slightly changed haircut."

"No. Wrong. Look again."

Maisie squinted and shook her head. "The eyes look different. Perhaps it's the angle—the way he's looking at the camera."

"No. Try again."

Maisie tried to disguise a sigh. She was tired. The week had tested her mentally, physically, drained her spirit—and now Thomas seemed determined to whittle away any confidence she had left.

"The need for accurate observation could save your life, Maisie," said Thomas.

"All right. Let's just say it isn't Leon Donat."

Thomas smiled. "Doubt has many faces, Maisie. It can trip you up or be your friend. Good. You're right. This is not Leon Donat. What about this one?"

"Yes, it's him."

"This?"

"Yes."

"And this?"

"No."

At last Thomas gathered the photographs and returned them to the envelope. Maisie had been tested on her recognition of Leon Donat until her eyes smarted and she felt herself fighting to keep them open.

"Now to the next thing on the agenda," said Thomas.

Maisie looked at the clock set on the mantelpiece. "It says on my timetable that I have a safety briefing in five minutes. In the gymnasium."

"Yes, that's right. But your briefing is not in the gymnasium, it's right here. With me."

Maisie met Thomas' eyes. She knew that beneath the scarf worn at her neck, the woman before her bore the scars of hand-to-hand combat. As a member of La Dame Blanche, she had sought to avenge the death of her husband, killing the man who had taken his life. She had been prepared to die in the attempt.

"I am going to teach you how to save your own life, Maisie. How to keep yourself safe."

B y the time the motor car arrived to collect Maisie for the journey to London, where she would lodge at a flat close to Victoria for just a few hours, the English language seemed almost alien to her, and she was tired to the bone. As soon as she was settled in the small flat, which was situated in the center of a nondescript mews just ten minutes' walk from the station, MacFarlane knocked at her door. With him was a woman who was to fit Maisie with a shoulder-length wig of deep coppery brown hair. She also carried a small suitcase packed with clothing that fit Maisie, and which she would probably have chosen herself if Priscilla had not recently insisted that she buy nothing without her sartorial advice. The garments were plain, of fine quality, and in dark or muted shades—a heavy tweed coat, a navy skirt, a pale blue silk blouse, another matching jacket and dress costume in a deep burgundy wool barathea. There was nothing to attract attention. Soft leather shoes that were a perfect fit had been slipped into the case; and a heavier pair of walking shoes had been provided for travel purposes, and to stand up to the weather in Munich, expected to be much colder than London. There would be no Prince Charming to slip a new slipper onto her foot and whisk her away to another life.

All travel documents provided were in the same name as on the passport MacFarlane handed to her, along with the papers she would be required to relinquish to the German authorities upon her arrival in Munich. There she would be issued with more documents to secure the release of Leon Donat—the man she would call "Papa"—from the prison in Dachau. She was now officially Edwina Donat.

"You're on your way, Miss Donat." MacFarlane nodded to the woman who had fitted Maisie's wig and demonstrated how to secure and style hair that was so unlike her own. The woman put away the brushes and combs, the wigs that were not deemed satisfactory, and left the room with an almost silent step. Maisie realized that she might pass the woman in the street and never recognize her; she was an everywoman, with no significant features to mark her as memorable.

MacFarlane pressed his lips together as if to stop himself uttering words he might regret. "You know what to do—stick to the plan we've given you, and you should have no problems at all. You just go in, say everything we've told you to say, then collect Leon Donat and board the train, all in double-quick time. I know I can trust you not to linger to see the sights. We want you and Donat in Paris and then in not-so-sunny London post-bloody-haste."

"Don't worry—I want to get back as soon as possible too."

"Are you sure you won't agree to an aeroplane out of Munich, hen? You only have to say, and it's done—we can make arrangements now, and believe me, Maisie, we would rather you—"

Maisie smiled. MacFarlane was almost going soft, she thought, calling her "hen."

"If my remit is as straightforward as you've described, the train will be as good as flying, and before you know it we'll have crossed the border into France. After that, it's only a quick hop to the finish line."

MacFarlane nodded. Then he opened a small attaché case he had brought with him. He reached into it and took out a revolver.

"This is for you. My own personal kit. Same revolver, slightly modified. It'll feel lighter in your hand, but handle it the same and you'll be all right. It's been lucky for me, and I expect you to return it personally.

I'll see you in Paris. On Thursday. All right, Fräulein Donat?"

Maisie laughed. "Paris. On Thursday. And you'd better have more than just a wee dram waiting for me."

"Hen, I will have a bloody great bottle of a good eighteen-year-old malt and a couple of glasses at the ready. Now then . . ." He faltered. "Now then—do your job and come home."

"Leave now, Robbie, before you go soppy on me."

MacFarlane gave one more nod and left. Maisie was on her own—except, perhaps, for the assumed character of Edwina Donat.

M aisie thought she might try to sleep for a couple of hours before she had to leave for Victoria Station to catch the Night Ferry train service to Paris. She lay down on top of the bed and closed her eyes, thinking of the journey ahead. The sleeper train would transport her across the Channel and to the French capital, where she would undergo a swift final briefing from Huntley, perhaps with new intelligence, before setting off again on the express train to Munich.

Sleep evaded her. She rose earlier than needed, walked across to the window, and looked out onto the street, where smog rising from the river swirled around the lampposts. A single policeman was pacing up and down—not a common sight in a small mews, but he was there to keep an eye on the flat, making sure the coast was clear when a plain black motor car arrived to take Maisie to the station.

She looked both ways along the street. One more hour, and she would be locking the front door and handing the keys to the driver to return to whoever was responsible for Secret Service properties in London. She turned away from the window and reached for her bag. Taking out MacFarlane's revolver, she lifted the weapon and aimed the barrel at a portrait hanging on the wall over the fireplace. She narrowed her gaze and then lowered her arm, looking at the gun in her hands. The barrel seemed shorter, and MacFarlane was right—it was lighter than the one she'd used in training. It bore the scars of use, scratches and a tiny dent, but there was not a speck of dust anywhere on the revolver.

She remembered something Strupper had said. *Look after your weapon. I'm sure your father taught you that you get to know a horse first by grooming it, by laying your hands on the creature, not just using the brush—that's how you form a bond. Same with your gun. Clean it, oil it, get used to it in your palm; finger every part of it. That familiarity might save your life.* And she'd wondered, then, how much he knew about her. Had he known she was the daughter of a man who had worked with horses?

Looking at the clock now, she hurried to get ready. She'd deliberately left little time, so there would be no lingering and waiting, no butterflies, no time for regret. She bathed, dressed in clothing that Leon Donat's daughter might have chosen, and, following the instructions she'd been given, pulled the wig over her own dark cropped hair. "Good job you've not got a lot of hair there," the wig mistress had said. "The difficult ones have long hair and don't want to chop it. We have to pack it in and hope for the best." MacFarlane had looked at the woman. She didn't say another word except to bid Maisie good-bye as she left the flat.

Hearing a motor car rumble at a slow pace across the cobblestones, drawing to a halt outside the front door, Maisie picked up a small leather case, along with a new leather shoulder bag, and left the flat. She handed the keys to the driver as the policeman held open the door for her.

"Good luck, miss," the policeman said as he closed the door, and she could have sworn he winked at her. He tapped the roof, and the driver maneuvered the motor car out of the mews and on toward the station. There he stepped from the vehicle and opened the passenger door for Maisie, nodding acknowledgment of her thanks. As she set off toward the platform, she looked back once. The driver touched his peaked cap in her direction and pulled away from the curb.

Soon Maisie—now Edwina Donat, she reminded herself—was making her way along the platform, carrying the small leather case she'd been given years earlier by Andrew Dene, the man with whom she'd had a love affair, before breaking off the courtship. She had been issued with a new, nondescript case to take with her to Munich, but had left it at the flat with her own clothing inside, and on top a note asking that it be delivered to the Dower House at Chelstone Manor in Kent. There was a comfort in bringing her new belongings to Munich in a case that was part of her real life. Dene was now happily married with two children and doing well in his profession as a leading ortho-pedic surgeon, teaching at two medical schools. A perfect life, thought Maisie. Each year she received Christmas cards from Dene, always with a note bringing her up to date with events in his growing family. As she came alongside the first-class compartments she felt a not unfa-miliar sense of isolation, of loneliness. If she were a wife and mother, a woman with a home, husband, and children, she would not be travel-ing from one dangerous situation to another. Her family would be all she wanted and needed. Instead, she was a widow—fair game, as far as those who needed her to work for them were concerned. Still, she could only look to herself. She had agreed to take on the assignment.

Having been shown to her private compartment, Maisie placed her case and coat in the stowage above her head, unbuttoned her jacket, removed her hat, and settled into her seat with a newspaper she'd bought from a vendor at the station. The wig had begun to itch, but she could not tamper with it in case she altered her physical appearance. In truth, she was rather afraid of the wig, perhaps more so than the revolver in her handbag. Both changed who she was; both challenged how she might conduct herself in the world. With both in her possession, she was another person—a woman on her way to claim her father from a prison known for brutality in the name of a regime that, according to Huntley and MacFarlane, threatened peace in the world. But she would have to become accustomed to the sweaty discomfort of the wig, and the gun she would only fire if her life or that of Leon Donat was in danger.

The wild card, of course, was Elaine Otterburn. Maisie hoped the young woman—if she located her—proved less wild than her reputation suggested.

The sojourn in Paris was just for a few hours, enough time for a final meeting with Brian Huntley, lunch, another check of her papers, and another briefing with an expert on the "German situation" and what she could expect when she presented her papers at the Nazi Party headquarters. She was cautioned regarding her available time in Munich, and instructed to conduct herself with care—only a little sightseeing. She might take a book with her, sit in a park, act as if she were the anxious daughter of a man about to be released following years of incarceration.

Given that the house the Secret Service used in Paris was part of Maurice Blanche's estate, and therefore now part of Maisie's property portfolio, she felt more on a par with Huntley. But she could not escape the memories of her first visit, when Huntley—then reporting to Maurice Blanche—had brought her there, after following her during her work on a case. The investigation had revealed many things, not least the intelligence work Priscilla's brother was engaged in during the war, before his death. Maisie had also discovered the truth about her beloved mentor's subterfuge in his recruitment of intelligence agents, and how he had effectively used her to gain information without her knowledge. The information had led her to feel responsible for Peter Evernden's death. That she had not been taken into Maurice's confidence earlier had pained her for a long time, though in time she came to understand his motives.

Now she was here with Huntley again—but this time, she was the agent.

"There is nothing more to say to you, Maisie. You have done well in your training, and you are prepared for as many eventualities as we could imagine. Your past—your training with Maurice, and your subsequent work—will stand you in good stead. This task should be straightforward, but it has to be said—if some aspect does not go according to plan, you must do all you can to save yourself. We have other people in Germany—in Munich, especially—who might be drafted in to help you, but this operation has thus far been conducted in circumstances of extreme confidence. Given the agreement leading to the release of Leon Donat, only a few have been brought into the circle, as I am sure you understand."

"Yes, I understand. For diplomatic purposes, if this goes wrong, I don't exist."

"That's the measure of it."

There was an awkward pause. It seemed Huntley did not know what to say next. Maisie came to her feet and held out her hand. "You were held in high esteem by Maurice, Mr. Huntley. I have every confidence in your planning and the preparation you've . . . subjected me to." She smiled. "Now I must leave." She picked up her coat and walked to the door, whereupon she turned back. "And you know that, should this plan not proceed as we hoped, Mr. Klein has my will and all instructions pertaining to this property, should they be required."

Huntley inclined his head to signal his understanding, but added, "Oh, we don't expect the Secret Service to be bothering Mr. Klein, Maisie. You'll be back soon enough."

CHAPTER 6

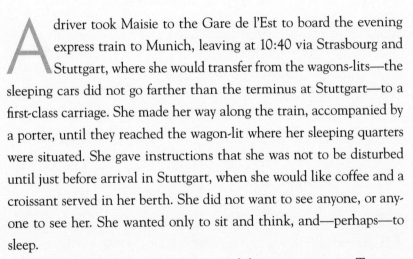

A driver took Maisie to the Gare de l'Est to board the evening express train to Munich, leaving at 10:40 via Strasbourg and Stuttgart, where she would transfer from the wagons-lits—the sleeping cars did not go farther than the terminus at Stuttgart—to a first-class carriage. She made her way along the train, accompanied by a porter, until they reached the wagon-lit where her sleeping quarters were situated. She gave instructions that she was not to be disturbed until just before arrival in Stuttgart, when she would like coffee and a croissant served in her berth. She did not want to see anyone, or anyone to see her. She wanted only to sit and think, and—perhaps—to sleep.

She dreamed that night of James, of their apartment in Toronto, and of sailing on Lake Ontario. It was a strange dream, as if a moving picture were being shown in her subconscious mind. Upon waking, she thought she could recount the conversation they'd had as they prepared to go out for the day. James had asked if she felt well enough, if she might strain herself in some way. She was carrying their child and, because she was not in the first flush of youth, had been advised to take care. The dream seemed to leap from the apartment to the lake, and the point where she felt buoyed along by the gentle lapping of small waves alongside the yacht, a sound that reminded her of thirsty dogs taking water. In the dream James decided to go for a swim, and soon she was alone on board, looking toward him as the vessel moved away—not with any speed, but as if the water itself were slowly bearing her back toward the harbor. She had called to him, but he had only waved and said, "Don't worry, Maisie. You'll be all right. I'll see you later." And then he was gone, and she was awake, the side-to-side motion of the train willing her to fall asleep again. She turned on her side and felt tears seep onto the pillow.

The knock was not urgent, but it woke her immediately.

"Madame. Madame!"

She stepped from the narrow bed, pulled on her dressing gown, and wrapped a towel around her head—she had removed her wig before getting into bed—before opening the door.

A waiter with blond hair and blue eyes, his uniform immaculate, gave a short bow. "Madam, we arrive in Stuttgart in three quarters of an hour. You ordered coffee and a croissant. May I offer you something else—a little fruit, perhaps?"

Maisie shook her head. "No, thank you. Here, I'll take the tray."

The man seemed put out that he was not able to discharge his duty properly by setting the tray on the small table, but he acceded to Maisie's wishes with a brief nod and closed the door. She placed the tray on the bed before reaching to open the curtains. As the train clattered along, Maisie looked out, wondering when the villages, fields, forests, and then factories flanking the route would give way to the beauty she expected to behold when they entered Bavaria. She shivered. Yes, it would indeed be beautiful, but she knew she would see little of that majesty as the next few days unfolded. She would see the darker side of Bavaria from the moment she arrived in Munich.

The coffee was good and strong, reminding her of Maurice, and the croissant was light, with flakes that dropped onto the napkin in her lap as she took a bite. She dipped it in her coffee and took another bite. She would have to hurry—it would take her a good ten minutes to get the wig in place. The clock was ticking; her countdown had begun. This time next week, she thought, she'd be back in England, safe and sound. In just an hour she would be in Munich, and then in a few days her journey would be over. She would be safe in Paris, then London. As that last thought occurred to her, she heard the echo of words unspoken. *God willing.* And she remembered her dream, and James calling to her. *Don't worry, Maisie. You'll be all right.*

The final part of the journey, through Stuttgart and on to Munich, passed with ease. Soon the train was slowing, entering the railway station. Steam obscured Maisie's view from the window. People who had made the long journey were already anxious to be on their way, perhaps to be met by family or friends not seen for a long time—a woman reuniting with her lover, parents with their child. Maisie knew one man would be waiting for her: Gilbert Leslie, a foreign service official from the British consulate. To him she was simply Miss Edwina Donat.

Stepping off the train, Maisie tried to hide her discomfort. Guards wearing the uniforms of Adolf Hitler's Nazi Party patrolled the station. Her papers had been checked as the train passed from France to Germany, and now she showed them again before moving out into the waiting throng. A young man—she thought he might only be about thirty years of age—approached her there. He wore a gray mackintosh and a darker gray hat, the brim still dripping from sleet outside.

"Fräulein Donat?" He smiled when she nodded and came closer. "I thought it was you, Miss Donat. My name is Gilbert Leslie; I'm from the British consulate here in Munich. Do you have everything?" He nodded to a porter behind Maisie, took the case, fumbled in his pocket for a coin, and pressed it into the man's hand. Turning back to Maisie, he added without waiting for a reply, "Right, come this way. I've a motor waiting, and we can take you to your hotel straightaway."

The man did not speak again until they were in the backseat of a black motor car. "I am here to brief you before you go to the headquarters of the Nazi Party. You are expected to present yourself and your papers tomorrow morning at ten o'clock on the dot. I will accompany you, representing His Majesty's government, and to see that our claim to secure the release of one of His Majesty's subjects is free and clear of any impediment. Much work has already been done, Miss Donat; otherwise your father would not be anywhere close to release."

"Thank you, Mr. Leslie."

"It should be fairly smooth, though these boys are a bit intimidating, all leather boots and black uniforms. And of course they are running torture chambers and calling them prisons." He looked at Maisie. "I tell you this so you know that your father will likely not resemble the man you last saw, though I am sure they will have tidied him up a bit."

Maisie was careful to look suitably crestfallen.

"Miss Donat," added Leslie, "I have to ask you one question. Please do not be offended. But your coloring . . . Your father has a British passport, British papers, and was born in Britain—but are you of the Hebrew faith?"

Maisie shook her head. "My father comes from Italian stock—our name was, according to my grandfather, originally Donatello. It was my great-grandfather who came to England and set up a business. We are most definitely British."

"Not Hungarian Jews, then? Or French of the same persuasion?"

Maisie laughed, though inside she was bristling. "No—rather we are very lapsed Catholics, which would horrify my great-grandmother, who set great stock by the Virgin Mary."

Leslie nodded. He ran a finger around his collar.

"If it's that bad, Mr. Leslie, why haven't you been transferred back to London? For surely you're at risk here, if places like Dachau are filling up with Jews."

Leslie shook his head. "I am an officer of the consular service, a loyal British subject. I am at no risk."

Maisie said nothing. Given all Huntley had told her about Leslie, the fact that he was here at all, and in Munich, demonstrated either a lack of attention or complete complacency on the part of his superiors. Or perhaps they wanted to annoy someone, and Leslie provided the means.

The motor car pulled up in front of the imposing and somewhat austere Hotel Vier Jahreszeiten on Maximilian Strasse, only a few minutes' walk from the Residenz, the grand and ostentatious seat of kings and dukes for over four centuries. The familiar red flag with the black swastika insignia flapped in the wind above the entrance. A porter came to help with Maisie's luggage, such as it was, and as he approached, his hand shot up in salute.

"Heil Hitler!" he said, glancing sideways at two men in uniform walking toward them.

Gilbert Leslie lifted his hand just a little and repeated the words, while Maisie fumbled with her shoulder bag, deliberately dropping it on the ground.

"Wie bitte," she said. *I beg your pardon.*

The men in brown uniforms went on their way, and the porter breathed a sigh of relief. Leslie accompanied Maisie into the hotel to ensure there were no problems when she signed the hotel register and that she was seen safely to her room. As he studied other guests going back and forth, leaving or entering the hotel, and the number of black-uniformed men in the vicinity, he seemed agitated.

"Are you all right, Mr. Leslie?" asked Maisie.

"Those thugs in the brown shirts on the street—they unnerve me. They don't care if you're a tourist from a friendly country or not, they'll usually knock you down if you don't give that salute. An American couple ended up needing medical attention last summer. They were minding their own business on a sunny day in the street, and the next thing along comes a column of those henchmen and they start attacking anyone who does not salute. Of course, if you're a visitor, you don't know, do you? But here's the interesting thing about them—they're all new recruits, bully boys brought in by Hitler's regime. They had to get uniforms for them pretty quickly, so a batch manufactured for the desert armies was commandeered—and soldiers in the desert wear those brown uniforms, to blend in with all that sand, I suppose! Now the brown-shirted thugs are a law unto themselves. And Adolf Hitler."

Maisie looked away and smiled as the young man returned with her key and her passport and gave directions to her room. Another young man was summoned to accompany her and ensure she knew where the well-regarded restaurant was situated. While he waited to one side, Leslie whispered instructions to Maisie.

"I will be here for you at nine tomorrow morning. It's not far to walk to the headquarters, so we might as well." He paused. "Oh, and it's likely that you'll have time on your hands for a day or so afterward—I doubt if they'll have your final papers ready to collect your father until late Wednesday, so you won't be able to leave until Thursday. If I were you, I would make sure I confirmed my train ticket for Paris as soon as I had the stamped papers for the release. Get out as fast as you can, before they change their minds."

"Do they?"

"The common wisdom is that no one gets out of Dachau—but there have been instances of men being bought out by relatives. In this case, it's not only the money involved, but the fact that your father has friends in high places. Hitler likes his associations among the British aristocracy, and your father's connections in the right strata of society have helped enormously. That letter from— Oh, I'd better go now. Your escort is looking a bit hot around the collar."

As Leslie turned to leave, he gave one last reminder. "Nine o'clock. Wrap up warm and wear those shoes—they're best for walking. Good day to you, Miss Donat."

Maisie watched as he made his way out, stopping briefly to exchange a salute with the doorman. The young man snapped his heels together in front of her and reached down for her small leather case.

"Fräulein Donat? Please follow me." His English was perfect.

Soon Maisie was in her room overlooking Maximilian Strasse. There were few people on the street. To a person they executed a perfect salute, arm extended, whenever a man in uniform walked past in the opposite direction. Maisie sighed. She stepped back from the window, kicked off her shoes, and lay down on the bed. On the one hand, she didn't like the idea of having a "bit of time to kill"—but on the other, it gave her an opportunity to see if she could find Elaine Otterburn, the needle in a haystack. And she realized she was glad she had time, though had she not, she would have reported honestly to the Otterburns that she'd been restricted due to a schedule set by the authorities. She could still make her excuses, if she wanted to avoid any responsibility for Elaine. Yet her thoughts turned to the "little man"—a child who was loved, but without the constant attention and affection of the woman most important to him, his mother. If she could reverse the child's fortunes, Maisie thought, then it was worth a try.

As she lay on the bed, staring up at the ceiling above, she was intrigued—and yes, troubled—by Leslie's comment that someone "on high" had spoken on behalf of Leon Donat. If all went well, he would be one of very few prisoners released from a Nazi prison camp because he had money and contacts. She had not been informed of that small detail, and she wondered who the mystery person in such an exalted position might be.

Following an uneventful evening—she had opted to dine alone in her room—Maisie read through her notes twice more and checked her weapon again, heeding Strupper's instructions to get to know the revolver, to handle it, to become accustomed to its weight in her hand. She laid out her clothing and had a hot bath before going to bed, but sleep eluded her until the early hours.

Though she had not rested well, the thought of what was to come during the next twenty-four hours diminished feelings of fatigue in the morning. She was served a light breakfast, again in her room, but could only eat a small piece of warm bread. When she made her way down to the hotel entrance, Leslie was already waiting. It was ten minutes to nine, and he looked as if he had been there for a while.

Before leaving her room, she had lingered with the revolver in her hand, wondering if she should take it with her. No, not this time, she decided. Even if she had cause to use it, there would be too many heavily armed men around her; she would stand no chance at all. And what could possibly go wrong if all she was doing was presenting papers? Huntley had said the worst that could happen would be a last-minute refusal, but Maisie suspected it might be more serious. She could be incarcerated herself. She was already on thin ice. Leon Donat's great-grandfather had indeed been a Jewish Italian immigrant to London. And of course, her own maternal grandmother was a gypsy—and there had been reports of Nazi brutality toward gypsies.

Maisie stood to the side of the reception desk for a moment. Before Leslie saw her, she touched her middle, just at the point of the buckle securing the belt on the soft burgundy fabric of her jacket. She wanted to remind herself to be steady, to be strong from the very center of her being. Maurice had taught her, years ago—in those early days when she was green and young, a sapling next to a mature tree—that there was a connection between the physical being, the spirit, and emotions. He taught her to be aware of her bearing, of the way she entered a room, sat down to her work, or reacted to news, good and bad. Strength in the very center of her body would lend power to every word she spoke, and every thought that passed through her mind.

She straightened her spine, broadened her shoulders, and walked with a precise, clipped step to meet Gilbert Leslie, who seemed an inch or two shorter than he had the previous day.

"Ah, good morning, Miss Donat. Ready?"

"As ready as I will ever be," said Maisie, reminding herself that she was Edwina Donat, daughter of Leon Donat, currently incarcerated in a notorious prison at the behest of Adolf Hitler's Nazi regime. She imagined how she would feel if her own beloved father were in the same position. At once the strength in her spine ebbed almost—almost—beyond control; then it returned, stronger than before. She was determined to carry out her assignment to the letter.

Leslie seemed nervous. He gave a running commentary every step of the way, pointing out various landmarks to her as if he were quoting a guidebook to Munich. After they had passed the grand Residenz and were walking on toward Odeonsplatz, he took her elbow. "We'll go down this little alley, not across the square."

Maisie looked around and noticed other pedestrians making the same detour. "What's in the square, Mr. Leslie?"

Leslie stopped. "Just there"—he pointed, then quickly lowered his hand—"that's where the Führer was almost assassinated in the Beer Hall Putsch. Sixteen men in his party were killed, along with four policemen. They are considered martyrs to the Reich. If you go past that square, you are required to stand and salute the party, to honor those killed. I doubt you want to do that—neither do a lot of people. So we take this little path to avoid the square."

Maisie stepped out along the alley behind Leslie. Why, she wondered, if the Führer was so fêted, did so many people dodge the requirement to salute his party? She was about to ask Leslie when he began speaking, though his voice was so low she had to move closer and lean in toward him to hear.

"If you're wondering how he has managed to garner such attention, it's twofold. One, he is a very, very powerful speaker. Put him on a stage, and it's as if he can mesmerize everyone—he's like a cobra, ready to strike."

"All right, I can imagine that—I've seen such people in—" She was about to say *in my work*, but caught herself in time. "What is the other reason for his popularity?"

"Fear. There was an attempt on his life—an explosion. It failed. But he managed to persuade the population that their lives would be at risk if certain powers—restrictions, if you will, and elements of what I would call surveillance—were not enacted. For the most part, the people went along with it. Fear can be used in all sorts of ways to control people, and that's what he's done." They took a few steps in silence.

"I think that, for the most part, Britain is hoping that if he has enough rope, he will hang himself." Leslie coughed. "Now I'm getting a bit beyond myself."

Maisie rubbed her hands together as she considered Leslie's commentary while studying the austere buildings along the street. Perhaps it was because it was the stark end of winter, with shafts of low yet bright sunlight slanting between buildings on a very cold day, but nothing seemed welcoming. People rushed along with their heads down. Though she knew this was probably due to a sharp chill in the wind, she thought that despite the beauty of the Bavaria she had seen from the train, the country held an undercurrent of something very uncomfortable. It was fear, she knew, sprinkled like dust across the landscape. What on earth could Elaine Otterburn have gained from being in such a place?

Leslie seemed to read her thoughts. "Of course you're not seeing Munich at its best, Fräulein Donat. We have to get you used to the 'Fräulein' now—we're almost there. Munich is a very vibrant city, you know—beer halls, music halls, theaters, that sort of thing. It's an interesting place to be stationed for a couple of years."

"When do you leave for your next posting, do you think?" Maisie asked as they strode toward the building marked by red flags with the distinctive white circle and black swastika.

"I'm hoping for the United States, actually, perhaps in a year or so. Washington is the plum in the pudding of our line of work, so fingers crossed!"

Nazi guards watched their approach. Leslie pulled a clutch of papers and an identification card from an inside pocket of his jacket, giving a half smile to the guard who met them. Maisie followed his fluent German as he addressed the man.

"My papers and identification. I am accompanying Fräulein Donat, who has come to present documents for the release of her father. All is in order—here is the letter of appointment."

Maisie handed over the papers she had carried with her, together with her passport. She said nothing, and lowered her head a little. She worried that her height—she was as tall as Leslie and not much shorter than the guard—might cause the guard to be aggressive. She had seen it happen before.

The guard returned the papers to Leslie and indicated that they were free to enter the building and proceed to the first floor, pointing as if to an office above the door.

This part of the procedure was supposed to be a formality. All the hard work had been done; this was the rubber-stamping required for Maisie to take possession of Leon Donat. All the same, she could not wait for the next hour to be over.

Another guard took the papers Leslie handed him, and they were instructed to wait, seated on a hard wooden bench in the cold entrance hall. Leslie's hands were shaking.

"Take some deep breaths, Mr. Leslie. And put your hands in your pockets. This is a nerve-racking place because they want to intimidate people. You have every right to be here, representing His Majesty's government and as a citizen of Great Britain. And I have every right to bring out my father, who should not have been sent to any prison."

Leslie shoved his hands into his pockets and was about to respond, when a man in a black uniform, with shining black boots, appeared in front of them.

"Fräulein Donat?"

Maisie stood up, giving a half smile to acknowledge the officer. He smiled in return.

"Come with me."

Leslie stood up to follow.

"Not you. Only Fräulein Donat."

Leslie sat down again. Maisie followed the officer up the staircase and along a corridor to a spacious but unembellished office, with a window looking out onto the street.

When Maisie entered, another officer of the Schutzstaffel was rocking back and forth on a chair behind a broad desk of dark wood. He did not look up, but continued rocking while flipping through sheets of paper until Maisie was standing in front of him. He allowed his chair to rock forward, the legs meeting the floor with an audible thump, and then stood up and held out his hand, inviting Maisie to take the seat opposite him. The officer who had accompanied Maisie pulled out the chair, waiting for her to be seated before taking up a place behind the man who would be conducting the interview, who was now inspecting her papers.

"Fräulein Donat."

"Yes." Maisie nodded.

The officer looked at her, then at her passport. He shrugged. "You have no brothers or sisters?"

Maisie shook her head. "No. And now my mother is dead, there is only my father and myself."

"You are aware of why he was arrested?"

"I have been given details, yes."

"And what do you say to that? Your father was accused of proliferating literature disrespectful to the Führer."

Maisie chewed her lip. She had gone through all the questions that would be asked. Time and again, at the house in the Cotswolds, she had been subjected to mock interviews designed to mirror what might be put to her in Munich. Almost every scenario had been anticipated, her answers commented upon and edited each time.

"I found it most hard to believe," said Maisie. "My father wanted only to represent the academic books and the professors who write for his company."

"He wanted to sell British books to German students?"

"In the fields that my father's company publishes—mathematics, physics, chemistry, and so on—British students read many German authors. Those scientists respect each other, so the books my father's company publishes are read by students in many other countries."

The officer nodded, as if she had passed a test. "Then why do you think he was involved in publishing subversive literature?"

Maisie appeared to give thought to the question, looking pained. "My father has always believed that we must be . . . that we must be . . . a support, I suppose you could say, to young people. It is my belief that my father might have been duped. He would never have knowingly supported any political activism. That was never his desire. He wants only to see students rise to the top, wherever they are and whichever country they come from."

"Laudable, I am sure." The man sighed, picked up her passport again, and looked from Maisie to the photograph. His eyes lingered on her, his stare focusing on her eyes, her mouth, her hair, then down to her shoulders. She did not flinch.

"Your father knows important people," he said.

Maisie felt a bead of sweat trickle under the wig. She reached up and brushed her hand across her forehead.

"My father has crossed paths with many important people—mainly scientists who author the books his company publishes. Through that work he has met others. He has found that people of a certain status are always interested in new discoveries." She clasped her hands. Surely these matters had all been addressed during the negotiations with the British government. But Huntley had warned her. *They will toy with you—and we have to prepare you for that eventuality.*

"Indeed," said the officer. His English was perfect. "Do you have a religion, Fräulein Donat?"

Maisie smiled and shook her head. "My father is not a religious man, sir. He is a man of science. My mother liked to go to church at Christmas, Easter, and for christenings and weddings. So no, I do not have a religion. It was never our way."

The man nodded and crooked a finger toward the officer who had brought her into his office. There was some muttering between them.

"The release of your father has been agreed between the Führer and your government. It remains only for me to ask a few questions and to confirm your identity." He held out the passport and dropped it on the desk before her.

Maisie reached for the passport and placed it in her bag. She could barely conceal a sigh of relief. "I am anxious to see my father, sir."

The man lifted a large metal stamp and brought it down four times, once on each document. The resounding thumps reverberated across the desk.

"You will have to wait, Fräulein Donat. Present yourself here on—" He flicked a daily calendar on his desk. "Present yourself here the day after tomorrow, on March the tenth. At the same time. Ten o'clock. You will be given papers, and you must go straight to Dachau to take possession of your father. Your consulate must provide transport to Dachau and then to the station, and your departure from Munich will be immediate. Is that clear?"

"Yes, that is perfectly clear, sir."

"And what will you do in our fine city? You have almost two days to enjoy our hospitality."

"Mr. Leslie, from the consulate, has told me that I should not miss the Residenz, and I would also like to visit a few museums. However, as you can imagine, I am very anxious to see my father, so it will be hard to concentrate on other things."

The man placed his knuckles on the desk, pushed back his chair, and stood up. He was not as old as Maisie had first thought, perhaps in his mid-thirties, his black hair oiled and combed back. As he held out his hand to her, she noticed how unlined it was—the hand of someone who had been coddled, who was not a worker. His nails were manicured, and when their fingers touched, she thought it was almost like touching the hand of another woman. There was something about that softness that gave her pause. She wondered if his heart had hardened in compensation.

CHAPTER 7

Leslie was waiting outside, along the street well away from the guard, who appeared to have been keeping an eye on him, looking over his shoulder as he marched back and forth. The man came to attention and gave a short bow as Maisie passed, inclining her head in acknowledgment. Leslie joined her, though they did not speak until they had turned the corner, beginning their walk back along the route they had taken to the Nazi headquarters.

"What did they say?" asked Leslie. "Did they give you a day to claim your father?"

Maisie smarted at the word *claim*. It was as if Leon Donat were a coat discarded as one entered the theater, left with the girl who waited at the cloakroom. Perhaps she should expect to press a few pfennigs into the hand of each guard when she reached Dachau, a thank-you for taking care of the man she would call "Papa" until they reached the seclusion of the train to Paris.

"They said the papers would be ready on Thursday, and they bid me an enjoyable time in Munich."

"Longer to wait than I hoped. And not good."

"Why?" asked Maisie. "It seems we expected a delay of a day at least—that some sort of game-playing might be on the cards."

Leslie clapped his hands together as if to beat the cold from his fingertips. "Yes, we did—but I had hoped for it to be quicker, especially now."

"What's happened? Is something wrong?"

"I'm not sure, though I believe I'll find out when I get back to the consulate. There was a bit of a buzz as I left, and I heard someone mention Austria. I think something new has come up with Austria, and you never know with this lot—they might have all sorts of clampdowns just because something has happened somewhere else. That maniac Hitler—you've no idea where you stand, and it's not as if we haven't been expecting trouble across the border. With any country neighboring Germany, in fact—we're very concerned about Czechoslovakia, and Poland."

Maisie said nothing. She wanted only to reach the next hill she had to climb, complete the ascent, and go home. She had been reflecting upon the circumstances of her recruitment for this mission. What had made her agree? Was it the need to be useful? To do something of worth? She could have said no, and now she was wishing she had. This was not her work. She was an investigator, a private inquiry agent. Yes, she had proved herself in other areas, and Maurice clearly thought she might—in fact, should—be called to service if Huntley saw fit. But now she realized that if she were to work again, it would be her own work. When this assignment was complete, when she had discharged her duties, she would give more thought to what she would do next.

"Miss Donat?"

"I'm sorry—I was miles away. Did you ask me a question?"

"Yes—I just asked if you would like company during the next day or so. What would you like to do in Munich? Despite all appearances, it is a very colorful city, and of course Bavaria is quite lovely."

"I think I will consult my Baedeker, perhaps go for a walk in the English Gardens, visit the Residenz, and then spend most of my time at the hotel. And please don't worry—I can manage on my own from now on."

"I will of course accompany you again to Nazi headquarters to obtain the papers, and then we can go to Dachau from there. I'll have a consular motor car ready for us to proceed directly to the station."

"All right. Then telephone me at the hotel tomorrow evening."

"Are you sure you don't want company tomorrow?"

"Positive. I am used to being on my own in an unfamiliar country."

"Right you are. We started to see women traveling alone or in pairs and small groups a few years ago. I suppose it was to be expected, what with fewer men to go around. I must say, you bachelor girls are all very brave when it comes to just going off on your own."

They had reached the end of the narrow street, taken to avoid saluting Nazi heroes.

"I know my way from here, Mr. Leslie."

"Are you sure you'll be all right?" Leslie looked at his watch.

Maisie smiled. "Oh, yes, I'll manage—I am one of those brave bachelor girls, after all."

Leslie blushed. "I'll be in touch, then."

In her hotel room, Maisie pulled off her coat, threw down her bag, and went straight to the bathroom, where she splashed water on her face, leaning over the sink and holding her hands to her eyes as the face-cloth dripped water back into the sink. She had not known what to expect during the visit to the austere Nazi headquarters that morning, but she knew the tension would not leave her until she was in Paris, Leon Donat at her side. She raised her head and looked in the mirror. It was something she'd found herself doing more in the past months, as if she wanted to see who she had become, to monitor change. She wanted to see if she looked like a widow, whether something in the way she carried herself revealed a woman who had lost a dear husband. Or did she resemble the young woman she had become after the war—one of so many "bachelor girls" who had, perhaps, lost a first love, spinsters for whom there would be no husband or family? She had been one of the lucky ones; her loss had been repaid, and she had loved again. That her husband had been killed and their child stillborn seemed to her a most unfair fate—as if a much-cherished promise had been rescinded, leaving an aching void.

She shook her head, reached for the towel, and made sure her wig was in the correct position. She would be glad to see it consigned to the dustbin as soon as she could divest herself of Edwina Donat. She put on her coat, hat, and gloves once more and checked the time. It was not even one o'clock. She could spend half a day today and much of tomorrow looking for Elaine Otterburn. At that thought she gave a sigh of relief. This was work she knew, even if it was in a different country.

There was one last element of preparation before she made her way back to the reception desk to ask directions to Schwabing. She reached into the leather case, unwrapped a cashmere cardigan with mother-of-pearl buttons, and removed a velvet pouch that looked as if it should contain toiletries. She slipped her hand inside and took out the revolver given to her by MacFarlane. With a deft hand she checked her weapon, used a cloth to remove any dust, and made it ready with ammunition. Running her fingers across the metal one more time, as if she were gentling a racehorse before a gallop, she slipped the Enfield into her bag. She could not have said why she thought she might need the revolver with her on a visit to Schwabing—an artists' enclave of bookstores, cafés, and nightclubs, on the face of it a benign place. But she knew she did not want to venture out without it this afternoon.

The desk clerk took Maisie's Baedeker guide, opened the map inside, and lifted his pencil. "May I?"

"Of course," said Maisie. "I need to know where I'm going."

Flourishing the pencil, the clerk marked the place where Maisie could board a tram and the point at which she should step off. He told her where to walk, and made a note in the margin of his favorite coffeehouse, where he informed her that she could buy a slice of the very best apple strudel. Maisie thanked the man and set off.

As the tram rumbled along the streets to Schwabing, Maisie watched people going about their afternoon—women running errands, children who looked as if they should be in school, and a couple she suspected were tourists, for they held a map and stopped a man in the street. He looked at their map, and pointed in the opposite direction to the one they had been walking. And men in uniform, usually in twos, or groups, receiving the inevitable acknowledgment from passersby, a salute to honor the chancellor.

Soon the conductress tapped her on the shoulder to let her know she had arrived; this was her stop.

"Danke. Guten Tag," said Maisie as she moved toward the door.

The woman lifted her chin as she turned to another passenger to issue a ticket.

Stepping off the tram, Maisie looked up and down the street, taking stock of her surroundings. When the tram had moved off, she glanced across the road. She had no idea where she should start. How would she ever find Elaine Otterburn? The task seemed ridiculous—it was as if she had been asked to go to Chelsea and locate a person. But she had to start somewhere. She scratched her forehead where the wig had chafed her, causing a rash.

Elaine was a woman who liked society. She liked going out, and she liked to be noticed. It was mid-afternoon. Where would such a woman go, if she was not at home? Where might a woman who liked to be the center of attention be found? Maisie began to walk along the street, pondering the question. She suspected Elaine was not a shopper, but would accompany her women friends on an expedition to look at new clothing if it meant a chance of laughter, of company. And of course she might be in a restaurant, or a bar—what did they call them? Beer halls? Maisie wondered if Elaine would go to a beer hall. She realized she could just imagine it. Leslie had described the beer halls to her—they'd been the chosen venue for Adolf Hitler to address the crowd in earlier years. On those occasions, most of his audience had been drinking for some time, and many harbored an opinion about their situation—a job or lack thereof. The man who was now the chancellor took advantage of the situation, his rhetoric mirroring the temper of the times, reflecting the mood of the people and milking it for all it was worth. According to Leslie, Hitler's eyes would almost pop out, sweat would pour from his brow, and spittle would fly as he barked out each syllable. The crowd devoured every word, more inebriated with drink and hyperbole as the minutes passed. "And he goes on for a long time," added Leslie.

Maisie took a photograph of Elaine Otterburn from her bag and prepared to cross the road in the direction of what she thought looked like a very good women's clothing shop. It was next to the café recommended to her on one side, and a gentlemen's tailor on the other. Along the street were other shops—a hardware store, a grocer's, then another store selling general goods. There was a shop selling artists' materials, a bookseller's, another clothing shop, a pub, a restaurant, and another café. She turned around again. From the look of streets close to the shops, it appeared to be a nice area—what Priscilla might call "bohemian," certainly, but not a slum. Not top-drawer, either. It seemed a place that would attract those who liked a bit of color in their days—and nights. She could see a couple of shuttered music halls and a nightclub. Leslie had told her there used to be more, but many had closed down. And there were once a good number of small publishers in the area, selling magazines, broadsheets, opinion papers, books—though most had closed now, and the people who had worked on them had all but ceased to exist. There were, he said, "underground" presses, daily or weekly news and opinion from those opposed to the Nazi regime, published by people who railed against the loss of freedom in the name of keeping the country safe.

As she crossed the road, Maisie felt a whisper of cold air across the nape of her neck—a familiar sensation, where a scar ran just below her occipital bone. A shrapnel fragment had caught her flesh when the casualty clearing station where she was working in France, in 1917, had come under enemy fire. The same attack had almost taken the life of Simon Lynch, her former fiancé. The scar was barely visible now, yet it served her in its way, giving a warning when there was something close that demanded her attention. It was all but calling to her now.

She turned around. A man had stopped to look in the tailor's window before stepping inside, the bell over the door clanging as he entered. Maisie watched as a woman crossed the street behind her; she was walking toward the grocery shop. There were others in the vicinity—it was not a deserted thoroughfare—but nothing she saw explained the sense she had that someone was following her.

Entering the recommended café, Maisie took a seat. When the young waitress approached, she ordered a coffee with hot milk and some apple strudel. She was very hungry. Soon the waitress returned to the table, using the palm of her free hand to smooth out the white embroidered tablecloth. She placed the coffee and strudel on the table and dipped as if to curtsy. Maisie smiled at her and held out the photograph of Elaine Otterburn.

"I wonder, have you seen this woman in your café?" she asked in German. "She is the daughter of one of my oldest friends, and though I know she lives here in this area, I have lost her address. I know I'm hoping for a miracle, but your café is just the sort of place she loves!"

The waitress looked at the photograph, shook her head, and apologized. No, she did not know the woman. Maisie thanked her and continued to enjoy her coffee, which was rich with creamy milk and hot. When she had finished, she gathered up her gloves and bag, left a few pfennigs for the waitress, and made her way back out onto the street.

She moved on to the dress shop. No one had seen Elaine. Then to the grocery shop—which she thought was rather a stretch; she couldn't imagine Elaine cooking anything. But it was here that there was a glimmer of recognition as Maisie paid for an apple and then repeated her story. The man smiled and wiped his hands on his brown apron before taking the photograph, squinting as he studied the image. The abrupt change from helpfulness to a sudden interest in the next customer was almost imperceptible.

"Nein. Ich habe noch nie diese Frau gesehen." *No, I have never seen this woman before.*

Maisie thanked the man, who was already addressing the next customer with a cheery smile. She left the shop, certain that the man had indeed seen Elaine Otterburn. Why had he lied to her? And something else was bothering her. The person waiting behind her, to whom the shopkeeper had turned when he claimed he did not know the woman in the photograph, was the same man she had watched enter the tailor's along the street.

The general store held nothing of interest for her, though she thought she might buy some souvenirs. Purchasing a couple of postcards might not be a bad idea; at least it demonstrated an interest in the local attractions. The bar—a wood-beamed pub—was still a few yards away. Maisie imagined a darkened interior, with brown paneling and gravel-voiced daytime drinkers in corners, furtively caressing a glass of schnapps, or a rowdy crowd ready to move on to another venue for afternoon entertainment. She sighed. Yes, she would have to go in, though she dreaded it. On the other hand, she was well versed in entering dark, dingy places in the interests of gathering information. Still steps away, she heard the volume increase, with even louder laughter, shouting, teasing. The doors of the bar seemed to crash open to more giggling as a motor car came from along the street and pulled up parallel to the open doors. Three officers of the Schutzstaffel emerged from the pub, accompanied by three women. It would seem they were all enjoying the afternoon, each woman dressed in expensive clothing, one with a fur collar, the others with coats draped around their shoulders. High heels clicked along the pavement, and a woman's laughter punctuated the air, like champagne bubbles rising in a fluted glass.

Maisie stepped back into the shadows of the encroaching dusk and watched the partygoers clamber into the motor car and the vehicle draw away from the curb. She turned away and began to walk back toward the place where she would board the tram bound for Marienplatz. It was as she approached the grocery store that she noticed the shopkeeper standing on the threshold. They exchanged glances, and he nodded. Now she knew where he had seen Elaine Otterburn, and why he'd denied any knowledge of her or her whereabouts. Maisie would have recognized that laugh anywhere. It was Elaine Otterburn who had left the bar on the arm of an officer of the feared SS.

Maisie remembered once, a long time ago, attending one of the Otterburns' parties at their Park Lane mansion. Elaine had skipped over to Priscilla, Douglas, James, and Maisie, champagne glass in hand, her dress clinging to her narrow frame, her hair a pixie cap of curls, her eyes wide with the knowledge that she was noticed. "Lucky, lucky lady," she'd said, teasing Maisie as she linked her arm through James' as if to draw him to her. Priscilla had raised an eyebrow as Elaine laughed, released James' arm, and moved away toward a clutch of young men clamoring for her attention.

"If I were you, Maisie, I'd watch that one," Priscilla had said.

Darkness had fallen by the time Maisie reached the tram stop close to Marienplatz. She made her way across the square, past the glockenspiel, looking for the route back toward the Residenz and her hotel. After a few minutes, she suspected she might have taken a wrong path. The pedestrians had thinned out, and she felt quite alone. She hurried her step, and felt her heartbeat quicken when she heard the echo of her own footfall. The scar at her neck was throbbing a warning. She ducked into a doorway, pressing a hand to her chest to still her breath. The footsteps came closer and then slowed. Whoever had been behind her was just one step ahead now. She slipped off her gloves, feeling the chill air on her fingertips. Pulling the revolver from its hiding place in her handbag, she took hold of the grip, stepped from the doorway, and held the gun to the neck of the man who had halted, as if wondering where his quarry was hidden.

"Wer bist du? Warum hast du mich verfolgt?" Maisie whispered close to the man's ear. *Who are you? Why have you followed me?* Now she knew her suspicions were well founded; she was sure it was the man who had first walked into the tailor's shop in Schwabing, and then to the grocery store.

The man answered in English, and with a distinct American accent.

"Mark Scott. United States Department of Justice, ma'am. Or should I say Fräulein D? That would cover both of you."

"I would like to see a means of identification. And move forward two paces."

As the man flapped back an olive-green overcoat to reach the inside pocket of his jacket, Maisie stepped around to face him.

"No." Maisie aimed her weapon at his heart. "Keep your hands out of the way." She reached into his pocket, removed a wallet, and stepped back to take advantage of the light from a window above. She flicked open the wallet with her left hand, aware of the man's every movement. "And please do not try anything, because—believe it or not—I can use this thing, and I have it on authority that I am not a bad shot. Mind you, anyone could be a good shot at this distance."

She checked the identification. Mark Scott. US Consulate General.

"Trust me?" said Scott.

Maisie shook her head. "No. I don't. For a start, it says here that you're with the Consulate. But I do want to know why you're here and why you've followed me." She gestured back toward the Marienplatz. "There's a busy pub sort of place back there. Walk alongside me—and remember, you are still at the end of my revolver."

She let down her guard a little when they entered the pub and found a table. The revolver was consigned to her pocket, though she kept her hand on the grip.

"Now you can tell me what you think you're doing, Mr. Scott—if that's your real name."

"I may have to shout."

"I'll lip-read if necessary. What do you want with me?"

Mark Scott raised his chin in warning as a waiter approached their table. He ordered beers for both himself and Maisie. Not until the waiter was halfway back to the bar, and then only after he had surveyed their immediate area, did he turn back to Maisie. "We want to make sure Leon Donat gets out of this country alive, though of course he might not be exactly fine and dandy, given where he's been. You are his ticket; you have his release papers—or you will have them the day after tomorrow. It is in the interests of the government of the United States of America that Mr. Donat reaches Great Britain in a timely manner. We don't want anything to go wrong."

"What has America got to do with this?"

Mark Scott grinned. "Let's just say we have a soft spot for your boffins."

CHAPTER 8

Mark Scott stopped a few steps from the entrance to the Hotel Vier Jahreszeiten. He turned to Maisie and tipped his hat. "Don't worry, I'm on your side, *Fräulein Donat*. I've got your six." He pronounced her assumed name in perfect German, and with a knowing smile.

"And what exactly is my six, Mr. Scott?"

"Sorry about that—I thought you would have heard the saying before. I was an aviator in the war. When you see your pal going in to take on the enemy, you let him know you're right there, looking after him from the back. That's having his six. You know, it's like a clock—twelve is right out there in front, three has the starboard, nine the port, and six brings it up from the rear. You want someone back there at your six when you're going in, so the bastards can't come up and take out your tail."

"Oh, I see." Maisie nodded, smiling. "Right you are then, Mr. Scott. I daresay I might see you again, if I look over my shoulder toward the six."

"You can count on it, ma'am. You can count on it." Scott touched a finger to the brim of his hat and walked away into the night.

Maisie was sure he was who he claimed to be—and that meant Leon Donat was a far more valuable man than she had been led to believe. But then, he would be. Why else would the British government go to such great lengths to get him back onto home soil? And if the German authorities knew how important he was—over and above having so-called friends in high places—would they renege on the deal to release him? Maisie looked around, wondering if anyone else was following her or had seen her in the pub. She could not help but wonder whether she had made a wrong move in apprehending Mark Scott.

Inside the hotel, Maisie bid the porter good evening and collected her key from the desk clerk. She went to her room and closed the door. In approximately thirty-six hours she would be able to claim Leon Donat from Dachau. One more full day in Munich to entertain herself—and perhaps to engineer an encounter with Elaine Otterburn. Was that wise? She weighed up the odds, then remembered the "little man" brought down to meet her, and how it felt when Lorraine Otterburn held out her grandson for Maisie to hold, to take him in her arms. She knew it was a deliberate ploy; the soft vulnerability of a child abandoned by his mother seemed to cling to her long after she had left the Otterburn mansion. And it had worked, strengthening her resolve to find Elaine Otterburn and talk some sense into her.

She also gave thought to the machinations at play in the arrest and incarceration of Leon Donat. How had the Nazis known where to find him, and who had tipped them off? What stood in the way of him proving his innocence? And was there room for doubt? She tried to put the thoughts aside. Her task was clear: bring Leon Donat home to England. It was not her place to question him.

Having breakfasted in the hotel dining room, Maisie once again dressed for a chilly but bright day and set off to board the tram that would take her in the direction of Schwabing. This time she really would be a tourist, first detouring to walk around Marienplatz, admiring the glockenspiel, and looking into shops at will. She wondered if Mark Scott would once more be in the shadows, monitoring her every move.

After a night's respite, she was once more wearing the wig, and a plain brown hat with a black grosgrain ribbon band. She was dressed in her austere navy-blue jacket and skirt and strong brown walking shoes. Quite deliberately she omitted to leave her key at the reception desk, thankful for a clutch of tourists surrounding the clerks as she made her way out of the hotel onto the street. Within another fifteen minutes she was in the center of Marienplatz. In another time— perhaps just a few years ago—this place might have been so different. Yes, there were people rushing back and forth—mothers with children, people running errands, going into shops—but she felt a certain tension in the air. She suspected that the locals might not have the same experience; the atmosphere had changed at a gradual pace, and she knew people would accommodate even the most troubling situations to avoid recognizing an oppressive development. "It's not so bad," or "It will pass," they might say, and cling to the ways life had not altered—but for some, there would be a call to arms. She knew from experience that many of the more vulnerable, those who knew themselves to be most at risk, had already left Germany. Those who remained believed they were safe because they were German. And she could see why—especially on a beautiful day—they would be loath to leave Bavaria. Tourists came at all times of year. British girls from wealthy families, women younger than Elaine Otterburn, trav-

eled to Bavaria to attend finishing schools and enjoy a year of freedom before a husband was to be found and life as a society matron
loomed. Perhaps that was one of Elaine's problems. She could not
leave her girlhood behind; the responsibilities of marriage were too
much to bear.

Maisie left the tram at exactly the same place as before, and made
her way to the pub where she had seen Elaine Otterburn emerging
from the shadowy, smoke-filled interior, her hand draped like fabric
across an SS officer's arm. As she approached the pub, she heard bolts
being pulled back inside, and a curse from a man with a gruff voice.
She stopped just in time to avoid the bucketful of water thrown out as
the doors bounced back on their hinges. Another curse ensued, and a
stocky man with a bald head emerged, a cigarette hanging from a thick
lower lip, his eyes like those of a bloodhound. His apron was coming
loose, and he tried to prop a broom against the wall as he struggled
with the ties below his girth. Satisfied, he cursed again and took up his
broom to sweep the soiled water into the street. Maisie wondered how
wise it would be to approach him. Yet time was not on her side, and
this man could well have the information she wanted.

"Entschuldigen Sie, bitte." Maisie smiled as she approached, squar-
ing her shoulders and walking with an obvious sense of purpose. She
did not want to appear apologetic, or in any way weak.

"Was wollen Sie, gnädige Frau?" The man squinted through reddened hungover eyes.

Maisie's German was feeling more fluid now, as she continued to
converse with the man in his native language. "Sir, I am looking for an
old friend of mine—I lost touch with her, but I believe she is living in
Schwabing." Maisie indicated the inside of the pub. "She loves a good
party, if you know what I mean. . . ."

The man gave a grudging smile, as if he wished he had avoided the last party.

"And this is just the sort of place she would enjoy." Maisie leaned closer, as if bringing the man into her confidence. "She's a bit wild, you know." She swallowed as the man's fetid breath sullied the air between them, but smiled encouragingly as she reached into her bag for the photograph of Elaine Otterburn. "Have you seen her?"

The man continued to squint, then raised his hand and pulled down the skin under his eyes with thumb and forefinger, as if to widen the aperture through which he could view the subject.

"Ah. Ha ha!" He gave a knowing deep chortle. "Yes, she likes a good time."

"Do you know where she lives? I am very anxious to see her."

The man cast his gaze toward Maisie and narrowed his eyes as if to focus again, this time to assess her attire.

"You must have been friends a long time ago," he said.

She shrugged. "Yes, it was. We are very different, which is why we were able to be good friends." She wondered if the lie would work.

"Yes, I can see that. She needs a sensible friend."

"Do you know where I can find her?" Maisie pressed.

The man nodded. He held up a finger and rested his broom against the door frame. "Wait here."

Maisie remained on the street outside the pub, moving a few steps so it might seem as if she were window-shopping in front of an adjacent store. Still, passersby took second glances at her, as if wondering what a good woman was doing outside a destination for the committed drinker.

The landlord emerged, clutching a piece of paper. "Here you are. This is where you will find her."

Maisie took the small sheet of paper and then looked back at the man. The red rims of his lower eyelids appeared to be sinking toward his cheekbones. "How do you know her address?"

"I did not say it was her address, madam. I said it was where you would find her."

Maisie nodded. She asked the landlord for directions, and he indicated with one hand that she should follow the street, take a third left and a first right, then another left and right. She thanked him, wished him a good day, and went on her way, knowing she would have to stop another pedestrian at some point to ask for fresh instructions. Though she did not look back, she knew the landlord was watching her as she stepped out along the pavement, her body braced against the cold air.

S ome forty-five minutes later, Maisie stood across the street from what appeared to be a plain apartment building, almost severe in its design. She had read about the very plain, simple architectural style that had become fashionable in Germany, a trend which celebrated the union of form and function, akin to other artistic movements in Europe wherein ornamentation was set aside in favor of strength and purpose. This modern sensibility was reflected in the property she'd bought in Pimlico, where Sandra now resided. The flat had been new when she'd purchased it some years earlier, yet the way its glass reflected light on even the most overcast day gave the building a warmth. The overall impression was of a stately ship on the sea, not the square box of a government office.

She thought back to the landlord's comment. *It is where you will find her.* But who lived in this building? She crossed the street. The door was locked, so she cupped her hands around her eyes to look through the metal-framed glass door. Two men stood at the back of an expansive entrance hall, as if they had just reached the bottom of the staircase and were finishing their conversation. She had seen those distinctive black uniforms before, when she presented her papers to support the release of Leon Donat. Before they could turn toward her, she crossed the street to gaze into the window of a shoe shop. In the window's reflection, she saw a black motor car draw up alongside the building, and the men left the entrance hall and climbed aboard. Maisie would have to wait. She walked up and down, stamping her feet to keep warm. She hoped she would not have to linger very long, and attract unwanted attention. She watched as more men left the building, in pairs and individually, sometimes on foot but more often in vehicles. She was about to give up when a younger man pushed open the door, looking both ways and across the street.

Maisie picked up her heel as if to remove a smut from her stocking. The man took no notice of her, but Maisie was in time to see him gesture with his hand, as if to say "Hurry." Elaine Otterburn ran down the steps, dressed in clothing more suited to a night out on the town. She pulled the officer toward her as if to kiss him, but he drew back. He hailed a taxi, took Elaine by the arm, and all but pushed her in. Instead of joining her, he closed the door and turned back into the building. The taxi set off, but at a slow pace. Maisie was wondering how on earth she would corner Elaine Otterburn when she saw the taxi draw to a halt to allow a line of schoolchildren, holding hands and walking in pairs, snake their way across the road. She ran toward the taxi. It would be her only chance, she knew, to talk to Elaine.

Maisie had not seen John Otterburn's daughter since that fateful morning when Elaine had failed to report for her promised duty at an airfield in Canada, ready to fly an experimental aircraft. Now Maisie would have to face the woman she blamed for her husband's death—and do her best to bring her home. She felt her knees weaken as she slowed to a walk. The line of children was almost across the street, but one of them tripped over his untied shoelaces and crashed to the ground, crying out in pain. Maisie watched as the passenger door of the taxi was flung open, and Elaine Otterburn clambered out to go to the child's aid, kneeling on the ground to press a white handkerchief to a scraped knee. Maisie was close enough to hear her now as she soothed the boy, her arm around his shoulders.

"Weine nicht, Kleine. Weine nicht. Lass mich dir helfen, mit meiner magie Taschentuch." *Don't cry, little one. Don't cry. Let me help you with my magic handkerchief.*

Maisie was almost alongside the taxi now. A teacher approached and scolded the child for holding up the line, throwing Elaine Otterburn a look that Maisie thought would wither a rose still in bud. She handed back the handkerchief with a curt word of thanks before hauling the child off by the arm. Elaine turned, tears in her eyes. As she stepped back into the taxicab, Maisie gripped the handle of the opposite passenger door, opened it, and stepped in. Elaine was about to scream when she realized who was sitting next to her.

"Let's go to your flat, Elaine," said Maisie. "I've come to talk to you about going home."

Elaine Otterburn shook her head, as if trying to disguise her shock at seeing Maisie. "I can't go home, and you have no business asking me. You don't understand."

"Then you're going to have to do your best to explain."

Maisie looked at Elaine Otterburn's hands clutching the blood-stained handkerchief, and a welter of conflicting emotions washed over her. What words of advice would Maurice give her? She knew that he would urge compassion. *May I know what it is to feel the weight on another's shoulders. May I know forgiveness in my heart. May I be given strength to extend my hand across the divide to pull another from the abyss, though that person has wounded me.* Maisie knew the abyss; she knew what it was to walk the perimeter of darkness. Though she could never have predicted that she would do such a thing, she reached out and took Elaine Otterburn's hand, and feeling the younger woman clasp hers in return.

"You don't know what you're getting into, Maisie. This is not what it seems. I am not what I seem." Elaine turned to her with kohl-stained eyes. "Believe me, you should not have come."

I am not what I seem. In the months following her husband's death and the loss of her unborn child, Maisie had felt in limbo. It was as if, having been denied a place in heaven alongside her fledgling family, there would be no place for her on earth, no comfort, and nowhere to rest. She went first to America, staying at the home of a friend from the war years, Dr. Charles Hayden, his wife, Pauline, and their two daughters. The family had welcomed her; Hayden, especially, understood that Maisie had suffered a deep psychological shock. But in time she left, making her way back to India, to the place where she had found a measure of solace, of peace and hope years before—to the place where she had at last decided to accept James' proposal of marriage.

There were those who wanted to know what had happened in the time between leaving America and taking up residence in a bungalow amid the tea gardens of an estate in Darjeeling. It was as if her family, her husband's family, and her friend Priscilla needed to color the blank spaces in their knowledge of her. But she had nothing to tell them; in her grief, she was between worlds. She could not even remember ports along the way, or the exact route she'd traveled. It was now a blur. She had engaged in conversations—none lengthy, and all in the interests of maintaining politeness—eaten meals, leafed through newspapers and books; she had even written letters. Yet none of this could she

remember. Then it was time to come home, summoned by her stepmother, who was concerned about the effects of Maisie's absence on
her aging father. But as she neared England fear had encroached upon
Maisie's soul, and she realized she was not ready to face the places
where she and James had courted, where they had become friends first
and then lovers. Both of their homes held cherished memories—of
laughter, of companionable moments, of passion and plans. And she
knew that others would want to tell her stories about James; of his boy-
hood and growing years, his struggle to leave the war behind, his success as a man of commerce. Each memory and every story would feel
like a knife through her heart—for James was gone, and she was alone.

Once she had disembarked in Gibraltar, a chain of events led her
to cross the border into Spain. It was there that she began to be whole
again, using her skills as a nurse at an aid station set up by a nun who
had remained behind in her convent to minister to wounded warriors
fighting Franco's regime. And it was in delivering a child—a girl—
that Maisie realized that she could, if she tried, perhaps be reborn herself. The sharp waves of immediate grief had begun to diminish, like
a slow ebbing of the tide. They were not entirely gone; sometimes the
seas of pain would crash against her heart again, and she would feel
her resolve weaken.

In the months following James' death, one thought had returned
time and again as she passed others in the street. What secrets did
these people hold? What had they endured? She wondered how many
people rushing in and out of shops, or on their way to their work, had
lost a love, or known deep disappointment or grief, fear, or want, yet
summoned the resilience to go on. Those lines across foreheads, those
mouths downturned—what were the ruts on life's road that wrought
such marks, those signs of scars on the soul? She knew she might have
seemed like any other woman of a certain type—well dressed, hair in

place, shoes polished and turned out nicely—but inside it was as if she were being eaten away. She had been in the deep darkness of the abyss, then, and she was lost, even to herself.

Now, with Elaine Otterburn clutching her hand, she thought of those months and years, and then of the job that had led her to Munich—and the words came to her again. *I am not what I seem.*

The taxicab stopped in the middle of a quiet, narrow street of older houses, each one neatly kempt, with fresh paint and clean windows. Some had empty window boxes, waiting for a spring when they would be filled with seeds and then blooms. But it was still a city street, not a country byway. In the distance Maisie could hear the throb of traffic, though there was a middle-of-the-day laziness in the air.

Elaine opened the passenger door and stepped out onto the pavement, followed by Maisie. She leaned into the window of the taxicab, exchanged words with the driver, and handed him a few coins. Then she smiled, stood back, and waved before delving into her bag for a set of keys with which she opened the front door of a house no different from any of the others, beckoning to Maisie to follow while holding a finger to her lips. As they climbed the staircase in front of them, Maisie heard a shuffling from the door to her right, which she thought might be the entrance to the landlady's rooms. Elaine took each step on tiptoe, careful not to make a sound.

Reaching the second floor, Elaine pressed a key into the lock of another door and pointed out two doors to her right and one to her left. "Kitty, Pamela, Nell. All English gels, don't you know!" She put on an aristocratic tone, opened the door, and beckoned Maisie to enter, adding, "And all doing very nicely, thank you—plus having a jolly good time into the bargain."

Elaine moved a pile of clothing from a chair to the bed, and pulled another away from a small writing table. Maisie sat down as Elaine threw her coat over a screen to the left of the window, where it joined a silk dress with a long tear in the skirt. A needle and thread were hanging from the fabric, as if Elaine had started to mend the dress herself but became bored, or didn't quite know how to complete the task.

"My entire wardrobe is behind that screen—well, when it isn't on a chair," said Elaine. "Our kitchen is just along the landing. Tea? We both need some fortification, and I have a thumper of a headache."

"Thank you, that would be lovely."

Elaine left the room. Maisie could hear clattering from along the landing, and wondered if Elaine had ever made tea before coming to Munich. The more she thought about Elaine Otterburn, the more she suspected that the young woman experienced something of her own sense of isolation at times.

Elaine had grown up on both sides of the Atlantic. Her clipped English pronunciation sometimes gave way to longer vowels that caused aristocratic matrons to look twice and wonder how the girl ever came out into respectable society. But no experience had been denied either of the younger Otterburns, though it was Elaine who garnered most attention, rather than her somewhat more reserved brother.

"There. As the British might say, 'A nice cup of tea, my dear.' " Elaine entered, carrying two cups of tea. No tray. No biscuits. Not even saucers. Just cups of tea. "Those ancient Britons probably put a kettle on the log fire to boil the moment they saw the Romans coming at them across the Channel—eh? I can imagine them saying, 'Never mind the bloody invasion, let's have a cuppa!' "

Maisie smiled and took one of the cups with both hands. "I daresay you're right there, Elaine."

Elaine brushed another pile of clothing from a straight-backed chair onto the floor and sat down, placing her cup on a side table. "We have ourselves a conundrum, don't we, Maisie?" She reached for a packet of cigarettes and a silver lighter, which had been left on top of a dressing table, its drawers open and silk underwear spilling out. She tapped out a cigarette, opened and clicked the lighter to hold the flame close to the tobacco, and drew on the cigarette while closing the lighter. "I didn't offer—you don't smoke, do you?"

Maisie remembered the last cigarette she'd smoked, in Gibraltar before crossing the border into Spain. She had been new to the habit, which gave her something to do with her shaking hands.

"Not anymore, no, Elaine. I don't—"

"Look, cards on the table," Elaine interrupted. "You are here to persuade me to go home, to take up the reins of wifedom and motherhood. I am sure you have other things to do here—I suspect you would not have come to Munich just to see if you could drag me back."

"I have business, yes. And I promised your parents that I would try to find you."

"Really? Well, that's interesting, because my father could find me at the drop of his hat if he wanted. They probably thought sending you would do the trick—a sensible woman to escort the wayward child home."

Maisie wondered where the Elaine in the taxi had gone. It was as if, while making tea, someone else had emerged and taken over from the vulnerable person who had clutched her hand as if ready to confess her sins.

"What's so much more important than your son, Elaine?"

Elaine's eyes filled with tears. She brushed a hand across her cheek and looked away. "I'm not exactly maternal material, am I, Maisie? Let's be honest, now—he's much better off with Mother than with me. Certainly I knew my husband's people would not want him—*yet*.

When he comes of age, doubtless they'll have a sudden need to initiate him into the tweedy ways of his forefathers. With a bit of luck he'll have no patience with that sort of thing, and will have made something of himself. If he's under my father's roof, he'll be an Otterburn through and through. He'll probably even like modern art acquired at great expense!"

"To your point about motherhood, Elaine—frankly, I think you owe it to your son to try a bit harder. If you can't stand the wilds of Northamptonshire, then move in with your parents or get a flat for yourself and your son, and a nanny if you want to continue to be at large in society." Maisie came to her feet. "I don't think you've been completely honest with me, Elaine, but frankly, I don't have the time to sit here trying to persuade you to do something against your will. I've done what I gave my word I would do—which was find you and speak to you. Now I have to leave." Maisie began to turn away, then looked back. "Oh, and if by any slight chance you see me again in the next day or so, on no account must you recognize me or show any sign of familiarity. You must not use my name. If you must communicate, a simple 'Fräulein' will do."

Elaine shrugged. "Well, seeing as James' death—"

Maisie's movement was quick. She stood in front of Elaine and looked down at the still-seated woman, who had frozen while reaching to extinguish her cigarette in the ashtray. "Do not ever, ever speak of my husband in my presence again. Don't you dare say his name in front of me. And you know why."

Elaine Otterburn's face registered shock, the half smile at the corner of her lips quivering. In that second, Maisie wondered if anyone had ever countered this young woman in her entire life. Stepping over the discarded clothing, she reached the door, then looked back. Elaine reminded her of a Greek statue, her silky evening dress clinging to her body. "Do you know something, Elaine? Do you know what makes me sick about people like you? If an inspector walked into an ordinary worker's house anywhere in London and saw this kind of state, he would make a report to the authorities. But for some reason, the wealthier a person, the more they can get away with living in a filthy heap. Pick up your belongings, Elaine, tidy this place—and perhaps you'll find it easier to pick yourself up from whatever mess you've found yourself in."

Maisie passed two of the "gels" on the stairs, rushing past her, laughing, calling out Elaine's name. They had not offered even a simple "Guten Tag."

She had done what was requested of her. She had located Elaine Otterburn, and she had asked her to return to her son. And she had also lost her temper. But other thoughts came to mind, not least her own final comment to Elaine. Yes, something was not at all right with Elaine. In the taxi it had seemed as if the woman had been ready to reveal a confidence, of that Maisie was sure. Was it about a love affair with the German officer? Was it connected to the reason for her flight from England, her son, and her husband? Or was she really in such a state that everything—from the smudged kohl around her eyes to the clothing, shoes, and wine glasses littering her flat—gave away her predicament?

Having made a note of the exact address, and the number scratched at the center of the dial on a telephone on the table in the hallway, Maisie left the building, setting off toward the main street, where she would ask a passerby how to get back to Marienplatz. Soon she was on a tram, the conductor having promised to tell her where to disembark. As she sat by the window, looking out at people once again, it occurred to her that even in girlhood she had watched people, paid attention to them in a way that perhaps others didn't. Long before James and the child had been lost to her, she had asked herself questions about people, even those she saw on the street, though she suspected her sensitivity to that which ailed other human beings was established after the war, when everyone had sacrificed so much. Maurice had always maintained that not only did individuals reveal the secrets of their inner thoughts and feelings in their everyday demeanor, but the mood of a mass of people was just as evident. Now, in the midst of a journey during which she did not stand out in any way from other passengers on the tram, Maisie knew there was a cloud across this city and that it bore down on its residents. Yes, there was still fun to be had, restaurants to enjoy, and parks to walk on a fine day. But a veil of oppression was seeping into every crevice of life. *I am not what I seem.* Perhaps that was a cry from Munich itself—yet Elaine Otterburn had spoken those words in what Maisie suspected was an honest confession. And if Elaine was not the dilettante runaway daughter of a wealthy man, a woman who had abandoned her firstborn—then who was she?

CHAPTER 9

Having spent the evening alone, once again choosing to have supper delivered to her room rather than eating in the restaurant, Maisie had fallen into a deep sleep, waking at half past seven. She'd not been besieged by nightmares or slipped into the mystery of her dreams. Before drawing back the covers and taking to bed, she'd meditated on the coming day, allowing her mind to be still and trusting that all would be well. Now, upon opening her eyes, for a moment resting her gaze on the vertical line of light where the curtains met, she knew that by this evening, if the carefully laid plans held, she would be on board a train for Paris, Leon Donat as her companion. She would tell him nothing of note before they crossed the border into France, and even then she would not feel safe until they were met in the French capital. She thought about Donat. It occurred to her that he might never be safe again. He was a wanted man—the British wanted everything that was in his mind. Every new machine he'd ever created with his clever engineer's brain would have to be drawn again, and then scrutinized against the needs of a country expecting to go to war.

But who were those people, the ones who thought war was inevitable? The populace believed their leaders would maintain a hard-won peace. She had meditated on that peace, had drawn a picture in her mind of claiming Leon Donat, of an easy journey to the station, and then to the train and freedom—for both of them. If they were intercepted, if her true identity was revealed, both she and Donat were as good as dead. And though once, after the death of James Compton, she would have welcomed that release, whatever the pain involved, now she wanted very much to live. It was a welcome revelation.

Readying herself for the day ahead, Maisie once again dressed in clothing that marked her as an unimaginative woman, one with no interest in the latest styles—which was not far from the truth. A dark burgundy jacket, a matching dress, the almost mannish walking shoes, and a black hat and tweed coat. Gilbert Leslie would be waiting in the hotel lobby, no doubt pacing back and forth. Mind you, this was an occasion to feel unsettled, though Maisie hoped Leslie would endeavor to act the part of a man with no undue concerns about the outcome of his day. Together they would walk to the same building, avoiding the same square so they would not have to offer a Nazi salute on their way. And in that cold building, she expected to wait for the documentation pertaining to Leon Donat's release, before they could depart for Dachau.

But she was wrong on two counts. When she entered the hotel lobby, stopping to pull on her gloves and already cursing the wig that scratched at her hairline, Leslie was pacing, as she predicted. But when she reached his side, he informed her that they would not be walking; a motor car from the consular service would convey them to the headquarters of the Nazi Party. He reminded her that the German officer had stipulated a British consular vehicle should be used to transport Leon Donat from Dachau.

"It's all been organized, Miss Donat. As soon as you have the authorization to claim your father, we will go immediately to the prison to present our papers, and then to the station, and you will be on your way."

Maisie nodded. "I have my luggage packed and ready here, Mr. Leslie."

"All right, then. We're off." He picked up the small case and extended his hand toward the door. "Shall we? Let's get this over and done with."

The second unexpected deviation from the plan was the presence of Mark Scott. As Maisie and Gilbert Leslie stepped out into the crisp, bright morning, Scott was standing to the side of the entrance, chatting to a porter. Both men were laughing, perhaps at a joke told by Scott, and though the American showed no interest in Maisie, he held out his hand to clasp that of the porter, said a few words, and offered a wave as he stepped into a waiting taxi. Leslie had shown no sign of recognizing Scott as he held open the door of a black consular vehicle for Maisie, but after he'd joined her, slammed the door, and tapped the glass partition between themselves and their driver, he looked over his shoulder out the back window and cursed.

"Those Yanks don't know when to leave well enough alone!" he said, almost under his breath, though Maisie heard every word.

For her part, she chose not to acknowledge Leslie's comment. As far as she was concerned, a little attention from Scott might mean the difference between success and failure. He was another person on her side—she hoped.

Once again Maisie showed her identification papers to the guard outside the Nazi headquarters, and once again she was escorted into the cold entrance hall and up the staircase flanked by dark wooden banisters. She almost feared to place her hand on the rail, imagining that another hand would clamp down upon hers and keep her from leaving this building. The very air seemed oppressive.

She was ushered into the same room as before to meet the SS officer who had interviewed her during her previous visit. The conversation was conducted in English. Maisie gave no indication that she understood anything the officer and his underling said to each other in German, but from their words, she knew they would not allow her to take Leon Donat from Dachau that day.

"Now, Miss Donat. Let me see. Yes, the paperwork is in order. Good. Yes." The man flapped pages back and forth, as if to unsettle her.

"That's wonderful," said Maisie, smiling. "I am so very anxious to see my father."

"Of course. But there are procedures to go through." He waved his hand, as if such procedures were like a fly to be swatted away.

"Procedures? May I inquire as to the nature of these procedures?"

The man seemed to glare for a second, and then smiled—a broad smile, a fake smile, a smile that Maisie thought she might see in a children's book, on the face of a Fagin or a Magwitch. Even the devil himself.

"Those procedures are not your business, Fräulein Donat. Now, I am a busy man." He pushed back his chair. "Especially today. Yes, it is a busy time." He gave another sudden, unsettling smile.

Maisie came to her feet. "I would like your confirmation again that everything is in order. Am I assured my father will be released to me?" She looked from the officer to the man she assumed was his junior.

"You may return tomorrow morning, at the same time. You will have your father's release papers then. Now, as I said, I am a busy man. It is likely you will see another officer tomorrow, as I am honored to be joining the Führer on an important journey." A split second elapsed before he raised his arm in salute. "Heil Hitler!"

The junior officer repeated the salute, shouting, "Heil Hitler!"

Maisie felt the bile rise in her throat as she closed her eyes and lifted her hand only as far as she needed to effect a response. "Heil Hitler," she said, without raising her voice. And in that moment, the deeper sense of cold that had enveloped her from the moment she entered the building almost overwhelmed her. She clenched her stomach to stop shivering, and a fingernail scratch of pain across her neck began to torment her. It was as if the very air in the room had changed, and she fought to retain her bearing in front of the German officers.

She lowered her hand and nodded, but the men remained at attention. Only when she turned did she realize that Adolf Hitler had entered the room and was walking toward the desk. He waved a hand as if to dismiss her and began speaking to the officer in a clipped, staccato tone. Maisie did not linger. Another official, stationed by the door, had beckoned to her, and she left the room with as much speed as she could without appearing respectful.

Leslie was waiting outside. "Did you get the release?"

Maisie shook her head. "No. He told me I had to wait until tomorrow, due to administration, or something like that." She hated herself for sounding so absentminded. She had been distracted by the entrance of the Führer, she realized—and she wasn't the only one. The two officers had appeared intimidated at the arrival of their leader. "I won't be seeing the same officer—he's embarking on a journey with the Führer, or so he said."

Leslie shook his head. "I'll have the time for your next meeting confirmed through official consular channels. Not to worry—it's just like these people to make us run around a bit. I'll take you back to your hotel."

"Thank you," said Maisie.

Nothing was said during the short journey back to the Hotel Vier Jahreszeiten, but just before the motor car cruised to a stop alongside the hotel, Leslie turned to Maisie.

"Look, Miss Donat, if you want to do something interesting this afternoon, pay a visit to the Residenz. It's worth looking at and might take your mind off things. I am sure everything will be all right—this has all been approved at the highest level, and the Germans aren't going to pull out now. It's just the boys in uniforms throwing a bit of weight around. Your father will be out tomorrow, I'm sure of it."

"I wish I felt as confident as you, Mr. Leslie, really I do. But I will wait to hear from you—and yes, I will go to the Residenz. It's just along the road, so not exactly an expedition. Thank you."

Maisie stepped out of the motor car and watched as it moved away from the curb, out into the light midday traffic. She turned just in time to see another motor car, a taxicab, pull up behind Leslie's vehicle. Mark Scott was following the man from the British consulate. She stood for a moment wondering why the American was following Leslie. Or was he? Perhaps he'd simply tailed them back to the hotel, seen her step from the motor car, and now his work was done. She sighed, but the sighting remained on her mind, nagging her. It was almost a physical feeling, as if a friend kept nudging an elbow into her side to draw her attention to something. She could not brush the insistent jab away.

Maisie had never been one to play the tourist. She preferred to merge with the locals, if she could, not to draw attention to herself with a camera, notebook, or sketching paper, though she might have a map in her bag. In the cities she'd visited since leaving England almost four years earlier, she would wander the streets, slipping along little-used paths and byways, stopping for a drink or a bite to eat at a place where only those who lived in the area might linger. It was as if she were walking into the vanishing point, a place where she might never be seen or found again.

But since arriving in Munich, Maisie understood that there was a division between her perception of the situation and the reality of life in the Bavarian town. Fine clothing was still sold to fashionable women, men visited their tailors, people rushed to and from work and school, men and women drank in the bars and clubs, stumbling out in the early hours. As she wandered the halls of the Residenz, the grand home of Bavarian aristocracy for almost five centuries until the end of the war, in 1918, these thoughts brought Maisie back to Elaine Otterburn. She had another day at her disposal. Perhaps she would visit one more time, make one final plea for Elaine to return home. She was considering what tack she might take when she heard someone approach, the snap of steel-capped heels echoing in the chambers around her. She almost did not respond to her adopted name.

"Fräulein Donat."

She turned around. "Oh, forgive me—I was so taken with the magnificence all around me, I was not paying attention."

The officer who had interviewed her at the Nazi headquarters gave a short bow. "I completely understand. To be here in this place is to be transported, is it not?"

Maisie smiled. She felt the clamminess of fear slick against her skin. "Is this your lunchtime, sir?" Had she been told his name? She tried to remember. "I'm so sorry, but I think the worry of the past few days has caught up with me—it's the waiting to see my father. Forgive me, but I cannot remember your name."

"That is because I never told you, Miss Donat. My name is Hans Berger. I have a military title that is almost impossible for an English-woman to pronounce correctly, but it means I am a major, though I am at the moment assigned to administration at the Führer's headquarters. I am honored to be of service."

"Yes, I would imagine so. Very fortunate to be chosen for the job of liaison with other consulates."

"Oh, that is not quite what I do, but in your case, it may seem so."

Maisie looked at her watch. "I want to see as much as I can before I leave Munich. I plan to do some shopping this afternoon—a few souvenirs to take home, I think."

"Come, let us look together—there is much to tell about the Residenz. Being here clears my mind for the rest of the day, so I come often. A few moments amid such beauty, and I am refreshed."

"I've no doubt," said Maisie.

Berger pointed out various elements of note as they walked together. To Maisie, the Residenz seemed to be touched by Midas himself, so abundant was gold everywhere one gazed. It was without doubt a place of beauty and magnificence, an opulent palace demonstrating untold privilege and wealth. Yet as she walked on, and as Hans Berger pointed out a painting, a mural, an embellishment of design, Maisie could not prevent her mind from returning to the fact that the Führer had come to power on a tide of public emotion based upon want and fear, and his promises to give the people their due. Once again she considered her deep sense of being surrounded by doubt when she passed people on the street—a vibration so subtle it was like a faint scent carried on the air, or the few drops of rain that fall before a shower. Why did so many people take the detour along the alley, avoiding the Nazi salute? And why did so many look aside or step into a shop if they saw soldiers in the brown uniforms coming their way? She suspected they were a people with a profound sense of honor torn between loyalty to their country and a feeling that something was deeply amiss. Maurice had taught her of the balance between opposites: that when thirsty, people might drink too much, and that when starved of love, they may bestow affection with no discrimination. Look at the child who clings if he doubts his mother's adoration, who feigns illness or pain if it brings his mother's arms about him.

"Shall we walk into the gardens? It is not too cold, and they are particularly lovely, I think, when fewer people are here."

Maisie smiled. "Perhaps for a short while. I would like to return to my hotel to rest before I venture out again today."

Berger led the way to the Hofgarten, again giving Maisie what amounted to a history lesson on the way. But as they entered the garden, his tone changed. "Miss Donat, you have been busy while in Munich."

Though she felt anxiety grip her stomach, Maisie revealed no sign of alarm. She wondered what information Berger had been given of her movements, but she replied with honesty, imagining her father in Leon Donat's place. "There has been a lot of waiting. I am very anxious to see my father, and to take him home. He is not a young man, and being in prison will have had a poor effect on his health." She paused, looking straight into Berger's eyes. "Prisons are not designed to enhance well-being."

Berger stopped, pointing out another aspect of the garden to which Maisie should pay attention. Then he returned her direct gaze.

"You have visited Schwabing, Fräulein Donat?"

Maisie shrugged. "I had time on my hands, and I heard it was an interesting area, full of artists in their studios."

"Yet you did not visit an artist or a studio. You visited a woman of poor morals."

Maisie continued to look straight at Berger as she answered, though in truth, she was unsettled. "I visited the daughter of friends of my father. They are people of influence who are worried about the young woman, and they want her to come home. I was asked to intercede on their behalf—women of her age are not always disposed to follow the dictates of their parents. Frankly, I had little faith in my ability to influence her to return to England—she likes it here. But I promised I would try." She took a breath. "And if you are about to ask how the parents knew I was leaving for Munich, when I have told no one and wanted only to come here to be reunited with my beloved father, then I can only tell you that the father of the girl is a powerful man who is very good at procuring information."

After what felt like a long delay, Berger responded, "Yes, I understand." Then he walked on, once more assuming the role of tour guide, an officer in a black uniform who knew so much about the wealth of past aristocracy, yet was acting upon orders from a man who claimed to represent the ordinary people. Maisie wondered what Maurice might make of the imbalance.

Berger accompanied Maisie on her return to the hotel, giving his signature short bow as he bid her good-bye.

"I did not specify a time for your appointment tomorrow morning, Fräulein Donat. I will ensure your consulate is informed that I expect to see you again at noon. As it transpires, I am not making the journey that was originally planned; I am needed here in Munich. You will have plenty of time to present your papers to the Kommandant at Dachau, to be reunited with your father, and to proceed with him to the station for the train to Paris. You must of course leave Munich as soon as possible following your father's release."

"I am looking forward to it, Major. Very much."

He clicked his heels, extended his hand upward, and repeated the words she had come to despise: "Heil Hitler."

He had turned before she could lift her hand in response. She closed her eyes and exhaled, pausing before entering the hotel. She wondered if his speedy departure had been deliberate, giving her the opportunity not to salute his leader.

"Maisie."

The voice was low, and came from her right.

Moving with speed, Maisie took Elaine Otterburn's arm and with a firm hand led her away from the hotel entrance.

"Never, ever do that again. You must not call me by my name in this country, ever."

"I'm sorry, I—"

Maisie looked Elaine up and down. She was ill-kempt, and as she pulled her coat around her, a flap of her dress peeped through, showing stains, as if some dark liquid had been spilled on the silk. Kohl was smudged under her eyes, and her hair had not seen a brush or comb that day. Her stockings were laddered, and she seemed unsteady on her feet.

"Elaine, we cannot go into the hotel. Wait—let me get a taxicab, and we'll go to your flat."

"No, we can't go there."

"What do you mean?"

"We just can't."

Maisie paused. She felt goose bumps across the skin at the nape of her neck.

"Elaine, everything tells me that we must return to the flat, now, before anyone else ventures in."

CHAPTER 10

Maisie slipped her arm through Elaine's.

"Talk to me about anything, Elaine. We must look like two friends meeting for a cup of coffee, or going about our errands for the morning."

She hailed a taxi, and had the driver drop them on a side street not far from Elaine's lodgings. After checking that no one was there—the other young women with rooms in the house were out, and the landlady appeared not to be present—Maisie followed Elaine up the stairs. At the top she had to take the younger woman's arm for fear that she would stumble.

"Elaine, try to have some control. Whatever happens, we must contain ourselves."

Elaine looked at Maisie, her head shaking—not to counter her words, but as if she were cold to the bone. She said nothing, but nodded, forcing some measure of dominion over her body. She passed her keys to Maisie, her fingers barely able to keep them in her hand.

Maisie slipped the door key in the lock, turned the handle, and took a deep breath, afraid of what she might encounter. She pushed the door open and gasped. The room looked as if a madman had been released within its walls. Bedclothes had been ripped from the mattress and thrown on the floor. Clothing was strewn atop the pile of linens. Cups left on a tray on the chest of drawers had been smashed. And across the mirror in red lipstick was scrawled the word *Hure*. *Whore*.

Maisie looked at Elaine, at the contusion across her cheekbone, her laddered stockings, and the blood on her torn dress. She asked no questions. "Close and lock the door. We must set about cleaning up."

"I was going to telephone the police, but—"

"It would be best if you didn't."

Maisie found a bowl, which she took to the kitchen along the landing, bringing it back filled with water. She had a cloth over her arm, pulled from a makeshift line over the sink where the young women had hung their silk stockings to dry. When she returned to the room, Elaine was sitting on the edge of the bed, the torn robe she'd picked up from the floor held tight in her hands.

"Who would have done this?"

"First, we must sort out your room," said Maisie. "Then you can tell me what happened. If I thought the police would have any interest, I would leave everything as it is. But I can tell there is nothing here to give us any clue as to the identity of the person who did this, except that." She pointed to the mirror. "And I want to get rid of it."

Elaine gasped, tears falling anew as she choked her words. "You think Luther is dead? Do you think he is dead?"

Maisie placed the bowl of water on the dressing table and put an arm around Elaine. "Until you tell me the whole story, I cannot say. Now then, there will be time for tears later, Elaine. We must get on, and then you can describe everything that happened. If you sit down to tell your story amid all this clutter, your ability to think back with clarity will be diminished by what is about you; you must be in a place that is clear. I cannot take you onto a hilltop or put you in a field, but I can get this room cleaned. Come, there is work to be done."

Maisie scrubbed the mirror while Elaine picked up clothing, folding each item and placing it in a drawer. Maisie kept an eye on the younger woman as they worked. She knew that the destruction of Elaine's home—and for better or worse, it was her home—was meant to undermine her, to make her feel unsafe—and with a bitter twist, given the slur writ large across the mirror. If Elaine now felt less than secure, it was with good reason. Sweeping shards of china cups into a paper bag, Maisie stopped to inspect a long seam of lipstick, powder, and kohl pressed into a floorboard, as if someone had ground the thick red substance into the grain of the wood, compounding the damage with the powder and inky kohl. This was not just destruction but a deliberate act of cruelty, as if the perpetrator wanted nothing more than to destroy Elaine Otterburn's charm—her wide eyes, big smile, and hearty laugh.

Soon the women had finished cleaning and stood back to survey the results. Elaine's face was streaked with tears. "It's never been this neat and tidy." She attempted a smile, but began to weep once again.

"Sit down for a moment, Elaine." Maisie left the room, emptied and rinsed the bowl, and refilled it with cold water. She searched the small kitchen until she found an unsoiled cloth, and returned to the room. She steeped the cloth in water, wrung it out, and gave it to Elaine. "Press this across your eyes—it will diminish the swelling. And now tell me what happened."

Elaine's chest heaved with sobs. She pulled away the cloth and turned to Maisie, one eye clear of kohl, the other still smudged, as if half her face were that of an angel, the other touched by darkness—a theater harlequin. "We'd been drinking, so I was rather squiffy, but we were always like that. Luther—his name is Luther Gramm—isn't much older than me. He never wanted to do what he was doing in the Schutzstaffel, but it was the right thing, he said. He'd been an apprentice architect before he went into uniform. He enjoyed a good time." She paused, wiping her eye and looking at the black smudge across the cloth. "We'd been to a club, lots of laughing, lots to drink, you know, and we danced the night away. I liked him, really I did. We got on well together." Elaine began to cry again.

"Go on, Elaine. Until I know the whole story, I do not know if I can help you."

"But you must. You must help me. I'm all alone, and now this has happened."

Aware that the woman was panicking, Maisie softened her own voice. "Tell me what happened, Elaine. You must go on. We might not have much time."

Elaine swallowed her tears and wiped the cloth across her mouth. "Luther told me he knew a place, an alley where lovers go. You see, the old *Frau* downstairs would chuck me out if she knew I'd had a man up here. I've been pushing my luck a bit, and we were taking chances going back to the house where the officers are lodging." She covered her face with the cloth, leaned into it, and then sat up, dropping the cloth into the bowl of water. "I was a bit scared, to tell you the truth. There wasn't much light, except a bit from the houses, and it was a damp place, smelly. I don't think I could find my way there again, to tell you the truth. But Luther insisted and dragged me down there, and we began, you know, to kiss." She stopped speaking.

"Go on, Elaine," said Maisie, her voice low.

Elaine sighed. "We were in a doorway. We didn't think anyone could see us. Then we heard a motor car, and there were headlamps coming toward us. Slowly. Really slowly. I wondered how the motor car could even get down the alley—there must have been only a foot either side of it, if that. And there was a man walking in front of the car—I remember thinking that he looked like one of those men they have at funerals, walking in front of the hearse as if to pace it out, so the horses don't gallop off and everyone remains respectful. What do they call them? Escorts? Something like that." She paused, reached for the cloth, wrung it out, and pressed it to her eyes, as if to block out the images that came with her words.

"I'm still listening, Elaine."

"Then everything seemed to happen very fast, except no one rushed. The man wasn't in a hurry. One minute we were there, in the doorway, Luther with his arms about me, and then the man was there—no farther away than you are now. And it was almost as if I were no one, as if I didn't exist. Luther was about to say something. He opened his mouth to draw breath, and then the man seemed to jam something into his ear. I tried to scream, but nothing came out. My voice had gone, so I went to hit the man to try to get him to stop hurting Luther, but he drew back his hand and knocked me hard, really hard, against the wall. Everything seemed to move before my eyes. I tried to come to my feet, but my legs had buckled under me and I just couldn't get up, I was so dizzy. But I could still see them. I could see everything, because the headlamps on the motor car were pointed right at the man and Luther. I couldn't move my arm, it hurt so much, but I kept trying to lever myself up to help Luther. That's when I saw him, the man, holding Luther's nose and mouth at the same time, pressing his lips together, sealing his nostrils, so he . . . until he . . . suffocated to death, I suppose. I saw him shudder, and his eyes, which were really wide, looking at the man as if he knew him, and then he stopped moving. Then the man let go, and I must have gone spark out. I came to eventually. It was still dark. Luther was gone, the motor car was nowhere to be seen, and there was no sign of the man. A couple of drunks passed, calling me names and trying to grab me, but I managed to get to my feet. I didn't know what to do, so I came back to my room and discovered it completely turned over. I covered myself with my coat and ran out. I waited for a long time in a small park near here, hiding until I could come to find you. I guessed you would be at that hotel. I don't know how—I just guessed. I mean, it's one of the best in Munich."

Maisie's tone was soft when she spoke. "Elaine, finish washing yourself and pick out some plain clothing—nothing bright, nothing to attract attention."

"How did he die?"

"I suspect an initial tight clasp to the neck weakened him, even though he was a young man and robust. Then a sharp object—something akin to a metal knitting needle—was pushed into his ear. You need a strong man to do that, but I believe either the shock killed Luther, or after rendering him useless and you unconscious, the killer disabled him enough to hold his nose and mouth closed, so he suffocated. I doubt there was much blood."

Maisie could hear Elaine pulling out fresh clothing, each movement marked by sobbing. She heard items being dropped. The young woman was losing control of her hands, the shock once more taking hold in waves. But Maisie was looking around the room, wondering why Luther Gramm, a young officer of the feared Schutzstaffel, might be a target. Perhaps it was not the man but the woman who had been in the crosshairs: the woman who was now heaving great sobs, gasping for air as if her lungs were compromised. If that was so, then time was even more limited than she might have imagined; Elaine could be framed for a crime she did not commit. *Or did she?* The words seemed to ricochet into Maisie's mind, but she brushed them aside. For now.

"Elaine, we must get out of here immediately."

"Why? Who do you think knows?"

"I think there is some connection here that I cannot quite see, and it's possible that you were the intended victim, but not in the way either of us might imagine. I have to get you out of here. Are you dressed?"

Elaine stepped out from behind the screen. She wore a plain dark green costume: a jacket and a skirt with a hemline between ankle and knee. A silk scarf was knotted at her neck; her blond hair was brushed back and topped with a hat, its brim somewhat wider than presently fashionable. Her polished black shoes were simple, and she carried a black handbag and a dull maroon and green paisley carpet bag, as if she were an office girl going to spend an evening with a friend.

"You have your passport and identification documents?"

"Yes, Maisie."

"Now, then, I want you to write a note to whichever of these friends is your favorite pal, with yesterday's date, and slip it under her door. Tell her you decided to go away for a few days, and to tell anyone who might come to the house to visit you that you are not at home. When you've done that, we leave."

Maisie checked her reflection in the mirror on the back of the door and took one more glance toward Elaine. Her head down, the young woman was finishing the letter as Maisie instructed.

"Right—now lock the door and let's get away from this house. We cannot delay. I want you on an aeroplane bound for London as soon as possible."

Elaine slid the letter under Pamela's door, and they made their way downstairs, tiptoeing past the landlady's rooms, and out into the chill Bavarian air.

"March winds doth blow," said Elaine.

"Come, let's walk to the bus stop."

"I don't think I have ever been on a bus here."

"Now's your chance to mix with the ordinary people, then."

Steering them to seats at the back of the bus, Maisie looked around and out of the windows, her eyes lingering for a second on each person on the street behind them. There was a street sweeper clad in old corduroy trousers, the fabric distinctive for the way it bagged around his knees. His jacket was patched, and he wore fingerless gloves and a knitted cap. His boots seemed heavy on his feet as he swung his broom back and forth, back and forth, marking the rhythm of his day. She saw shop girls and soldiers, men in suits and women with their coats wrapped around them, scarves pulled up. March winds indeed doth blow, even in Bavaria, thought Maisie, wishing her day could have been so ordinary. A good dose of ordinary would be welcome.

"Before we go any further, Elaine, if you say my name, or refer to me, I am Edwina Donat. Is that clear? Do not expect an explanation—do not think for one moment that this is a game. I want you only to remember that name, and forget that I am Maisie Dobbs."

"Not Maisie Compton, then, or Mrs. James Compton? And what about Margaret, Lady Compton? I bet I got that wrong—these darn English titles befuddle the little Canadian girl." Elaine's voice had an edge to it. "But I would have thought you would be proud to bear your husband's name."

Maisie looked at Elaine, aware of the lurching of the bus as it stopped and started and took on new passengers. "I was more than proud to bear my husband's name, Elaine. But after he died, it was another knife to the heart every time the words left my lips, because he was no longer there." She looked away for a moment. "Elaine, can you remember anything about the man who—"

She looked around. Other passengers were reading, or just looking out of windows, or chatting to their neighbors. The nearest were some three rows away, out of earshot. "Who did that to your friend?"

"The man was very well covered—a mackintosh, a hat drawn over his eyes, and he had something over his face. He could see, but I would never have been able to identify him." She bit her lip.

"What is it, Elaine? What is it you're not telling me?"

Elaine pressed her lips together. "I—I—I cannot tell you, Mai—I mean, Edwina."

"Elaine, you've put me in a difficult position. I just had to listen to you haranguing me for the name I use, when you have no knowledge of the agreement between my husband and myself. Now you give me a fraction of a piece of information. I deserve better—much better."

"I didn't stay here in some self-indulgent capacity, you know. I've been trying to be of service to Britain."

"To Britain? How?"

"There's a man called Mark Scott, an American, and—"

"Mark Scott? Oh, Elaine—of all people . . ." Maisie shook her head, placing a hand on Elaine's. "Later—tell me in a little while, Elaine, when we are in a more private place. I want to know exactly what you've told him. For now, I need to think."

M aisie knew she had to get Elaine Otterburn out of her hair—and the country—at the earliest opportunity. Relations between Britain and Germany were on an even keel, and aircraft came and went daily between the two countries. Her fear now, though, was that she might have been followed. Being known to have helped the lover of a German SS officer, who would surely be reported missing in the next twenty-four hours, would prevent Maisie claiming Leon Donat, and might well lead to her own detention. She nodded to Elaine to get off the bus at the next stop, exiting by the rear door. She was thankful that more passengers had come on board, rendering their departure harder to observe in the driver's mirror.

Maisie led the way along the street without any destination in mind. Walking cleared the mind. Walking allowed her to think. She walked faster, as if to marshal her thoughts with the utmost speed.

"Elaine, you have to get out of the country as soon as you can. If you sent a telegram to your father, would he send an aeroplane for you?"

"He might, but that takes time. Perhaps I had better go to the airport and see if I can board a flight for anywhere other than somewhere else in Germany today. I might even be able to hire something small. I can pretty much fly anything, you know."

"All right. Look, you had better go straightaway. We should part ways now. Go quickly and keep your head down—don't do anything to attract attention. Do you need any money?"

Elaine shook her head. "No. I've plenty." She held out her hand. "Thank you. I never expected help from you—you were my shot in the dark. The other girls are too silly to know what to do."

"I never expected you would need this much assistance either, Elaine. Go now, go on. Leave this country as soon as you can."

The women parted on the street. Maisie turned away as their hands separated, and walked to a tram stop. She looked back once, but Elaine was gone. She wished she had questioned the young woman about Mark Scott. And she wished she had delved into the killing of a man who had now, to all intents and purposes, vanished. But perhaps it was best she knew no more on either count. What she did know was that she had done far more than she should for the daughter of a man she detested. Perhaps, with Elaine Otterburn gone, she could separate herself from this family. Their presence in her life had brought nothing but sorrow.

At the hotel, Maisie made her way to her room. She regretted ever accepting the assignment. The risks were escalating with each delay in securing Leon Donat's release—and now those risks were almost entirely upon her head. As soon as Luther Gramm was reported missing, and his dead body found, there would surely be a search for Elaine Otterburn—and when it was confirmed she had left the country, Maisie would be questioned, along with the woman's other friends and associates. Hans Berger knew of their connection, so he would pull her in—and perhaps delay Leon Donat's release. Maisie prayed for another twenty-four hours. Just one day.

"Don't be alarmed." The voice was low, yet the accent unmistakable.

"How did you get into my room?" Maisie stood still, looking toward the silhouette of Mark Scott, sitting by the half-closed curtains.

"It's a way I have with locks."

Maisie pulled off her gloves, unwound her scarf, and removed her coat.

"You have some explaining to do, Mr. Scott."

"Not as much as you will, if Berger discovers that his boy Luther is dead and Elaine has gone. Pity about that—Luther was very useful to us. Amazing what even the younger officers know, without really knowing they know it—forgive the tongue-twister. Give them a pretty girl and more drinks than they can handle, and it's only a matter of time before they're gabbing away merrily."

"You've put her life in danger, Mr. Scott—and mine, and that of the very man you say your government wants you to ensure is released into the hands of the British government. *Safely* into the hands of the British government, I might add."

"I didn't actually murder anyone, Fräulein D."

"Mr. Scott, I—"

"I will tell you enough."

"Well, you'd better start, then."

"As I explained, we don't have a formal intelligence service in the States, so it's down to me and some other fellows at the Justice Department. When I came here, I looked around at how your chaps work— let's face it, you British have been in the intelligence business for a very long time. Even your Good Queen Bess had her Walsingham. Anyway, I thought it might be an idea to nab me an informer or two—and you British girls do seem to find your way into the most interesting places. The younger ones love a party, and—despite all indications to the contrary—so do the Germans around here, so they're keeping a few for themselves. In the meantime, Hitler's henchmen have closed down more places where people can have some fun than were ever open in the city I'm from."

"Which is?"

"Best you don't know, eh, Fräulein D?" Scott completed his retort with a grin. "Elaine Otterburn, it appears, decided to trust an American more than she did the Brits, who seem to think she is a bit of a fly-by-night. Indulged and spoiled, yes, but it didn't take me long to realize that this woman did not just have a desire to do something useful for the old country—she had a need. Call it an atonement . . . of sorts." He seemed to leave the word *atonement* lingering in the air.

"She brought you information. Yes, I know that, Mr. Scott," said Maisie, refusing to take the bait.

"Each little piece she brought back to me—she was like a cat dropping a mouse on the doorstep—fitted in with something another of my contacts reported. And as you know, it's like a puzzle, looking at all the pieces and seeing where they go together."

"And where do they fit, Mr. Scott?"

"Ultimately, Fraulie D, they indicate that your government is being lulled by a cobra into thinking that all will be well."

"You're not telling me anything I don't know—though it's clearly something *you* didn't know, or you would not have put Elaine Otter-burn's life at risk."

"Oh, Elaine would have been just fine and dandy, had she not led on the artist with the hangdog look."

"Which artist?"

"A man who has more heart for the beauty of life than the ugliness, although, like many of the men of Himmler's SS, he has a tendency to veer toward the extreme. I think you know that too. One of those people who cannot just join a club—he has to run it."

"Berger?"

"Yes, Berger. Formerly an artist—and a better one than his boss, that's for sure!"

"Berger and Elaine?"

"No, not exactly Berger and Elaine. Just Berger. The river ran one way. Make sure you get your documents tomorrow, Miss Dobbs, and then you and Leon Donat get out of Munich as fast as you can. They still don't know exactly what they have in Donat, so once he's on the train, those Nazis will just count their money and have a big old party."

"Money?"

"Yes, money. And for the record, your Leslie is no small fry in the British consulate, Miss Dobbs. He is a bigger fish, though he may swim at the bottom of the pond to stay out of the light. Don't underestimate him—I learned everything I know about intelligence gathering from watching that man work. And I don't doubt he could give you a list of my every move into the bargain—but I hope not this one." He paused and came to his feet. "Now then, Miss Dobbs—I should say Fräulein

Donat, sorry about that. Better use the right name, now I'm leaving. And don't worry—no one will see me."

Maisie stood up. "Be careful with your overconfidence, Mr. Scott. As one of my teachers once told me, a healthy spoonful of fear will keep you from harm."

Scott laughed. "Fear? Oh, I am scared. Every day in this place, I know fear—but not just for my own safety. I'm scared for all our futures every time I see Herr Hitler pass in his motor car, or hear the messages he broadcasts to the people on the radio. I know fear for everyone when I see his brown-shirted henchmen on the streets, or those poisoned souls of the Gestapo strutting into a bar, pulling girls like Elaine Otterburn into their web—although with her it was a case of 'Or so they think!' And frankly, I cannot wait to go home. At least on the other side of the Atlantic I am on safer ground. The United States of America plans to keep its distance if the old country goes to war again. We lost too many boys the last time, over here."

"And so did we, Mr. Scott—it's why I'm here. But let's not split hairs."

Scott touched the brim of his hat, turned, and stepped without a sound to the door. A splinter of light from the corridor shone through into the room, and then he was gone.

Maisie stood for a moment, thinking of his words. *I am on safer ground.* "Or so you think, Mr. Scott," she replied in a soft voice, as if he were standing next to her. "Or so you think."

For several hours she sat alone in the dark by the window, the curtains opened just a few inches. She looked out at the street below in the still of the night, thinking of the many times past when she had taken up such a post, a vigil in the peppery darkness, looking back across time and wondering about the future. In the empty apartment in Toronto, after James' death, sitting by the window, paralyzed in her grief, willing time itself to move backward so she could run to James and say, "No, please don't. Don't fly today . . . remember us." In other places she had stationed herself by windows, looking out onto the world from a lair she had drawn around herself—in Darjeeling, in Gibraltar, in Madrid, and then, finally, in the small village near Spain's Tajo River. So many nighttime hours looking out into darkness, as if the stars could map her route to safe harbor.

In time she meditated, envisaging herself collecting the papers with ease. She imagined a trouble-free journey to the prison, and a Kommandant who gave her documents only a cursory glance before nodding to an assistant, who would call for Leon Donat to be brought to the guardroom. She would run to Donat, clasp him as if he were her father, and say, "I have come to take you home, Papa. I have missed you so much." Hands would be outstretched and shaken with the Germans in a passing moment of goodwill. They would depart for the station in Munich, for an agonizing wait before boarding the train that would depart for Paris at five minutes to four. They would take their seats in a first-class compartment—there would be no sleeping accommodation available on this train; not until the much later Orient Express came through Munich from Budapest with its wagons-lits would private quarters be available—and count down the hours until they reached the border. Her tension would not ease until they reached Paris—at eight minutes past eleven the following morning—and she saw Brian Huntley and Robert MacFarlane waiting for them on the platform. Then she would go home. And never, she vowed, would she give Brian Huntley and Robbie MacFarlane the time of day again. She was done with them.

Information from Mark Scott—if it could be trusted—suggested that a vital piece of intelligence had been played down during Maisie's briefings in London and the Cotswolds. No one had emphasized the complicity of wealthy industrialists in Germany, men who had seen an opportunity to get Leon Donat out of the way because they believed his businesses would collapse without him at the helm. Had a word here or there led to the police raid at a certain time when Donat could be captured? But why was she not told? For surely both Brian Huntley and Robert MacFarlane knew. Perhaps it was because, in truth, there was nothing she could do about such men and their activities against another businessman. What they had done could not be undone. But what of John Otterburn?

Scott might have been trying to cause trouble with his insinuations, but the suggestion that John Otterburn might have played a part—along with his business contacts in Munich—in the arrest of Leon Donat seemed like a plausible scenario. Maisie would bet that none of them expected that Donat would end up in Dachau.

She considered the circumstances of Otterburn's request to help bring his daughter home. She was still uneasy about the apparent break in the wall of secrecy that should have surrounded her assignment, but knowing how deep the tentacles of Otterburn's power ran, it was more than possible that a contact in Whitehall privy to Huntley's plans had informed the industrialist of the development. Maisie vowed never, ever to entertain an approach from John Otterburn again, even if he was holding an olive branch. She had sworn such a thing before, yet been drawn back in. No. This was enough. No matter how important he had become, how untouchable he might be—and, indeed, no matter how much her experiences in Spain had changed her mind, made her believe him right in predicting a devastating air war in Europe—she wanted to be as far from the Otterburns as possible.

As she lay waiting for sleep to come, as she tried to exert a semblance of control over her thoughts, it occurred to Maisie that the reason she had not been informed that there were important German

businessmen who wanted one of their main competitors out of the
way was that she might not have accepted the assignment. Already
she had looked hard at the truth behind their decision to earmark her
for the role of Edwina Donat. She was a known entity, true, and had
worked with both men on highly sensitive cases—but beyond that,
they thought she had few connections of true worth to her now.

But now Maisie knew she would prove them wrong. As her father
and Brenda, Priscilla, and the Comptons had shown since her return
from Spain, she had everything to live for. And as soon as they were
alone, on their way to Paris, she would persuade Leon Donat that he
had everything to live for too. With his beloved daughter ailing, she
knew that might well be her greatest challenge.

CHAPTER 11

Another bright, cold morning greeted Maisie when the alarm woke her at half past eight. For all her early wakefulness, when it seemed rest would be hard to claim, she had at last slept soundly, no dreams to disturb her. Now she had time to consider the morning ahead, envisioning the day as a jockey might imagine every hurdle in the steeplechase before taking to the saddle.

Maisie thought about Elaine Otterburn too. She should be back in England by now, safe, when the body of the SS officer was found. *Elaine Otterburn.* How great had been the weight of her guilt after she didn't report for the flight that killed James? Maisie suspected she was living with the remorse only those who have survived when others have lost their lives can know. Elaine might spend her life trying to prove herself, whether by filtering information to people like Mark Scott, or joining do-gooder committees, following in her mother's footsteps.

Maisie shivered as she rose from the bed, realizing that she could not imagine Elaine Otterburn as an older woman.

She ran a hot bath and allowed herself to soak, going over each move, each journey and possible interrogation, in detail yet again. She took one telephone call from Leslie, who confirmed he would pick her up in a consular motor car at eleven thirty. If all went to plan, he estimated, they would have the completed documents by half past twelve at the latest, and then proceed to Dachau—depending on traffic, they would be there by approximately a quarter past one. All being well, they would be leaving with Leon Donat at half past two and would proceed directly to the Munich railway station first-class waiting room.

As Maisie knew—and she hoped as far as Leslie did not know—every moment she was not on the train was a moment when the body of the young SS officer could be discovered. Without a shred of doubt, a warrant for her apprehension would be issued at once, given her perceived friendship with Elaine Otterburn, who would be considered a fugitive. She pushed away the image of black-uniformed men storming the station searching for her—and at the same time wondered if Elaine was already in England. She might not care for the Otterburns, but if Elaine had been detained, then the quest to take Leon Donat home would doubtless fail, and all would be lost. And she wanted to go home so very much. If nothing else, the assignment had brought the truth of her feelings into sharp relief. When Leon Donat was brought into the guard room, she would hold him as if he were Frankie Dobbs. The very thought of her own father being in such a brutal place brought tears to her eyes. She missed those she loved and who loved her in return so very much, and she wanted to be close to them.

Maisie ordered a light breakfast and dressed in her plain clothes, absorbing the persona of Edwina Donat. She was soon ready once more to step out onto the boards of risk, to watch the curtain open and then play her part.

The telephone rang again. She picked it up on the first ring.

"Edwina. It's . . . it's Elaine."

Hearing another click on the line, Maisie faltered, then spoke clearly. "Oh, hello, Elaine—look, I cannot talk now. I'm expecting another call, and I have a lot on this morning. Do give my best to your parents when you speak to them. Must dash—"

She replaced the receiver in its cradle and put a hand to her mouth, closing her eyes. *Think. Think.* She pressed herself to make a plan. She had meditated on a perfect outcome to the day's challenges—the documents, the journey to Dachau, the release of Leon Donat . . . to the train . . . crossing the border . . . Paris. What she had not accounted for, and perhaps quite deliberately, was that Elaine Otterburn had not left Munich. The sound of a train pulling into a station and steam pushing out across the buffers had punctuated the woman's call. She must be at the railway station, in a public telephone kiosk. It occurred to Maisie that perhaps she should wonder who else might have been the beneficiary of late-night conversations fueled by drink and dancing. She'd received no assurance from any quarter that the sharing of information had gone in one direction only. Could Elaine have been passing information back to the Germans? And could she—Maisie felt almost lightheaded as her thoughts took her in this direction—could Elaine Otterburn have been working on behalf of her father from the beginning? Whatever might ensue, Maisie's innermost thoughts warned her not to give Elaine the benefit of the doubt.

The telephone rang again. It was Leslie.

"Miss Donat. I'm waiting for you by the registration desk. Let's not be late."

"I'm ready, Mr. Leslie."

Maisie took up her small leather case, her handbag, and her coat. In the mirror by the door she checked her hat and the wig underneath. *Does it look the same as yesterday? Does it seem natural? Do I resemble*

Edwina Donat? And as she made one last check of the room, she knew Maurice would approve. In that moment she felt fear envelop her. Fear might well be her shield against failure, and she could only trust that it would keep her safe—along with the small revolver in the bag, which now seemed to carry all the weight of Robert MacFarlane behind it.

The drive to the Führerbau of the Nationalsozialistische Deutsche Arbeiterpartei on Arcis Strasse seemed to take longer than before. Leslie talked through the plan again. He asked Maisie questions as a teacher might test a pupil, and Maisie became aware that his demeanor had changed, that he was no longer playing the part of a somewhat nitpicking civil servant but a seasoned professional engaged in foreign affairs.

Then he surprised her.

"Of course, just to shift the elephant in the room a bit, Miss *Donat.*" He seemed to emphasize Maisie's assumed last name. Had she imagined the tone, or were nerves getting the better of her? Could he have guessed that she was an agent for the British government charged with a sensitive assignment, not the somewhat naive daughter of a wealthy industrialist?

Leslie continued. "There is the problem of Miss Otterburn. Clearly you had your own reasons for paying her a visit, but it was most ill-advised, given her position. And of course there is the pressing question of her missing paramour."

Maisie said nothing.

"I think you should prepare for the fact that the major might well ask you a few questions about her liaison with the SS officer."

"I understand."

"Be vigilant, listen to his questions with care, and do not fall into any traps."

"I will, yes." Maisie wondered if Leslie knew she was armed.

"You will, to all intents and purposes, be on your own with your father once you are on the train." Was Leslie divesting the camouflage now, revealing the full extent of his knowledge? Or was Maisie imagining each sentence to be a hint that he had her number? "We believe the Germans are so convinced that Leon Donat has nothing at all to offer, they will not be positioning an agent on the train—and definitely not across the border. We're not yet sure why they aren't more worried. Stupid requests such as stipulating that he can only be released to a family member, when the protocol is for the foreign service to receive the prisoner in a negotiated release, right down to this messing around with papers—it's all been designed to rattle our cages. It was only to be expected. We poke sticks through their bars every now and again, and they poke sticks through ours. It could of course be an attempt by the Führer's boys to present him in some sort of compassionate light, though that won't last long. Anyway, I think we will know more when Donat is released to us."

Whether he knew Maisie to be working on behalf of the Secret Service or not was not important now, though she knew she would feel safer if he was in the dark.

"Mind you," he continued, "I would like to have a pin in the map for Elaine Otterburn. She could upset the whole apple cart."

"I'm sorry, Mr. Leslie."

"It's done now—and you were quite careful, though that meeting with Berger in the Residenz rather rattled us."

"He just turned up there."

Leslie turned in his seat to look directly at Maisie. "No one in the

SS just turns up." He faced the front of the motor car again and continued. "I have no doubt of our success today. However . . ." He did not continue.

Maisie's voice was low as she filled the gap. "However . . . if it does not go to plan, the most important thing is to get *my father* out of Munich, to London. I think it's evident I know that much, Mr. Leslie."

They sat in silence for the remainder of the journey, Maisie resting her hand on her bag, feeling the now comforting outline of the small revolver, her short meditation not on the outcome of the day but on her training with MacFarlane, and a bullet striking the bull's-eye with her very first shot.

The guard outside recognized Maisie and Leslie, gave their papers a cursory look, and waved them into the building. Leslie remained in the cavernous entrance hall while, ten minutes after being allowed entry, "Fräulein Donat" was summoned by another guard and shown into the same office as before. She was taken aback to be greeted by Berger. He gave a short bow, and held out his hand to the chair in front of his desk. The same junior officer stood to attention on his right. Berger shuffled some papers.

Maisie spoke first, as she took her seat. "How very nice it was to see you at the Residenz. I enjoyed hearing about it from someone who has studied every facet. Will you be long in Munich?"

"Thank you, Fräulein Donat. And I depart tomorrow—today is a busy day for the Führer's staff. Now, Fräulein Donat, to business. Let me see—yes, all the papers are here for the release of your father into his loving daughter's embrace." He gave a tight half smile as he looked up from the papers.

Maisie thought of Frankie, and tears came to her eyes. "Thank you,

Major. Thank you very much—I am so anxious to see him, and to take him home. He is not a well man, as you know."

Berger looked at his junior officer, and they both began to laugh.

"What is it?" said Maisie. "What about my father's health do you find worthy of mirth?"

"Mirth?" The men laughed again. Berger spoke in German to the boyish man in uniform behind him. "Warten Sie, bis sie sieht, was unwohl sieht aus wie nach Dachau!"

Maisie understood every word. *Wait until she sees what unwell looks like after Dachau!* She frowned. "Is something wrong, Major?"

"Oh, no, nothing, Fräulein Donat. Just a little joke between men in uniform—we have to let off a little steam on occasion."

He looked down at the papers, countersigning each page, checking a word here and there, running his finger along a line and nodding. It's all a game, thought Maisie. A man's life had been trampled, and it was all a game.

Berger looked up again. "Just one more thing, Fräulein Donat."

"Yes, of course."

"Your friend, Fräulein Otterburn."

"You already asked me about her. I tried once to get her to return to her parents, at their request. I'm not sure if she decided to heed my advice, but I believe she was thinking about it."

"Then she must have left Munich."

Maisie feigned surprise. "Well, at least I have managed to reunite one daughter with her father. I just wish I could be reunited with mine."

"Patience, Fräulein Donat. Patience." Berger leaned forward. "Our concern is not that she has returned to England to see her very rich father, but that one of her young men, a fellow officer, has not reported for duty."

"I—I beg your pardon, Major, but I don't understand."

The officer made a point of looking at Maisie's clothing, at her dull jacket and her plain hat. "No, you probably wouldn't. I am sure you were never a frivolous young girl."

"I would never have disappointed my mother and father, Major," said Maisie. She wondered if his changed attitude toward her, so different from their meeting in the Residenz, might be bravado in front of the junior officer.

There was a pause, during which Berger turned every single page again before finally shuffling them together. He slipped them into an envelope and passed the envelope to Maisie.

"Present these to the Kommandant at Dachau. He will be expecting you. But be warned, it is his job to check every document again before relinquishing the prisoner. Is that clear?"

"Yes, it is." Maisie stood up.

"And one more thing, Fräulein Donat."

"Yes?" said Maisie.

"Thank your government very much. On behalf of the Führer, we wish to extend our gratitude to you for paying Herr Donat's fines, and for their generous contribution to our wounded soldiers' fund."

Maisie nodded and tapped the papers she held to her chest. "Thank you, Major." She turned and walked to the door already held open by the junior officer.

"Oh, I almost forgot, Fräulein Donat." Berger was standing now, putting on his cap. "If by any chance you see Miss Otterburn, do ask her to be in touch. We are concerned about our brother officer."

"Of course. But I doubt I will ever see her again, Major. She was never a friend of mine."

"Thank God. Now let's get out of here and on to Dachau. You were longer than I thought." Leslie checked his watch, took the papers from Maisie, and ushered her from the building. The driver was holding open the official vehicle's door, and they stepped in. Almost before she was settled, the motor car had moved off into traffic.

"This all looks in order," said Leslie.

"I should hope so," said Maisie.

"Any problems?"

"He asked about Elaine Otterburn."

"He knows you saw her, so not surprising. Let's try not to worry about that—at this stage I would hope the Otterburn woman presents nothing more than a distraction, now we are on the way to Dachau." Leslie placed the papers back into the envelope. "Hopefully they might assume the pair have gone off for a nice long dirty weekend."

Maisie said nothing at first. The driver was negotiating traffic with speed, weaving in and out between slower vehicles, pressing down on the accelerator when the road was clear. "I'd tell him to calm down a bit if I were you," she said. "We don't want any problems at this stage, and reckless driving isn't the way to respect our hosts."

Leslie tapped on the window separating the passengers from the driver, and made a hand signal to slow down.

"So, the British government paid to have my father released."

"It's not unusual, just not widely known. Not sure it will go on for long, but money talks between nations whose leaders are still in somewhat polite conversation—though the issue with the Sudetenland is going to be a bit of a problem."

Maisie was quiet again, only breaking her silence to speak her mind. "There's something wrong, Mr. Leslie. I cannot put my finger on it, but this is all too easy. I'm worried."

"Three visits to those Nazis? Easy?"

"No, it was all show. They were playing us as if we were marionettes with strings to tweak. I just know they think we have paid money for old rope. Never mind that the Führer is impressed by my father's aristocratic connections—there is something else going on. There's not exactly a search party out looking for Elaine Otterburn—it could be her father's associations here, and she is a socialite, after all. But I keep thinking they are giving us all enough of that old rope to hang ourselves."

"If I may say so, Fräulein Donat, you are not sounding very much like the shy daughter of a wealthy man."

She turned to Leslie. "Call it a woman's intuition, then—and what a woman looks like has nothing to do with it."

The motor car jolted to a halt, and Leslie tapped on the window again. "Get around this holdup, Boyle. And forget the bloody traffic police—just get us to Dachau by the quickest route."

Maisie held on to the leather strap above her head and looked at Leslie. His skin had become more taut.

"There's something else you should know, Miss Donat, and this is in extreme confidence—not that you have anyone to blab to, thank goodness, and the papers are already on fire with speculation. We absolutely cannot have another delay in gaining your father's freedom. We have received intelligence that within the next forty-eight hours Herr Hitler will effect an invasion of Austria, though as far as he is concerned it is a reunification. He has long wanted to annex the land of his birth and bring it under the rule of the Third Reich, and to that end he has undermined the leadership of that country. In short order, his henchmen will be in positions of power and his Gestapo will be rounding up anyone who does not meet the Aryan ideal of the perfect citizen. Needless to say, Czechoslovakia is hot around the collar."

He paused, looked at Maisie as if to gauge her reaction to his news, then continued. "What that means for us is that this diplomatic fly in the ointment could either be to our advantage or against us, dependent upon how our hosts react to the news. The Kommandant may be doubly magnanimous—we have to assume he is aware of political developments—or he may be so full of himself and Nazi power that he makes life difficult. With luck he will display only enough hubris to toy with you a little, as the major did earlier. That we can surmount. Do not rise to the bait. Smile along with him. Greet your father with joy, and then let's get both of you out of this place before we all end up in chains."

It was as Leslie uttered the words *in chains* that the motor car turned the corner and the entrance to Dachau came into full view.

The guardroom was a low building, its ground floor divided by an archway, with doors to the left and right. In the rural comfort of the Cotswold manor house, Maisie had seen photographs and been advised that she would enter by one door and leave via the other. The interview would take place on the first floor, not the ground floor. Two armed guards stood watch in the square turret above the archway, which reminded Maisie of a widow's walk she'd seen on a house near the coast in Massachusetts. It seemed odd to her that such a memory should come to her then, of being in Boston with Charles and Pauline Hayden, and how they had welcomed her after James had died and she could not remain in Toronto. They had taken her to a fishing village one day, and she had asked about the small square room that seemed to be set into the roof of a captain's cottage. They had explained that it was a widow's walk, a place where a woman would go to look out for her husband's vessel on the sea, as if she could will him home. She thought, then, that any room she occupied would be akin to a widow's walk, for it was a long time before she stopped hoping for the nightmare to end and for James to come walking home toward her.

Watchtowers with armed guards were situated to her right and left, and barbed wire seemed to run everywhere—along the top of fences, and even beyond, more barbed wire deterred escape. As the motor car came to a halt Maisie located the door to the left, where they would enter before being taken to the building's first floor. She turned to Leslie as two guards made their way toward the vehicle.

"Let's get this over and done with, Mr. Leslie. I want to go home."

CHAPTER 12

The guards separated as they came closer to the motor car, one to stand alongside Maisie's door, the other by Gilbert Leslie's door. Maisie thanked the guard as she stepped out of the vehicle onto the hard, cold ground. Feeling a few nuggets of loose gravel and ice underfoot, she held on to the motor car to steady herself. The guard reached as if to assist, but instead used his hand to instruct her to follow him. She looked across to Leslie, and nodded.

As they approached the door to the left of the archway leading into the prison, one guard took the lead and one remained behind Leslie. Maisie framed a silent prayer in her mind: *May this be over soon.*

The door was opened by a guard inside, and they were led past what appeared to be some sort of staff room for officers of the Schutzstaffel. The guards accompanied them to another room where the Kommandant was seated, alongside another man who was not in uniform but whose dark clothing and black leather coat gave him an aura of authority. Maisie felt her tension increase, and knew Leslie's otherwise calm demeanor was strained; he rubbed his forehead several times, and clasped and unclasped his hands. She wondered who the second man was—she had not expected anyone bar the Kommandant or a guard or two until Leon Donat was brought to the room.

Leslie took the Kommandant's proffered hand. They exchanged what might have passed for pleasantries in another time or place. A comment on the journey, the traffic, the weather. Maisie—*Fräulein Donat*—was introduced. The second man gave the briefest nod by way of a greeting, and instead of offering his hand, held it high.

"Heil Hitler," he proclaimed, his eyes on the visitors.

Maisie felt sick. Her skin grew clammy as she raised her hand and uttered words she most detested. As a child she had witnessed her grandmother, upon hearing a boy swearing on the street, take the urchin by the scruff of the neck, pull him inside the house, and proceed to wash out his mouth with carbolic soap. "I'm going to clean that mouth for you, my boy, and your mother will thank me for it," said Becca. Maisie wondered how she might ever banish the taste of those words from her mouth. Perhaps it would take a good brushing with carbolic soap.

The Kommandant spoke. "May I present my colleague, Untersturmführer Acker, chief of the Dachau Political Department. It is Untersturmführer Acker's job to hear all cases at Dachau. His presence here is an important formality, as you can imagine."

Maisie nodded, biting her lip. Acker looked at her, drawing breath as if to speak—yet she felt compelled to say something before either Leslie or Acker uttered a word.

"I have all the documents to secure my father's release. I am very anxious to see him—it has been almost two years. Please, gentlemen, . . . please." She took the sheaf of stamped, signed, and countersigned documents from her bag and laid it on the table between the two men. "I only want to go home with my father." She thought she might stutter, yet played her hand. "I am his only family, but as you know, he has dear friends at home who want only to see him safe in his own country."

Leslie's discomfort was palpable. She had no need to look at him to know he was afraid.

Acker leaned over the papers, turning each one at a snail's pace as he appeared to read. Maisie suspected he was not reading at all, just taking his time, as if turning a hidden screw in the room to ratchet up the tension and thus render both the man from the British consulate and the daughter of a prisoner even more ill at ease. Maisie took a deep breath, imagining an impervious circle of strength encompassing and protecting her. She pulled her shoulders back and stood taller, as if to counter the officer's intention, which she believed was to make her feel small, insignificant.

Acker bore a half smile as he looked up. It was not a smile intended to demonstrate kindness, or a friendly outcome to the morning's events. It was a smile worn to invoke fear. He spoke in German, and Leslie translated. Maisie suspected the officer could have conversed in English, had he wished.

"Yes, indeed, all the papers are in order. I can see that." He looked up from the desk, sat down, and pushed the open folder toward the Kommandant, crumpling the sheets in the process.

Maisie heard an almost inaudible gasp from Leslie.

"Naturally, in my position, I am always reticent to release a prisoner, especially when I know that man to be guilty." He looked at Maisie as if daring her to counter his words.

There was silence in the room. Leslie cleared his voice to speak. Instead, Maisie stepped forward.

"Sir," she said in halting German. "My father is a man of the world. He has respect for the people of the many countries he has visited during the course of his work. He can speak several languages, and in fact was disappointed that I have little of his talent—as you can hear, my German is very poor indeed. However, out of respect, I am doing my best. My father, as you know—and as his testimony maintained—was here in Munich only to do business. He was a victim, and has been proven innocent—hence the many papers you have in front of you. Now I want to take my father home."

Acker came to his feet once more, staring at Maisie. He raised an eyebrow. "Then let us bring him to you." His smile was now unnaturally broad.

Acker nodded toward the Kommandant, who instructed the guard to take the two English visitors to another room. The guard followed instructions, leaving them in a small square room. He said nothing as he closed the door and left them alone. Leslie spoke almost as soon as he heard the lock turn.

"Miss Donat, I really must—"

Maisie silenced him, placing a finger on her lips. With her other hand she gestured to two points on the wall where the plaster was mottled. Leslie flushed.

"Good Lord," he whispered. "Do you really think they . . . How on earth did you know?"

"Didn't you ever do that when you were a child, Mr. Leslie?" Maisie whispered. "One of the boys in my class at school drilled some holes in the wall between the parlor and the kitchen in his house, so he could listen to his parents' conversations. I think he used some wire and an old tin or something to give a bit of volume, and he probably didn't hear anything important, though he must have felt like a spy. I am sure our guards here are doing much the same thing, but they have more sophisticated tools at their disposal." She kept her voice low. "The Germans are great engineers, you know—one day I am sure they will invent something that will do the job nicely. Anyway, let us take a seat here and wait in silence for my father, shall we? We are both rather tense, and it's best we do our utmost to contain any doubt. I do not want to be weak in the face of his interrogators, and those who may have caused him harm."

"We have been assured—"

She looked down at the ground as she spoke, so that Leslie had to strain to hear.

"I don't care what you have been assured, Mr. Leslie. I paid attention when we walked toward this building, which I hope very much to leave soon. I looked beyond this guardhouse into that vast expanse of concrete and those bunkers. I noticed some of the men out there, working, and for the briefest moment I knew that those are men subjected to terror. Now, silence, please. I want only to go home now, not to be here for any longer than I have to. And I want my father with me."

Leslie nodded, his gaze focused on the two mottled spots on the walls.

Another twenty minutes passed. In that time, Maisie struggled to draw upon everything she had been taught by Khan, the teacher to whom Maurice had taken her to learn that "seeing is not something one necessarily does with the eyes." Despite relentless cold drafts that seemed to seep from the outside and through the bricks, she cleared her mind, concentrating only on her breathing, tempering the sound of an inner voice that tested her, that gave her reason to feel fear. She envisaged all that she wanted to return home to—her father, Brenda, Priscilla, the Evernden boys, and those she loved at Chelstone. As time went on, she found her heart filled with renewed admiration for her dead husband, for his willingness to give his life in the service of his country, though only a handful of people knew the truth. She wondered how many men and women would risk their lives in ways that would forever be unacknowledged because, like James, they worked in a place unknown to all but a few. And when she returned with Leon Donat to England, he would enter into that same dark world—the quiet corridors of secrecy surrounding Britain's defense of her realm.

Maisie and Gilbert Leslie looked up toward the door as the key turned in the lock. Their eyes met, and they came to their feet in unison, as if there had been a prearranged agreement to appear impervious before the German guards.

"Kommen Sie mit mir jetzt, Sie beide."

Come with me now, both of you. The words seemed to snap from the guard's mouth. He stood back as they left a room that felt more like a cell, then pushed past to lead them to the office where the meeting with Untersturmführer Acker and the Kommandant had taken place.

Both officers were staring at Maisie—*Edwina Donat*—as she regarded the man standing in the corner of the room. He held out his hands to her as she began to run toward him. Then she stopped.

"Meine Tochter. Meine Tochter. Komm zu mir. Komm in meine Arme."

As Maisie heard the words—My *daughter. My daughter. Come to me. Come into my arms*—she stopped and looked at the man, feeling as if her heart would break into many parts. His skeletal hands and sockless feet drew her attention more than the small pyramids of bone that were once full cheeks. His eyes seemed burned into their sockets, and she could see the points of his clavicles prominent through the fabric of his collarless shirt and the threadbare jacket draped over his skeletal frame. The trousers he had been given seemed as if they would not even fit a twelve-year-old boy, and as he moved toward her, the soles of his shoes flapped away from the cracked and worn leather.

And then, before she said a word, she wondered how she might save this man. She dropped her head, instead seeing the face of Francesca Thomas. *Know him, Edwina. Know your father. Is this he?*

She turned to Leslie, then to the two officers. Time had become suspended, so still she could hear her heart beating, the blood coursing through her veins, the reverberation in her ears. Beyond herself, she was aware of the pleading of a frail man who was now taking her hand, placing it on his shoulder as if to persuade her to hold him, to give him comfort. She was aware that only one second, then another had passed, yet she knew she must speak her truth—if only for Leon Donat and his daughter.

Maisie turned to Gilbert Leslie, then to the two officers who waited. "This man is not my father," she said. "This is not Leon Donat."

And then she put her arms around the man and held him to her as she wept. "Es tut mir leid. Wahrlich, ich bin so sehr traurig."

Her German was perfect.

I am so sorry. Truly, I am so very sorry.

Two guards dragged the man from the room, and Leslie—the white pallor of fear now gone from his complexion, replaced by heightened color—stepped forward to gain the officer's attention.

"On behalf of His Majesty's gov—"

Maisie raised her voice above the cries emanating from the corridor as the man was dragged away.

"Sirs, as you can imagine, I am very distressed—and I want to know where my father is. But, please, show clemency toward that man. He really does not know what he is doing or has done."

"Fräulein Donat, this is a very serious matter," said Acker. "We must establish what has happened, how this man has been successful in appearing to be your father, and indeed locate your father, dead or alive. I say again, this is a most serious matter." He nodded to Leslie as if dismissing him, and along with him, the issue of a British citizen who was now unaccounted for.

"Gentlemen!" Maisie felt herself on the verge of shouting. Leslie reached out to place his hand on her arm, as if the movement would stop her speaking. "Gentlemen, as I was about to say—show some clemency, for I believe the man who was brought to me is indeed a man who fought for your country in the war, and now has a . . . a . . . compromised mental capacity." She felt herself hesitate, as if her lips could only fumble over her words, which she spoke in English. Leslie translated. Maisie continued, making up the details with each second, melding her own experience with a new story for Edwina Donat. "I . . . I . . . my father, during the war, insisted I help in some way, so I visited men who had been shell-shocked, just to talk to them, read to them, to bring some comfort. So, you see . . . so you see, I know what I have seen. That man has, I think, been used by someone and, because he knew no better, was a willing puppet. You have given him new clothing, so he knew, somewhere in the outer reaches of his mind, that someone must be coming from beyond the prison. And that was I—so he called me 'daughter' not because I am his child, but because it was a safe word to use." She paused, looked at Leslie, then at the officers. "This I believe. And now I must ask— do you know where my father is, or is this as much a shock to you as it is to me?"

Leslie intervened. "Miss Donat, let us deal with this through dip- lomatic channels. I am sure the gentlemen will observe protocols with regard to the identification of the man we have just seen, and get to the bottom of why he is here—and why your father is not here." He looked toward the officers, who were both standing at attention.

"You will leave now," said the Kommandant. He turned to Maisie. "As stated, we will conduct an investigation." The men turned and left the room, and were replaced by guards who accompanied Maisie and Gilbert Leslie to their motor car.

Maisie watched Dachau grow smaller and smaller as the vehicle drew away, beyond the bounds of the camp. The two guards were still standing to attention, watching them depart. They did not move, even when the motor car began to turn to join the road once more.

"For goodness' sake, Miss Donat, what the hell just happened in there? Are you absolutely sure that man was not your father? Because he looked like every photograph I have seen of Leon Donat since I was handed this case."

"That man was not—I repeat, not—my father. Mr. Leslie, my father would not have greeted me in German. He might be proficient in the language and able to conduct business, but we're British—we speak English. I don't know how you can question me—I thought it was obvious. Yes, he was of the same height, the eyes are similar, and at one point he would have had my father's build. But please do not assume I would not know my father because time has passed while he has been incarcerated in one of the most terrible places on earth."

Leslie rubbed his forehead. "This is going to cause an enormous amount of trouble, Miss Donat. We've managed to keep this whole agreement with the Germans under wraps, and while dealing with their nasty SS boys, and now diplomatic machinations are going to swamp us. There's the situation with Austria, the question of the Sudetenland. The last thing we need is this situation to distract us from matters of policy. The Prime Minister would be furious if he knew."

She took a breath, closed her eyes, and then spoke again. "Mr.

Leslie, just for one moment, let us consider the horrors that await the man I just had to dismiss as not being my father. I have consigned a human being to more torture, and I am sure he has endured a terror beyond words in that place. Yet I could not pretend, as I would have liked to, just to get him out of there. I had to tell the truth, because I have to find my father. Now I will have that man on my conscience for the rest of my life—because I denied him his freedom."

Leslie rubbed his eyes. "What do you mean, you have to find your father? I daresay you will be required to leave Germany soonest. There will doubtless be a veritable brick of paperwork waiting for me at the consulate."

Maisie turned to Leslie. "I am not going anywhere until I know what has happened to my father. I want to know if my father is still in that prison. Frankly, I don't think he is. How did that man come to be mistaken for my father? Make no mistake, those two thugs in uniform were as shocked as we were that he was not Leon Donat. They are now in the position of having received funds from the British government in exchange for a British citizen who was wrongly imprisoned—and they've lost him. My father could be dead, but if he isn't, then where is he? And why did he not come home? I want to know all these things, Mr. Leslie."

"But really, Miss Donat, you do not have any experience of these things." His half laugh was dismissive, reminding her of Acker. "You should go home to England now, instead of waiting for news here."

"I don't intend to wait for anything, Mr. Leslie." She looked out of the window. "I may not have the experience, but what I lack in experience, I will make up for in tenacity. I do not intend to take a backseat any longer."

"The matter of your continued presence in Munich is something

I have to discuss with my superiors. It will be a diplomatic embarrassment."

"Discuss it all you want. I will do what I have to do." She knew the insolence in her tone would not endear her to Leslie, but at the same time, she could only respond as if it were Frankie Dobbs who was unaccounted for.

Maisie turned away, looking out once more to the winter-barren trees lining the streets as the motor car wove through Munich traffic. Already a plan was forming in her mind, a plan that encompassed Elaine Otterburn, who was unaccounted for, and Mark Scott—who she hoped really was in her wake, the enemy in his sights.

Then there was the matter of the missing—presumed dead— Luther Gramm. Maisie wondered if the man's murder was intertwined with the disappearance of an English businessman. Or was it just a distraction from the heart of the matter?

Where was Leon Donat?

Hurried plans were made for Maisie to spend the night at the consulate, in a room designated for visiting foreign office dignitaries. She requested a new reservation be made at the Hotel Vier Jahreszeiten for the following day. When the consular clerk, an assistant to Leslie, asked how many nights she would be staying at the hotel, she replied, "Three," not wanting Leslie to know she might be in Munich longer. The bill would be settled by the consulate upon receipt; she would change the date of anticipated departure when she signed the register.

The room where she would spend the night was well appointed in an almost Gothic décor, with heavy velvet curtains and thick Persian rugs on a carpet that, before it faded, would have been the color of crushed blackberries. The furniture seemed cumbersome, and she wondered how many men would have been required to move just one piece. As she stood on the threshold, she thought the room might serve well for a moving-picture show starring Bela Lugosi.

She was informed that the driver would take her to the hotel the following day, after lunch, and that Mr. Leslie would see her in the morning, when he'd had sufficient opportunity to speak with his superiors in London. Another visit to the Nazi headquarters might be necessary—"Though in the circumstances, they should come to us," said the clerk, his voice tinged with contempt.

Yes, I bet he'll be doing a lot of speaking, thought Maisie as she imagined Leslie rattling off instructions to get this or that person on the telephone. She checked the time: late afternoon. Leslie would have spoken to Huntley and MacFarlane without delay. Huntley would deal with foreign office liaison, using whatever tactics were necessary to keep the truth of today's outcome from spreading along the corridors of Whitehall and Westminster. Maisie and Leon Donat were small fry in terms of the greater political maneuvering at present under way—but like a tiny pebble in a shoe, the truth about them could be crippling if revealed. And how would Robbie MacFarlane respond to the businessman's disappearance? *Oh, please, please, keep him away from Munich.* She uttered the words as if offering up a prayer to be answered.

Sitting at the mahogany writing desk, Maisie made a list. Locating Mark Scott was imperative—she was not sure she trusted him, but without doubt he had his finger in a few pies, and he seemed to have knowledge at his disposal. Was Elaine Otterburn safe in England—or was she somewhere in Munich? Maisie had heard nothing more about the dead SS officer. That problem had gone to ground—but for how long? Then there was the place where Leon Donat had been arrested, a workshop of some sort. It was likely locked up by now, the doors chained, but she had to locate it, as well as to find someone who knew Ulli Bader, the man Leon Donat had tried to help. He was supposedly the son of a good friend. Who was that friend, and where was his son, the man who had apparently evaded capture?

And was it true that Leon Donat had tried to help? Had he tried to assist the young man, or had he become involved somehow in producing propaganda against Hitler's Reich? Had he really been arrested in error, or had he committed a crime against the Führer's regime? But how could he have? He'd only been in Munich a matter of days. Unless . . . unless he'd wanted to stay.

Maisie leaned back in the chair, feeling the unforgiving wood press into her spine. She sat forward again and looked over her notes. She had brought no documentation with her from England, other than the papers required to release Donat. She'd had only a short time to memorize all the reports, photographs, letters, and transcribed interviews she was tasked with reading before her departure from England. She closed her eyes as if to envision each sheet of paper, each image.

A knock at the door heralded the arrival of a late lunch. She had asked for only a sandwich and a cup of tea. As she ate, she formed her plan. There was not much time before nightfall, but she hoped something could be accomplished before the end of the day. Had all gone well, she would be at the station by now, as good as on her way home. Now she could only speculate on when that journey might take place. Before doubt could claim her, she made ready to leave the consulate, put on her coat and hat, and walked toward the door. Only as she passed the mirror did she realize that she had forgotten to put on her wig. And of more crucial importance, she had answered the door and taken in the tray without it, having taken it off almost as soon as she was left alone.

The momentary terror passed as soon as she replaced the wig, after rubbing in cold cream to soothe the welt along the top of her forehead. She would carry on as if nothing had happened. But the woman who brought her lunch might have seen her when she arrived at the consulate, wig in place. Would she see her again? And would she mention—possibly to Leslie—that the lady in the guest room had very short hair indeed?

Perhaps she should wait until tomorrow to begin her search for Leon Donat, when she was fresh and rested. She could not afford another slip.

Fatigued and despondent, she removed her coat and hat and pulled off the wig again. Throwing them all across a leather chair, she lay back and stared at the ceiling, where a garland of alabaster leaves encircled an ornate glass chandelier hung to resemble a flower, as if crystal were growing down from above her head. She thought about the man she had denied freedom. She felt like a Judas. But how could she have saved him? She suspected the man had been used, but had she accepted him as her father to save his life, how could she have traveled through Germany and France with him, a man who apparently spoke no English and thus was clearly not the man she had come to receive on behalf of herself and her country? Could she have taken him and just put him on a train for France and freedom? Perhaps. But if the SS officers were party to the subterfuge, then she would have been revealed as an impostor.

She'd had to make a swift decision in the guard room, and for better or worse she had told the truth. How could anyone have guessed, when the man was thrown in prison, that Leon Donat's captors would begin to play cat and mouse, stipulating that a member of the prisoner's family should be present for his release? After all, a family member would be able to identify him.

Maisie stood up and walked across to the window to draw the curtains. The room faced a side street, which was empty save for a couple of people walking toward the main thoroughfare as if to catch a train at the end of the working day. She was about to reach for the cord to draw the curtains when she noticed a man lingering under a lamp across the street. She looked down; below her window a guard patrolled the building. It was not a display of might, simply one guard assigned, she supposed, to answer questions, direct travelers to the entrance around the corner, and help the odd person who had mislaid a passport.

When she glanced back toward the lamp, the man was still there but had now retreated into the shadows. She smiled. If she was correct, Mark Scott still had her six.

CHAPTER 13

M aisie ordered breakfast in her room, though this time she was careful to replace her wig long before she heard the maid's knock at the door. As she opened it, she noticed the woman looking at her twice, as if trying to pinpoint what was different about her.

Maisie smiled. "I had my hair tied back last night—I'd just washed it, and couldn't find a hair dryer. I wonder if you have such a thing here?"

The woman smiled. Her English was perfect. "We don't have hair dryers—most of our guests are men, and if they're accompanied by their wives, the maid attends to their hair."

"Of course. Thank you. Anyway, it's dry now, and a few curlers always do the trick."

The woman nodded and left the room.

Maisie breathed a sigh of relief, though she wondered if the woman believed a word she'd said.

A sealed envelope bearing her assumed name had been placed to one side of her breakfast tray.

Miss Edwina Donat

Timetable, March 12, 1938

09:15 hrs Collected by Peter Stamont

09:30 hrs Library

Briefing with Mr. Gilbert Leslie

10:00 hrs Take private telephone call from London

10:15 hrs Depart for Nazi headquarters

10:45 hrs Briefing on investigation

11:15 hrs Proposed departure from Nazi headquarters

11:45 hrs Arrive at consulate; debrief in library

12:15 hrs Luncheon in consular dining room

13:00 hrs Depart for Hotel Vier Jahreszeiten

Miss Edwina Donat must submit daily timetable to the consulate for approval.

"Well, we'll see about that." Maisie ran her finger down the page, where she tapped her fingernail against one word: *approval.*

At the appointed time, not a minute too soon or a second too late, a man who introduced himself as Peter Stamont knocked at the door. Maisie was ready for the briefing and the journey to Nazi headquarters: she wore her plain burgundy costume and her stout walking shoes, and carried her coat over one arm. Her hat was already pinned to the wig, which for once felt secure on her head. Or perhaps she was simply getting used to it.

Stamont was what her stepmother would have called a "long, tall drink of water" in a blue pinstripe suit. He had a stoop to his shoulders, as if from childhood his height had caused him to lean forward in an effort to hear and be heard. She was sure he had no need of amplification, but whenever she spoke, he cupped his ear with one hand. His dark eyes and brows suggested an earnest approach to life, and she thought, he might be one of those people who always tried to please. She wondered how he felt when a column of men with brown uniforms raising their hands in a Nazi salute marched toward him on the street. He was too tall not to be noticed. Did he make a quick detour into a shop or down an alley? Or did he do as was expected in his host country? She suspected the latter. She could not blame him for it—he was too much of a target.

Stamont guided her to the library, where Gilbert Leslie waited, a black telephone on the table before him. As she sat down, Maisie realized there was a lock at the side of the telephone. Calls could neither be made nor received from it without the key on the table next to Leslie.

"Miss Donat. I trust you had a good night. Sleep well?"

"In that room, I suppose one expects to sleep like the dead."

Leslie looked up, giving a brief smile. "Didn't take you for one with a quick quip at the ready, Miss Donat—but I suppose it is a bit like an anteroom at an Italian mausoleum, not that I have ever been in one." He pressed his lips together. "Right, down to business. First of all, I've been in touch with London—with a Mr. Brian Huntley. Not sure if you've heard his name, but he was one of the more important negotiators with regard to your father's release."

Maisie frowned. "The name is a little familiar." She told the white lie with ease, continuing in the same vein. "I had a briefing from a woman, though I was not informed of her name. I was simply told I would meet you here in Munich, and off we'd go. Of course there was some indication of what I might expect when I relinquished the papers to be counterstamped by the Nazi authorities, that sort of thing."

Maisie pulled her chair in closer to the table, as if earnest in her words. "It's all rather like being swept up into a nightmare, actually. I keep thinking I will wake up and find myself on a train to Paris with my father sitting next to me, asking me if I could possibly bear another game of cards."

"Yes, quite. In any case, I've been on the telephone this morning to London, and my instructions are to assist and encourage our hosts—the term 'hosts' is loose—to search for Mr. Leon Donat. You have been given leave to remain for some three days, considering the toll this must have taken on you. We understand how difficult it would be for you to depart Munich, under the circumstances. You will want to know any information as it comes in."

"All the time I do not know where my father is, I will be anxious for news."

"Indeed." Leslie consulted his notes and looked back at Maisie. "Now, we have been summoned to Nazi headquarters. Apparently, this whole thing has put them into a bit of a spin, and—"

"How do you know they're in a spin?"

"Miss Donat, not only would we be in a spin if the boot were on our foot—losing citizens at a diplomatically sensitive time is not generally a good idea—but we have our sources."

"I see. Of course you do."

"One thing might be in our favor, though it will certainly draw manpower away from the investigation. It has to be said that the SS administrators and their Gestapo brethren are nothing less than vipers when it comes to seeking out prey." He tapped the table. "Events have moved on apace in Austria. German troops entered the country, and we have word that Kurt von Schuschnigg, the Austrian chancellor, has been replaced by the Nazi Arthur Seyss-Inquart. The Gestapo and Waffen SS will be swarming across Vienna—you can count on that." He turned a page of typewritten notes. "We have word that Herr Hitler will be making a triumphant entry into Vienna tomorrow. However, whilst all this is going on—and we can only hope it puts the men we see today in a good mood—I must assure you that we have certain resources of our own here in Munich, and will conduct a parallel investigation into your father's disappearance. Though such searching has, of course, to be carried out in a somewhat, well, careful manner."

Maisie nodded. "And you will keep me posted daily?"

"We will do our best, though you understand there are certain formalities here that cannot be divulged to a civilian, no matter how deeply concerned with the welfare of the subject of the investigation."

"Yes, of course."

"Now, let me brief you on what we expect at Nazi HQ. Frankly, they cannot bully you. You have been as shocked as anyone could be, given the circumstances—but they will ask about your father's associates here, and will ask you again about his intentions during what should have been a sojourn of just a few days. They may try to intimidate you—in fact, at some point, you can count on it—but simply be yourself, and all will be well."

Maisie nodded.

Leslie looked at his watch. "The call should be coming in soon. Again, nothing to worry about, Miss Donat—some foreign office bod over there wants to check up on you, in private. A word to the wise, though—all calls received and placed from this telephone in this room are, we hope, unable to be overheard by any listening devices employed outside the confines of the consulate, and indeed inside the building. However, one can never completely trust anyone. Frankly, I remain circumspect in all telephone conversations. Mind you, you're safer than you would be on an ordinary telephone." He took the key, slipped it into the lock, lifted the receiver, and turned the dial once for the operator.

There was a click as the call was answered, and Leslie cleared his throat to speak. "Yes, thank you. Ready when London comes in." He nodded, as if the operator were in the room. Then he replaced the receiver, pushed back his chair, picked up the sheaf of papers, and took one step toward the door. The telephone rang. Leslie did not look back, but kept walking. Maisie waited for the door to close behind him, and picked up the receiver.

"Are you there?"

"Yes, I'm here."

"Well, you've been having some fun, haven't you, lass?"

"Just so I know you're who I think you are, tell me your favorite pub."

"Oh, for heaven's sake." MacFarlane paused. "We've trained you too well. It's the Cuillins of Skye."

"Right. As you can imagine, Mr. MacFarlane, I wouldn't mind a swift visit there right now."

"Mr. MacFarlane, is it now? All right, Maisie. Get it off your chest."

"In the few days since I arrived in Munich, I have been followed and engaged in conversation by an American—from the United States Justice Department, I might add—who maintains, with his hand on his heart, that he has my six. Elaine Otterburn is in all likelihood under suspicion for the murder of an SS officer, though I also have a suspicion about that little problem." Maisie took a deep breath to keep her voice steady. "More to the point, in the course of my duty to bring Leon Donat home to England, I may have consigned a poor sick man to torture beyond belief—that's the one breaking my heart, Robbie, and I have to live with it. Now then, what's all this about having to give Leslie a list of my plans for each day? I have a job to do here, and that is to find Leon . . . *my father* . . . and if he's still alive, bring him home. Given what I've heard about what's happened in Austria, I suppose we're going to need all the boffins we can get. And one more thing—does Leslie know who I am? Or are we two being moved around like puppets?"

"One thing at a time, Maisie. Here's my colleague for you."

There was an audible click on the line, and Brian Huntley spoke.

"Due care, Miss Donat. Due care. Do you understand?"

"I may have slipped up a bit with Mr. M."

"I am by nature a very careful man."

"Tell me what's going on. I'm being allowed to remain here for three days—I intend to search for my father."

"Right you are. Amateurs have been known to be lucky, but do remember that the German government is beholden to search for Mr. Donat, and there are other resources being deployed to help."

"I take it my intentions meet with your approval."

"I see no problem, Miss Donat—as long as you don't tread on any very sensitive toes. I look forward to your regular reports."

Maisie paused. "Has Miss Elaine Otterburn arrived back in England?"

"No. You had a most regrettable meeting with Miss Otterburn."

"It was a difficult situation. I made a promise."

"Difficult situation!" Robbie MacFarlane's retort in the background was loud enough for her to hear. "You knew better than that, Maisie."

"Indeed," said Huntley, in response to Maisie's explanation, and—Maisie suspected—to Macfarlane's comment. "We remain troubled by the fact that plans regarding your journey to Munich were so readily available. However, that leak has been stemmed." Huntley cleared his throat. "Please keep me apprised of your progress. I take it you will be looking for the people—professors and the like—your father visited before his disappearance."

Maisie avoided confirming Huntley's assumption, commenting, "I'm hampered by the fact that tomorrow is a Sunday—but I will keep you informed."

"Very good. And do take care, Miss Donat. We will be working from this end in the search for your father."

The meeting at the Nazi headquarters was a formality. Security was as intense as before, but there was an urgent jubilation in the air. Men rushed back and forth; motor cars drew up and left, filled with black-clad officers of the Schutzstaffel. Maisie answered one familiar question after another, none posing a challenge. Once again she assured Hans Berger that the man at Dachau truly was not her father.

For a moment a silence fell. Berger dispatched the junior officer on an errand—a ruse, Maisie suspected, so they might have a private conversation.

"Our fellow officer remains missing, Miss Donat." Berger's English was flawless, as before.

"I beg your pardon? I don't understand how that has anything to do with me—or the search for my father."

Berger leaned forward. "But you visited Miss Otterburn, and now she's also disappeared."

"We already discussed the problem of Miss Otterburn. She might well have taken my advice and returned to her family—or she could have absconded with your colleague. I really don't know—and at the moment, if I may say so, there is nothing I can do about either of them, because I would not know where to start."

Maisie felt the strength in her voice, and she feared she'd been too forthright. But to her surprise, Berger appeared to withdraw. He rose from his chair, stepped to one side, and took up a place by the window, his hands clasped behind his back. Maisie remained in her seat, silent.

"I know you have no information for me, Miss Donat. But if at any point you do, please see that I receive word without delay."

Maisie was about to reply when Berger turned. His eyes, she saw, seemed red. She cast her gaze down toward the handbag on her lap, as if searching for a handkerchief or a pen, then met his again.

"Yes, of course." Her answer was firm.

The junior officer returned, handed another clutch of papers to Berger, who nodded. "See Miss Donat out to meet Mr. Leslie," he instructed his assistant. He did not look up again, and she did not offer a formal word of departure. Soon she was in the motor car with Leslie, recounting to him every detail of the meeting—with the exception of the tears she had seen in Berger's eyes.

"Well, that's a relief," said Leslie. "Nothing of note, everything in order—with a bit of luck, we won't have to see this place again."

Maisie said nothing. Though there was no indication of what had happened in the days since his death, she felt sure Luther Gramm's body would not be found—and suspected Berger had orchestrated the removal and disposal of the young man's remains. Berger's attempt to hide his emotions while discussing the disappearance of the couple pointed to a deeper connection with either Luther Gramm or John Otterburn's daughter. Hadn't Mark Scott intimated as much? Or perhaps it was fear itself that had affected the officer—even if he was not implicated, perhaps he guessed that his colleague was dead.

But in truth, Maisie admitted to herself, she had no evidence that Berger knew anything about Gramm's disappearance. All she had was conjecture—and Mark Scott's innuendo.

"Stimme der Freiheit." *Voice of Freedom*. Maisie saw the words torn to shreds, scattered across the floor as she peered through the lower ground-floor window into the darkened interior of an almost derelict house, flanked by others of the same age and in a similar state of repair. With her hands cupped around her eyes, she squinted, trying to see if there might be another way into the building.

Following the interview at Nazi headquarters, Maisie had been taken to the Hotel Vier Jahreszeiten, where a room had been reserved for three nights. She asked the clerk if the room might be available for an additional two nights, should they be required. Yes, he said, thus far the room was not booked beyond the Monday night.

Now she was free to do as she pleased—to a point. Without doubt someone would be charged with keeping tabs on her. In order to foil any surveillance of her movements, she took one bus after another and walked along byways she did not know, hoping they might lead her back to her map, and on her way. She had the name and address of the press for the journal Leon Donat had been accused of supporting, in a poorer district known as the Au, and though she knew it might be clear to anyone following her that this would be her destination, she wanted just a little time on her own to look around.

Maisie picked up the solid padlock again, felt its weight in her hand, and rolled it on its back. She let it drop in frustration. Leaning toward the window, she peered in, again searching for a way in. It was then that she noticed movement at the corner of her eye. She gasped, straining to see. A cat emerged from a corner of the room and stretched out, yawning. It clawed at the sheets of paper strewn across the floor, then sat down to lick its paws. Maisie stepped back.

She listened to the street above and then made her way up steps flanked by moldy green walls oozing freezing water, and looked both ways along the street before stepping out. At the next corner she turned into a cobblestone alley. Which of these back doors led to the former home of the *Voice of Freedom*? The rear entrance of one of the houses was boarded up—the planks of wood rotten, the nails rusty. *Verboten!* The warning was clear. Maisie stepped toward the planks, pulling one back. The door was in a similar state, the wood soft and worm-ridden.

Maisie stopped for a moment. One of the elements of life in Germany that had impressed her was its citizens' attention to detail, as if every job worth doing—whether that job was building a house, cleaning a street, or boarding up a disused property—must be perfect. This work might have been good enough when it was completed, but it had not lasted—and that struck Maisie as unusual. But there again, the whole of Munich seemed to shout a warning, that you dare not cross the Reich.

The alley remained quiet, not a soul in sight. Wishing she had worn trousers, Maisie pulled away another plank, tried the lock, and pushed against the door. As she continued to apply pressure, she felt it begin to give. The lock was shearing away from the wood, but she needed something else to make the final break. She looked around and picked up a piece of old metal with which she might lever the lock from the door. It was rusty, but strong enough. She pushed the metal between wood and lock and pulled back, feeling the wood splinter. With a sound like a firecracker, the door fell open.

Maisie looked both ways along the alley, then up at the windows of the neighboring houses. A shaft of daylight from behind fell past her through the open door as far as the steps within. She opened her handbag, pulled out a box of matches, and struck one. It burned long enough for a glance around a room now revealed to be a scullery, with a large square sink to the left, an old cast iron stove to the right. Shelves hung on the walls, and the door to a larder stood open. The floor was wet, with water seeping from a leaking pipe under the sink. It was so cold Maisie felt as if she were turning blue from head to toe. She lit another match, located an inner door, and stepped toward a narrow passageway. In the light of a fresh match, she saw dark brown smears across the wall. She drew closer, and as the match flickered and died, she knew it was blood. Plaster fallen from the ceiling above crunched underfoot. She reached out toward the door she knew was to her right, and pushed it open.

Two bright eyes peered at her. Light from the window at the front slanted across the black cat. Its coat rippled, and with a yowl it leaped past her and into the passageway. She turned back to the room. Enough light filtered in from the street to show her what had come to pass here. Copies of the *Voice of Freedom*, torn to shreds, were strewn across the floor. She suspected the remnants had been left as a warning to others who were thinking of crossing Hitler's regime. Fragments of cast iron were piled in the corner. She lit another match and brought the flame closer; they were parts from what had once been a small printing press. Ink had been poured across the floor, mixed with the reddish-brown stains that could only be dried blood.

It was all Maisie could do to remain on her feet. She held out her hand to steady herself. As if she were being taken back in time, she could see before her what had happened in this place. A small cadre of like-minded men and women had gathered here to write and publish what they believed to be the truth about Herr Hitler's Third Reich. They had been discovered, and they had paid the price. Were they all dead? No, not all. The young man to whom Leon Donat had offered a job had escaped, according to reports. But had Leon Donat been here? As she stood in the room, she believed he had—for no other reason than it was something she wanted to believe. Given all that she had seen in Munich, she wanted to believe that Leon Donat had supported the dissidents who dared to speak out. She wanted to believe that he had, in fact, escaped with his life—or died because he was a man committed to truth. She shivered.

The meager light had begun to fade. She knew she should leave and return to the hotel.

As she stepped into the passageway, a feline sound, a squawk almost birdlike, caused her to stop.

"What *are* you doing here?" She bent down to run her hand across the sleek black coat. "I think you're a witch's cat."

The creature wrapped its body around her ankles, so she chivvied it away with her hand. "Go on now, don't trip me up."

Holding on to the now-broken door, Maisie stepped with care onto the rough ground that led to the street, only to be met by the screams of two little girls.

"Haben sie keine Angst. Ich werde dir nicht weh tun—ich war gerade auf der suche am Haus." *Do not be afraid. I will not hurt you, I was just looking at the house.*

"Bist du ein Geist?"

She laughed. She was not a ghost, she assured them, or a witch—even though a black cat was following her.

One of the girls had hair the color of wheat, her pale blue eyes mirroring the color of her coat, which had a dark blue velvet collar. A blue dress and leather lace-up boots peeked out beneath the coat, a blue scarf was wrapped around her neck, and gloves secured with tape hung below her sleeves.

The other girl's thick brown hair was tamed in two braids. She too wore a coat, with a matching hat pulled down almost to her eyes. Her gloves were secured to the sleeves of her coat in a similar fashion to those of her friend, and she wore almost identical lace-up boots.

"Is this your cat?" Maisie asked in German.

The dark-haired girl shook her head. "No, but we bring him food when we come."

"I see, so that's why you're here. But it will be getting dark soon, and this doesn't look like a safe place."

"This is my friend, Rachel," the blond girl explained. "We can play together here. No one can see us."

"And what's your name?" Maisie smiled to encourage the girls.

"Adele."

Adele leaned toward Rachel and whispered in her ear. Rachel nodded.

"We've seen a ghost here," said Adele.

Maisie widened her eyes and stepped closer. "You have? Goodness, that is a very scary thing to see." She cupped her ear as if to hear a secret. "Tell me about the ghost."

Soon both girls began talking at once, their words tumbling out to form a story. They explained that they came to the street to play together so Adele's parents could not see them, and on two different occasions they had seen the ghost going in through the door, but they'd never seen him leave.

"Though he might go back to his grave after we've gone home."

The girls nodded in unison, as if in agreement about the ghost's final destination.

"Do you think he comes often?"

The girls shrugged. Maisie could see they were losing interest.

"We have to go now," said Adele. "Rachel shouldn't really be here, because it's Shabbat. She has to go home before her mother finds out she's playing."

"Well, take care on your way home." Maisie watched as the girls held hands and began to run away. They skipped toward the corner, dropping their hands as they entered the main street.

Maisie pressed her lips together and looked up at the now-darkening sky. She would have liked to go back into the basement, or at least look for whatever it was the "ghost" had come for. But it was time to return to the hotel. Time to go back to her plans.

As she walked away, she thought of all she had seen since arriving in Munich—of the veneer of ordinary life overlaying something much darker, a mood among the people that pressed down upon her heart so she felt the weight of it on her chest. At times she thought it might stop her breathing. And she knew she had seen something she would never forget, an image that would come back to her unbidden throughout the days of her life: two little German girls, playing in the rubble behind a derelict building because no one would be there to see them meeting.

CHAPTER 14

aisie made her way back to the hotel by tram and on foot. She was surprised at how easily she was finding her way around, as if the geography of a place were another language and she was developing her ear for the sounds, oft-used words, and the way in which movement echoes speech. She had come to know that every city has its ebb and flow, its tide pools, rivers, and still waters; the time she'd spent wandering had aided her immersion.

She would return to the Au the next day and spend more time in the old building. She was not sure what she might find, but the pull to go back was strong. And Sunday would be a quiet day, though there might be celebrations to mark Austria being brought into the fold with Herr Hitler's Third Reich. In any case, she'd make the journey; she knew she had missed something. In addition, she wanted to return once more to the house where Elaine Otterburn had lived. More than anything, she wanted to find Leon Donat, though now even more she wondered if he was still alive.

In her room, she set to work. She pulled a large paper liner from one of the drawers in the dresser between the windows and placed it on the table. It was just the right size for a case map. On it she wrote Leon Donat's name and circled it, then those of Gilbert Leslie, Mark

Scott, Elaine Otterburn, and Hans Berger. Sitting back, she began to write notes across the sheet of paper, using a lipstick to make a cross here or circle another name or idea. She had a feeling that whoever the girls had seen coming to the basement where the *Voice of Freedom* was printed had been there to collect something—but what? She'd hardly been able to see the first time she stumbled into the building. She would need a torch. How would she obtain such a thing on a Sunday, when shops were closed? She would have to ask for one at the hotel, and come up with a good excuse for needing the *Taschenlampe*.

As she sat at the table, tapping her pen against the wood, already new thoughts and possibilities were coming to mind, and she suspected that if she managed to find out who was coming to the house—and why—she would in turn find out what happened to Leon Donat.

Maisie was thirsty and hungry. She sat back and decided to go downstairs to the restaurant for supper, and perhaps a well-deserved glass of wine. She thought of Priscilla, and wondered if after all that had happened, a gin and tonic would not be such a bad idea. A woman dining alone was already subject to enough attention, though. One enjoying a cocktail without a companion might inspire whispered speculation from other patrons. She rooted through her bag until she found a book Priscilla had given her to read during her journey. *Gone with the Wind*. She sighed. It would not have been her first choice, but any book was a good book for a woman alone who did not want the attention of others.

Entering the restaurant, Maisie noticed a copy of the *Times* on a chair set to one side. She picked up the newspaper and asked to be seated at a table in a corner of the dining room. She sat with her back against a banquette, where she could watch other patrons coming and going. With her newspaper folded to the first page—though she had to lean toward a wall light to see the print—she placed her order for a glass of white wine and a fish dish with vegetables and potato. She took one look around the room, trying to establish whether anyone had followed her, then pulled out her book, placing it next to her on the table, ready to open as soon as her meal was served. For now she continued with the newspaper.

"If you can read it, you can speak it." The voice was familiar.

Maisie looked up to the man staring down at her. She shook her head.

"English, I mean," said Mark Scott.

"That sounds like a very bad line in one of those pictures at the cinema. What are you doing here?" She kept her voice down, her eyes scanning the room in case their conversation had attracted interest. "You of all people should be more circumspect."

"Probably, but strange as it may sound, I am one of those guys easily forgotten by people in my midst. For some reason they don't remember me." He set his hat on the banquette next to Maisie and drew back the chair opposite her. "Mind if I join you?" He continued to sit down without waiting for a reply. Once seated, he reached for her book and slipped into an accentuated drawl. "*Gone with the Wind?* Miss Donat, if the best you can do is a bit of southern romance, why, I do declare, you aren't the woman I estimated you to be."

Maisie shook her head and looked away.

"Oh, come on—even at the worst of times, we must have something to smile about."

"It's hard to forget what the worst of times can really be like, Mr. Scott, especially in the midst of another of those times." She pushed the newspaper toward him, with its headline in bold letters: "Hitler Announces Union with Austria." She looked up as a waiter approached with her glass of wine. "I'm not sure you should be seen here, Mr. Scott—or with me."

"I'll make it quick, then." He shook his head when the waiter asked if he would like to order a beverage. "What happened when you went along to see your friend Berger? Was he tap-dancing, trying to explain the disappearance of Leon Donat?"

Maisie shook her head. "No." She sipped her wine, casting her gaze around the room once more. She wasn't sure Scott was as invisible as he considered himself to be. "Let's just say it was all very light and cordial—or as light and cordial as one would expect in that place. I'm allowed to stay here for about three days, which I will use to find Donat. They won't like me looking—the Germans *or* the British in Munich. But . . . there's something very amiss here."

"Be careful—you have no idea how complex this situation is."

Maisie sat back. "Oh, I think I do, Mr. Scott. I'm just surprised no one has found either Donat or the young man he was supposedly helping. Mind you, the Germans thought they had him. I cannot believe they were fooled."

"Maybe they weren't."

Maisie kept her voice low, took another sip of wine, and set down her glass. "That had crossed my mind."

"It's a web, Miss . . . Donat." He smiled as the waiter approached again and set a plate in front of Maisie.

She declined additional condiments, and the waiter left. Scott waited until he was out of earshot.

"Don't be the fly who gets caught in that web, Fräulein D. We're all skirting the edges—your friend Leslie too. Did you see anything interesting today? I lost you just as the tram made it to that stop close to the river."

Maisie looked at Scott, folded the newspaper, and lifted her knife and fork. "That's annoying—I thought I'd managed to get rid of you before that." She sighed, at once grateful for someone to talk to beyond the stiff Leslie and officers of the SS. "I saw two German girls playing. They must have been seven or eight. Both wrapped up warm and looking for the stray cat they'd befriended, to give it some food. Then they went on their way."

"That sounds riveting, Fräulein D."

"Give it a little while, and it might be: one was Jewish, and the other wasn't. They were playing where they might not be seen, because one set of parents had forbidden their daughter to play with her friend—perhaps for the safety of both children, who knows? Given the climate here, one must be careful before pointing the finger of blame. But that's the great sadness of any act of discrimination, isn't it? When children cannot play together." Maisie reached for her book. She wanted to be alone.

"Well, ma'am, I guess I had better take my leave." Once again Scott sounded as if he'd come straight from America's Deep South. He stood up and was gone, passing into the shadows of the dimly lit dining room. No one looked up. No waiter paid attention to his leaving. He might never have been in the room.

Before going to bed, Maisie worked on her case map. She had identified two points to which she would direct her attention the following morning. She wanted to return to the place where the *Voice of Freedom* had been published, and to revisit the house where Elaine Otterburn had lived with the other girls. And where was Elaine, if not in England?

In the morning, on her journey toward the Au, Maisie thought about Elaine and how she'd come to the Hotel Vier Jahreszeiten to find her, her clothing in shreds, blood on her dress, with barely an ounce of dominion over her thoughts. Was it real terror? Or an act? Maisie had at once responded to Elaine's predicament. Her decision to help the young woman now seemed to be a poor choice—but there had been few options. She could hardly alert the police—Elaine would have been under immediate suspicion, and in all likelihood incarcerated. Had John Otterburn's daughter left Munich for another city—if not in Germany, then perhaps one of its neighbors? And if she was still here, then why had she remained? *I am not what I seem.* Then what was she? Was she more than Mark Scott's sometime informant? Maisie thought about the woman's character, the way she'd reacted when asked to recount the events that led to the disappearance of Luther Gramm. It was as if she were a doll dropped and broken in many pieces. She seemed to do well when told exactly what to do, but in this instance she'd shown no ability to retain her presence of mind, no fortitude under pressure. It occurred to Maisie that Elaine was only able to present herself as a certain type of woman—devil-may-care, lighter than air—when she had a safety net beneath her. On the ground it was her father's money. In the air it was her training. Maisie considered the relationship between Elaine and her mother. Lorraine couldn't cope with a daughter who had lost control of her emotions because the man she had a crush on was married to someone else. Maisie felt little shame when she whispered to herself, "She should have had Becca for a mother."

The edge of the Au was as quiet as she'd hoped it would be on a Sunday. No children played, and the street in front of the former home of the *Voice of Freedom* was empty. She dispensed with looking through the glass-paned door that marked the entrance to the basement at the front of the building. But as she walked farther along the street, turned the corner, and stepped along the narrow alley that led to the back entrance, she wondered why people who played a dangerous game of risk would choose to house their press in a cellar accessible via a door half-paned in glass? Or had it been disguised as something else—a small-time lawyer's office, perhaps? The workshop of a woman who took in mending? Or a tailor? But a printing press was not a small thing—unless there had been a disguise she had missed. Perhaps there was something so blatant about running an illegal press in a room with a part-windowed door that it would seem inconceivable to the authorities that anyone would take a risk in a place so vulnerable.

She stopped some way back from the rear entrance to study the boarded-up door she had breached the day before. There were three upper floors, all of which appeared empty—perhaps abandoned when the lower floor was raided, although one resident had of course left a cat behind. As Maisie looked up at the windows, she felt a soft touch on her ankles—the stray cat had returned to press its body against her, weaving a figure eight around her ankles. The animal stared up into her eyes and squawked a meow, so she reached down and ran her hand from its pointed shoulders to its tail. The thick throaty purr was loud, signaling pleasure—or a call for food. She had come prepared. Unwrapping a table napkin which was inside a paper bag she'd brought, she knelt down and laid out a feast of leftover fish. She observed the cat crouching, ever watchful for a predator in his territory, eating in ravenous mouthfuls.

After leaving the restaurant the previous evening, Maisie had asked the hotel desk clerk if he had such a thing as a *Taschenlampe*. She had nightmares, she told him, and sometimes awoke frightened in the night, so she liked to have one by her bedside. He smiled, informing her that one would be brought to her room without delay. And it was. Now she stepped toward the door, pulled back the boards once again, and used the torch to illuminate the rooms beyond.

She flashed the light around the kitchen, seeing clearly what had only been in outline before. It seemed strange that there weren't more utensils, more pots and pans—if the place had been abandoned in a hurry, how would there have been time to collect those things? Of course, the area was far from well-to-do; people might well have pillaged the abandoned property for anything they could use or sell. She opened two cupboards above a table set against a wall—there was nothing inside—and another tall, wide cupboard, like a pantry, to the left. She turned on the tap; a trickle of brown water choked its way out. The pipe behind the sink shuddered, and more water came out in thick filthy spurts, then cleared and flowed into the sink. She turned off the tap. She moved forward into the corridor, again casting the beam up and down the walls. Squares of lighter plasterwork revealed places where pictures or notices had been removed. She looked down, stepping over the detritus of life in the basement. On the floor she noticed a broken pair of pinking shears, and pins spread across the boards. Perhaps the place had indeed been disguised as the workshop of a tailor or someone who took in clothing alterations and repairs.

The front room was spacious, larger than she had thought at first. She stepped toward the remains of machinery, moving the beam across the abandoned ironmongery down to the floor, stained dark with dried ink and blood. Looking closer, she noticed that underneath the broken press were several sewing machines, the cumbersome sort that might be used in a small factory. The whole mass of metal sat on top of torn rags. Maisie directed the torch up to the ceiling, where a rod extending from one side to another still held a few brass rings. Ah, that was it—from the front entrance all anyone would see was a clutch of seamstresses toiling away, yet behind the curtain a small press operated. The rattle of the sewing machines would disguise the sound of the press. The curtain played its part too—any visitor could have concluded that it was there to protect the modesty of customers who came for a fitting, or to protect garments awaiting collection. There would have been little risk of the place being raided. There were so many small workshops of this type in any city, and not all could be policed.

But someone had tipped off the Gestapo.

There was nothing else of note in the room, apart from the broken sign that must have once covered much of the door, and which indicated that this was indeed the workshop of a tailor who took in all manner of work. Maisie's thoughts turned to the young needlewoman she had become close to in Gibraltar. Miriam Babayoff. She wondered what had become of Miriam, now that she was married. She pictured the small house on a narrow street, the way the sun cast its midday light across the cobblestones, and the warmth on her skin as she made her way from one place to another during her time there. She pictured the small kitchen; the table where Miriam worked, the stove with a kettle on the boil, ready to make tea. And then she remembered the narrow door that led from the kitchen to the upper floors of the white-washed house. It hardly seemed like a door from one place to another; it was more like a larder. If she remembered correctly, it was even disguised with a curtain.

Maisie stepped back into the corridor toward the kitchen. Once again she moved the beam of her torch up and down and across the walls. She directed the light onto the door to what she had assumed was a large cupboard, and opened the door. It was indeed a cupboard. Flour spilled from an open bag; the shelves were sticky to the touch, and when Maisie brought her hand away, her fingers were covered in a thick, black moldy syrup. She pulled a handkerchief from her pocket to clean her hands and began to turn away toward the sink, but instead returned her attention to the cupboard again. It was almost a reflex action that led her to rap her knuckles on the back of the piece of furniture. And the sound echoing back to her told her that this was one thing she had missed. There was no wall behind the wood.

Maisie thought back to her first visit, and what she had observed as she stood outside before making her way down the slippery green steps to the basement. There'd been nothing to indicate that this was more than a three-story building sandwiched between other three-story buildings in a row of ten. There was nothing to indicate that the basement rooms would have a means of access to other floors. At first she had wondered why there was a corridor along the lower ground floor at all; then she realized that at one point there might have been two rooms and a kitchen, with the corridor allowing access to both without walking through one to get to the other. But a wall had been taken down at some point—perhaps for the first artisan. It was along that seam in the ceiling that the curtain had been hung. She suspected that, if she looked hard enough, she might find evidence of a small cot having once been situated in the corridor.

The house had no indoor lavatory—she'd seen outhouses in the alleyway where the young girls had played. Now she thought she knew how to gain access to another part of the building.

She washed her hands in cold water, dried them with her handkerchief, and brought her torch back to the cupboard, paying attention to the sides, and running her fingers along the line of wood where it met the wall. She looked inside the cupboard again, trying not to retch as the smell of rancid food and dead rodents wafted up. Then she found it—a small lever. She pushed down, and the cupboard moved toward her, almost knocking her off balance.

She pulled back on the wood of the cupboard to reveal bricks and a narrow platform—just enough room to provide a hiding place for two or three, perhaps at a pinch four people. She flashed the torch up and down the walls. They were cold and damp to the touch. She aimed the light up toward the roof of the hideout and gave a knowing smile. Small ledges had been cut out of the bricks to form a ladder of sorts, leading to the floor above. She could not climb the stairs today, nor would she need to—but she'd found an escape route for anyone who had been in the workshop when it was raided. Except for the one person who had been required to remain and close the door, to secure the lever, to disguise the hideout and draw attention away from it.

Maisie stepped off the platform and into the kitchen. She was about to close the cupboard and leave it as she found it when the torch caught something in its beam. It was not easy to see at first, but Maisie removed the small triangle of fabric snagged on a corner of rough brick, ran the cream silk with the remains of an embroidered red rose through her fingers, and knew she had seen it before. Of course, she could not be completely sure—but if she was right, Elaine Otterburn had taken refuge in the hideout. And Maisie had no doubt that she had been very, very scared.

Another piece of the jigsaw dropped into place as she retraced her steps. It was speculative, of course, but it was a thought inspired by experience. When she had worked as a nurse among shell-shocked men during the war, a doctor had advised giving the men a purpose, something to do—learning a new trade, perhaps. One of those trades was tailoring, learning to wield a needle and thread, and later, if the mind could bear the noise, a sewing machine. It was a job that could be done in solitude, that demanded one work only at one's own pace. There was much to recommend it. What if, she wondered . . . what if the man at Dachau had learned his trade following the war—or returned to it once his battles were over? What if he had allowed a press to be set up at the back of his workshop—and what if he had either volunteered to be the scapegoat or had been instructed in his role? What if he had believed that his army service on behalf of his country might save him? She closed her eyes, the what-ifs coming and going, as if stepping forward for consideration, then vanishing when they didn't hold water in the face of scrutiny. What if the young Ulli Bader had known of the old soldier's affliction, and taken advantage of it? Perhaps the man was lonely, after all. And perhaps the man did not reveal everything to those who imprisoned him, because he'd forgotten. Perhaps his mind had cordoned off the workshop because it was a place where men with guns and a brutal way about them only sparked images of battles that were still too close. Maisie had known the man at Dachau had suffered a trauma to the mind—had speculated that he was shell-shocked. Now she was sure he had played a role in helping the others escape. Had Leon Donat been among them? He was not a young man, but not an old man either. He was not slim, but fear could have helped lever him up the notched ladder in the wall. Now she wondered if Donat had known exactly what he was doing, and taken the risk anyway.

As she took one more look around the basement, another thought struck her. It had been assumed that Leon Donat was an innocent caught up in the propaganda war against the Führer. But what if he wasn't? What if he had known exactly what he was doing, and come to Munich specifically to assist those who published the *Voice of Freedom*? What if . . . what if . . . Maisie's mind raced.

What if Leon Donat was not who she had thought him to be?

She'd allowed herself to imagine him as a somewhat avuncular character, a sort of father figure to workers and customers alike; a sharp but ethical self-made man, a man of commerce, but with something of the absentminded professor about him. An inventor with a touch of genius.

If Donat was not who she had believed him to be, he might well have heard about her, and known she was not who she'd claimed to be when she arrived in Munich. It was an unsettling thought. She might be in far graver danger than Brian Huntley had led her to understand.

CHAPTER 15

t was a strong hand that took a firm hold of Maisie's arm, dragging her into a doorway. The cold metal pressing into her neck took
her to the edge of fear, as if she were looking over a precipice, not
knowing what was below. The voice was thick, guttural, as if uttered
through clenched teeth. Now the man—for surely it was a man—had
her arm twisted behind her back.

"Do not cry out, do not try to summon help—no help will come."

Maisie felt nausea grip her, but without a second's delay, with
no conscious thought, she twisted her heel into the man's foot and
brought back the elbow of her free arm. Though she did not connect
with the man's body, the unexpected movement was enough to loosen
his grip. She took her chance, pounding on his foot harder with her
heel as she turned. Her arm came free, and taking hold of his hand,
she twisted his little finger backward. Not three seconds had passed
since he first uttered a word.

"You speak very good English, sir," said Maisie, facing her attacker.
She did not have the advantage over him, but he was subdued and did
not fight back.

"Who in hell's name are you?" he asked.

"You first."

"Ulli. My name is Ulli."

"Ulli Bader?"

"How do you know?"

Maisie loosened her grip on the man's little finger. He shook his hand and grimaced.

"Where did you learn to do that? It hurts." Bader put the side of his hand into his mouth, as if to suck away the pain.

"Never mind that. Your finger is only strained. Don't be a baby, Mr. Bader."

Bader had been slouching against the wall, but now straightened. He wore what appeared to be a shabby black suit underneath an overcoat a good size too big for him, threadbare at the elbows. His leather shoes were cracked and worn, and he had not shaved in a day or two. A black fringe of hair flopped across his forehead, and his eyes were red-rimmed and sunken.

"So how do you know who I am, Fräulein?"

"It was your illegal press that my father was supposedly imprisoned for supporting."

"You're Leon's daughter?"

"Yes, and I have come to take him home."

"What were you doing in that building?"

"I was searching for anything that might help me find him. I expected to collect him from the prison at Dachau, but another man had been incarcerated in his place."

There was no indication that this news was a surprise to Bader—no flicker of the eyes, no lifting of the chin or shrug of the shoulders. He looked both ways, then up to the windows of the nearby houses, seeming satisfied that no one had seen them. Maisie wanted to look around too, but dared not take her eyes off Bader.

"So where is he, Mr. Bader? I understand I have you to blame for my father's disappearance, and for the fact that our Nazi friends believed him guilty of supporting you, and then imprisoned a man they thought was Leon Donat. Another innocent man took his place, either willingly or because he'd been set up—and I would hazard a guess it was the latter."

Bader shook his head. "Not quite, Miss Donat."

"You speak English very well—where did you learn? In England?"

The man nodded. "I was schooled there for a while."

"Where's my father, Mr. Bader?"

The man looked to the left and right again and stood up straight. He crooked an elbow for Maisie to take, but she shook her head.

"It might serve you to have it seem as if we are a couple on a Sunday afternoon walk," she said. "But I would rather depend upon my own sense of balance, if you don't mind. And wherever we're going, we must take care—I was not followed here, but someone may be looking for me."

"The SS?"

"And a few other people."

"They're looking for me too—but come, make haste. I will explain, though not here."

Maisie lingered. Should she go with the man who claimed to be Ulli Bader? What was the risk, and should she take it? But she had to find Donat, and get him back to England.

She nodded to Bader and stepped out alongside him as he beckoned her toward a path between the houses across the street. Soon they arrived at another house, where Bader knocked at the door. The man who let them in did not offer a greeting, and looked away as Maisie passed, as if he did not want her to remember him or be able to identify him in a crowd. Bader opened a door. It led down to a cellar. Another cellar, thought Maisie, descending the stairs into darkness.

Bader lit a lamp and pointed toward what looked like a tunnel. After several moments they came up into another house, where Bader let them out onto the street, and then toward yet another house, this one set on its own and not part of a terrace.

The process was repeated. As they descended a staircase into another cellar, Maisie thought that if someone were observing her from the sky, she would resemble a mole, going into a hole, coming up in another place, then boring down into the ground again. Finally Bader led her through a short tunnel into the basement of a house where the sound of machinery rattled into life.

"It's all right, Ulli—I think I've managed to get it going without that part from the old mach—" The man addressing Ulli Bader stopped speaking abruptly, seeing Maisie. "Who's she?"

"Leon's daughter. She came to Munich to take him home from Dachau."

The man looked at Maisie. "Did you see Klaus?"

"Ah, so the man who was imprisoned instead of my father has a name. Klaus. Was he a willing replacement, or didn't he know what might happen to him if he was captured in my father's name?"

The man looked at Bader, who nodded. "It's all right, you can talk to her."

"How do you know she's Leon's daughter?"

Bader flushed. "I—I . . ." He hesitated.

"Here," said Maisie. "You can look at this." She delved into her bag and brought out the passport bearing the name of Edwina Donat. She held it out for him, the feel of cold metal lingering on the back of her hand, where it had brushed against MacFarlane's pistol as she reached into the bag.

The man wiped his hands on a rag and took the passport. He held it to the light, looked back at Maisie, flapped it closed, and handed it back to her. He stared at Bader.

"That was lucky for you, Ulli—she's who she says she is. This is a real passport."

"I'm a writer, not a soldier, Anton," Bader muttered in his defense.

"You have to be both. I'm not an engineer, but I've had to learn." He turned back to the machine and sighed. "The parts you scavenged the last time seem to have done the trick. I've managed to get it to run, though I still think it's too noisy. Let's just hope it holds up, eh?"

Maisie stepped forward. "You speak very good English too—were you also schooled in England?"

"I *am* bloody English. One of King George's subjects. Trouble is, with a German father and English mother, and a nice German name, it was a bit tricky being in England when I was a child. My father was interned during the war, and my mother and I were ostracized." He stopped, pausing for a moment, then sighed. "We came back here after the war, when it was hard for my father to gain employment in England. Neighbors who liked and respected us before the war were not so friendly after all. My father did not bear a grudge, nor did my mother—they understood, but it broke their hearts. So here we are—a little English boy with a German name, an Englishwoman, and her German husband, living in Munich. I met Ulli at the university, and we became friends, but now—well, we are brothers in arms, with a few helpers, and we know what we have to do."

"You're both taking a dreadful risk," said Maisie. "They'll kill you if they find you."

"Some things are worth dying for. My father loved England, and was planning to return. But he and my mother were killed in a motoring accident a few years ago. They'd lingered because they wanted to be sure they would not be shunned, though they knew what our Herr Hitler was doing to this country, and they desperately wanted to leave."

"Would you have gone with them?"

The man Bader called Anton shrugged. "Yes, I would—they were my family, and there are cousins in England. I told my father we would have to be the Smith family if we went back. We'd have to rid ourselves of our German names. It was good enough for the king and his family to drop their German ancestry, and everyone conveniently forgot about the Saxe-Coburg-Gothas." He shook his head. "I would have been Anthony Smith in England, not Anton Schmidt, but now I am doing this, and I'm committed. I will die before I give up, and so would Ulli."

Maisie said nothing at first, allowing a silence to descend upon Anton Schmidt's declaration.

"You're very brave, both of you," she said quietly after a moment. Then she looked from one to the other of the young men. "But where is my father? And what happened in the shop where you ran the old press?"

Bader sighed. He looked around, pulled up a chair, then left the room and came back with two more. He nodded to Schmidt, who moved a small table strewn with papers and photographs so that Bader could set the chairs in a cluster.

"I'm sorry I can't offer you anything to eat or drink, Fräulein Donat. We subsist on very little." Bader pulled a crumpled cigarette pack from inside his jacket and shook out the last three cigarettes. Maisie declined. Schmidt and Bader each took one before Bader returned the packet to his pocket. Schmidt reached for a box of matches on a shelf, picked out a match, and struck it on the wall. The two men lit their cigarettes and drew deeply on the tobacco, seeming to hold on to the smoke until it filled their lungs, before exhaling.

"I don't know how much of the story you know, or even if it was the correct and true story, but here's what happened." Bader took another draw on the cigarette. "Leon contacted me when he first arrived in Munich. He knows my father—my parents lived in Berlin, but they've moved to Geneva, where my father runs a business. It seems Father voiced his worries about me—as far as he is concerned, writing is not real work. Leon said he thought he might have something for me. I could continue with my writing, as the work had an element of leeway. Anyway, when we met, he explained that he was only here for three days, maybe four, and he wanted to discuss a job he thought I might be interested in. I wasn't making enough to get by, reporting for a newspaper. It was all parochial news, you know the sort of thing; births, marriages, deaths, meetings. But in the meantime, we had founded the *Voice of Freedom*, and every pfennig I earned was going into spreading the truth about our beloved Herr Hitler, and how our freedom of speech, freedom of movement, even our freedom to think as we wanted, were being crushed under his jackboots. He had shown our people that they should fear insurrection in their midst, that there was terror afoot, and he enacted draconian new laws supposedly to protect his people, but that only put us more securely under his thumb."

Though she was taken by the young man's passion, Maisie was anxious to move Bader back to the issue of Leon Donat. "Yes, I know this, but how did my father fit into your plans?" She looked at Anton Schmidt. He had closed his eyes, but was not asleep; he continued to smoke his cigarette.

"The job he offered seemed a good one. I would visit our seats of advanced learning—universities and so on—discuss the company's library of books, and hopefully the teachers would tell their students to go out and buy them. I also had to find some translators for a number of the books, and would work on building the company's ability to publish in this country. Leon told me that next time he would send the head of the publishing company to talk to me, to set up all matters concerning translations. I wanted to work for him. As he described the job, I realized it would give me some, well, room to maneuver. I would be working for myself and wouldn't have to go to a formal office; I would be responsible for my own time, as long as I did the job. I imagined that, in due course, the company would set up an office here, so it seemed to be a good position, with good money. More than anything, though, it would give me enough time to work on the *Voice of Freedom* with Anton, and the funds to support us."

"Then what happened?"

"I suppose someone tipped off the Gestapo. They knew where to find the press. Klaus had already volunteered his rooms, using his business as a cover. He wanted the *Voice of Freedom* to flourish—he said he never wanted to see another war. And he was prepared for the worst."

"Weren't you afraid he would crumble if he was captured and interrogated?"

Schmidt's eyes were open now. "No. The poor man becomes mute under any kind of pressure. Fortunately, this level of angst does not usually happen in the quiet life of a tailor—the job he came back to after the war—but I have seen him pushed too far during an altercation with one of Herr Hitler's Brownshirts, when he was unable to lift his hand in salute—he'd had problems with his shoulders due to the work he was doing, hunched over the machine. Klaus was shouted at, shoved against a wall, and could not hold his water. He was ridiculed by the men, and others joined in the humiliation."

"Let me be clear on this." She looked from one to the other. "Anton, Ulli—this man, Klaus, knew that he could be caught, and you took the chance because you knew his condition—caused by the war—would render him useless to his captors."

Schmidt shrugged. "And, well, we know all old people start to look alike as the years begin to tell on them. So when the time came, and we knew we were minutes away from being raided, we pushed Leon's papers into his pocket and made our escape."

"So my father was with you in the room with the printing press?" The men nodded.

"Yes. Yes, he was," said Ulli Bader.

"He knew all about the press, then, and your publication?"

"Yes."

Maisie shook her head and folded her arms, looking away from the two men. Then she brought her attention back to them. "And he gave you money to continue your work?"

Again the two men looked at each other.

"He gave us money, but not when we were seen in the café," said Bader. "No, he passed it on before that, as he was instructed."

"As he was instructed?"

"Yes," said Bader. "Well, perhaps 'requested' would be a better word. I mean, he was quite genuine in his offer of a job, but he was also bringing us funds from another source."

"What other source?" Maisie was beginning to feel uneasy in the confined space. She knew, intuitively, that her presence in Munich was about to become more complicated.

"I don't know his name," said Bader. "But he has a printing company in England, and some overseas, I think. And they're not small—big concerns."

A feeling of dread washed over Maisie. She shifted her gaze from one man to the other. "Do you know a woman named Elaine Otter-burn?"

"Just tell her the whole bloody story, Ulli—you might as well. It doesn't do any good dropping in a bit here and a bit there and giving us your life story into the bargain. Just tell her—and if she gets caught, well, we'll keep on with our work until they come to get us."

"I won't get caught anywhere, Mr. Schmidt. I just want to know what I'm dealing with." Maisie looked from Schmidt to Bader. "Now just go on and tell me everything."

"All right," said Bader. "The money came from Elaine's father—well, to tell the truth, it was her mother. Her father knows nothing, but her mother would do anything for her, so she asked her for money. Anyway, her mother sent the money. Leon brought it to Elaine, acting as the postman as a favor to her mother. I know Elaine was not on good terms with her family—that's her business. She used another address for their letters. I think they were sent poste restante or via friend; Elaine didn't want her parents to know where she lived. But money was different. You can't just send cash to a post office to be collected by the recipient, but it was safe if Elaine knew where Leon was staying, so she could collect the money."

Maisie frowned. "Enlighten me, if you will—how did you all know each other? How did you know Elaine, and how did she get involved with the *Voice of Freedom*?"

"A mutual friend." Bader looked away as he spoke. "We have other supporters of the *Voice*. And Elaine mixed in all sorts of circles—she had a way of finding out many things, so she knew about us, and we'd all met. And when she learned we were about to be raided, she came to our aid."

"Then what? How did you all manage to escape?"

"Elaine came to the shop to let us know we'd been betrayed—

possibly by a neighbor; you never know who's watching, and who wants to cover their own back. They all want to curry favor with the Nazis. She'd learned the news through a man she knew, an officer in the SS. She thought we would have time, but Anton tried to save the press and Klaus. It was Klaus who told us to use the old escape route—I'm not sure, but it had been there for years; probably used by smugglers ages ago, I would imagine. So we went in. It was terrifying. There was no air, we were treading all over each other, and it's a wonder no one heard us. Leon is old and could hardly reach up to the footholds. Then the worst happened—Leon slipped and broke his ankle and wrist. We all managed to escape—except Klaus."

"And where is Leon—my father—now?"

"At a safe house. Someone we know who has a motor car took him, and he's been moved a couple of times since. It's best if he's taken by different people each time, so if anyone's picked up, they know as little as possible. And it's hard to move a lame elderly man. Although he seemed robust for his age, the injuries caught up with him, and he became infirm. In fact, he's quite ill. Now he wants to go home."

"I want to see him, and I want to make arrangements to get him out of Munich." Maisie stood up, as if to underline her intentions with action. "Do you know where Elaine Otterburn is?"

The men looked at each other as if each thought the other might know. "Probably still living in the same place with the other women, I would have thought," said Bader. "Elaine is always wherever she needs to be—that's one thing you can count on."

"What do you mean?" asked Maisie.

"Ah, Elaine—a free spirit to all who *think* they know her." There was an edge of sarcasm in Schmidt's voice. Then his demeanor changed. He stood up, reached for a can of oil and a spanner, and stepped toward the machine again. He turned to Maisie. "Elaine can fly, you know—that should tell you a lot about the kind of woman she is. It takes a lot for anyone to fly an aeroplane, but if you ask me, it takes even more gumption for a woman to do it. She's a brave girl." He turned away and began winding the handle on the machine.

Maisie turned to Bader. "All right. I think I know enough now, and I want to get my father home to England. You must take me to him."

Bader and Schmidt exchanged glances again, though neither spoke until Bader reached the doorway to lead Maisie out.

"I need some words on paper from you, Ulli," said Schmidt. "There is no *Voice of Freedom* unless you get to work and give me something to publish. Talk to the others, see what they have."

As Bader led Maisie from a tunnel to a flight of stairs, then out onto the street, where he looked in all directions before beckoning her toward another alley that would doubtless lead to another street and another house with a basement, it occurred to her that Anton Schmidt might be in love with Elaine Otterburn. Had they been lovers? It didn't seem important at that moment—but what if he had been a jealous lover? How might he have felt, if he had tried to tame a free spirit in vain?

Ulli Bader left Maisie at a street corner where she could board a tram to Marienplatz. Then he was gone. If she'd been asked to lead the way back to the place where the printing press was housed, she would have only had a vague idea, so complex was the route, both above- and underground. In truth, what had felt like long tunnels were probably much shorter; it was as if the changes in level played tricks with the mind, giving the impression that more of the journey was underground. Tomorrow morning they would meet again, at the same place where she boarded the tram. In the meantime, there was still some light left in the day, and Maisie wanted to think.

She entered the Hofgarten via the Residenz. She craved the peace and quiet offered by a walk in the garden, and there would be just enough time before dusk fell. It might have been faster to walk around, but she did not want to pass the Odeonplatz, where she would be required to give a Nazi salute.

Maisie found a seat underneath a tree in bud. The Bavarian air was so clear; even within the city, it seemed to bring the promise of finer weather to come. She wondered who had brought Elaine together with Ulli Bader and Anton Schmidt. Perhaps she should not set too much stock in this—Bader had been schooled in England, and Schmidt was British; they were drawn together by a shared experience. She knew from living in Canada, and from her travels, that people away from home seem drawn to others from the same country, as if by magnetic force. As much as people might want to be immersed in life abroad, there was at times a comfort to be found in the familiar, and only too often she would be introduced to someone who would say, "Oh, you must meet so-and-so, she's British too," as if by dint of one's place of birth, you were bound to become lifelong friends. At the time she had often been grateful to hear another accent she recognized, even if the person might lean towards her and say, sotto voce, "They just don't know how to make a decent cup of tea here, do they?"

Maisie sighed. She felt at sea with the task she had been given. She yearned for the familiar, wondering if she shouldn't have just boarded the train for Paris as soon as it was clear that Leon Donat was not in Dachau. But a true daughter would not have done such a thing. If it were Frankie Dobbs, Maisie knew she would have been rattling the prison gates from the moment of his incarceration. And as much as she truly wanted to go home now, she had given her word. She had committed herself to finishing the job, and finish it she would. But it would be good to be in London again. In the sleepless small hours, her thoughts had lingered not only on Leon Donat and how she would get him home to England but on her own life, and what she might do with it.

A plan was beginning to take shape in her mind. She only hoped she was not pushing the boundaries of fate, and could remain alive to put it into action.

She rose, and pulled up her collar. It was time to return to the hotel. She knew she should speak to Gilbert Leslie soon—but she would go to the consulate tomorrow, after she had seen Leon Donat. With her plan for the following day made, she stepped out along the path.

It was as she was walking back toward the Residenz that she stopped, and stepped back into the shadows. On a bench farther along, an SS officer was seated, his eyes closed, as if he were deep in thought. Maisie recognized him; without doubt it was Hans Berger. Had he followed her there? Or was he in the Hofgarten just by chance? Hadn't he told her how much he enjoyed the peace of the Residenz and gardens?

Should she approach? No—after all, what could she say? She began to step back, ready to turn around and exit in another direction, when she saw Berger pull a handkerchief from his pocket and draw it across his eyes. Perhaps he was tired. Or a man shouldering a deep and wounding grief.

As Maisie began to walk away, she realized that the only exit available to her was straight onto the Odeonplatz and the memorial to the martyrs, the men who had died to protect Hitler. Her arms felt leaden as she pressed her hands down into her pockets. She prayed dusk would conceal her deliberate lack of respect.

CHAPTER 16

The sound of rain hard against the windowpanes woke Maisie from an unsettled sleep. For a moment she thought she was back in Spain, where the endless spitting of gunfire peppered the night, and bombs and incendiaries dropped from aircraft flying so low, they looked like seabirds descending to snatch prey from calm waters. Her memories snapped back and forth: at the convent, waiting for the wounded to be brought into the makeshift casualty clearing station—and then to Canada, and another aeroplane swooping low over the escarpment, the *ack-ack-ack* of the aircraft's gun, and then the long spinning down to earth. Memories streamed over her, and she sat up, images converging in her mind's eye, the sneaker wave of grief catching her in its riptide pull once again, leaving her washed ashore, bereft, with two deep desires: to sleep forever, or to live life for them both.

"Oh, James." She turned her head into her pillow. And even though she continued to question why she had ever allowed herself to be talked into this assignment, she knew that it was in part an effort to please James, as if he were still alive, as if she could go home and re-count everything that had happened, and hear him say, "Oh, Maisie— well done. You're doing your bit." As he had done his.

She dressed, choosing the navy jacket and, this time, not a skirt but woolen trousers with turn-ups. The long coat would do much to disguise the trousers—she had only seen one woman wearing them since she arrived in Munich, but she suspected the ease of movement they offered would be a good idea, especially if more tunnels were involved. She stood in front of the mirror to position and fit the wig. As she pushed and prodded it into place, she saw how much it changed her. For a second she stared at herself. *Who am I?*

She lifted her hand and allowed a finger to trace the outline of her face as she watched in the mirror. Other Maisies seemed to be reflected, taking her back into the past before returning her to the present. Maisie, the daughter of a dying mother. Maisie, a girl who keened for hours through the dark night of loss, then steeled herself to become a maid in a grand house, never—she thought—to hold a book in her hands again. But life changed; the girl before her was a student at Girton College. Then war came, and instead of wearing a wig of hair so different from her own, she'd pulled back her hair each day and placed the veil-like cap on the unruly mass, carefully checking the exact position of the white linen points that made her look like a nun. Maisie closed her eyes, as if to push against the images flooding back to her. She'd fought them so many times. She'd almost lost her life when the casualty clearing station was shelled, and then she recovered, choosing to become a nurse in a secure ward for shell-shocked soldiers. But in time she had to move on, into her apprenticeship with Maurice Blanche . . . then her own business, then . . . then James, and marriage, and at last the feeling that she could trust someone with her heart. And all too soon, after the joy, the anticipation of motherhood, she was a widow. In Spain she'd come full circle, a nurse again. She shook her head as if to shake away these thoughts. Picking up a small compact, she began to dab powder on her cheeks, across her nose, and down to her chin, gazing into the mirror as if to see her future. *If I am in a circle, then I know what comes next.*

Looking at her reflection, she hoped that, of all the things she was at that moment, she wasn't a pawn in Huntley's game. And she remembered something Maurice had said, so long ago. "Never fear going in circles, Maisie. The next time around, you'll see something you missed before—that's if your mind is open. And you will be different, and it will be better. Experience, Maisie. Knowledge of yourself. And when you have knowledge, you have wisdom. *If your mind is open, and your heart is willing.*"

Maisie met Ulli Bader at the prearranged place. He said nothing to her, gesturing with his hand to remain several paces behind him. He led her to a tram stop, where they boarded the tram—Maisie thought they might be going back toward the Au, alongside the river Isar, but when they stepped onto the pavement, Bader set off along the main street and then detoured into what was little more than an alley. A motor car awaited them. Bader moved with speed; opened the back door and beckoned Maisie to climb aboard, speaking only one word. "Hurry."

Maisie was not introduced to the driver of the motor car; she had not expected the formality. She looked out of the window as they made their way along little-used thoroughfares.

"Don't look—it's best you have no idea where you are."

"Even when I look, I have no idea where on earth I am, Mr. Bader," said Maisie. "But I take your point. I'll forget any landmarks I see."

"There are men in Himmler's Gestapo who could make you

remember those landmarks in the time it takes your heart to beat once." He turned to face forward.

There was no conversation between the two men—Maisie guessed that Bader was keeping in mind that she had some understanding of the German language, so he was being circumspect.

Soon city streets gave way to houses with large gardens, and in time the motor car pulled off onto a track running through an area that, while it did not fulfill an image of bucolic Bavarian landscape, seemed more rural. The driver parked the vehicle behind a house on what Maisie imagined was a smallholding. A few goats and some chickens ran around in front; there were a couple of pigs in a pen beyond the house, and a swaybacked mare in a field, with a donkey for company.

Bader took Maisie into the house, entered through a lean-to with hooks for coats and paper laid out on the floor where wet boots could be left to dry. An old dog, gray at the muzzle, looked up but made no sound. He sniffed at their ankles as they passed and then rested his head, as if his duty for the day were done. A woman working at the sink acknowledged Bader's entrance with a nod, then turned back to the task of peeling potatoes. Bader opened a door that led to a staircase, pointed up, and beckoned to Maisie to follow him. Neither said a word.

On the narrow landing, Bader opened the door to a bedroom, where he drew back a curtain to reveal another, narrower door. Maisie was reminded of the cupboard at the back of the tailor's shop where the press had been housed.

"It's not perfect," said Bader.

"It's like an endless game of cat and mouse. Tunnels, curtains, cupboards that become staircases. I feel as if I am caught in a bad dream."

"A very bad dream is what it has become, Fräulein Donat." Bader reached above the door for a key, then turned it in the lock.

Maisie had prepared herself for this moment, for the time when she would have to make Leon Donat understand that he must accept her as his daughter. She thought of James and how much he would have hated what she was doing in Munich, would have argued against the risk. *But why you? Why can't someone else do it?* She had heard it many times before. And she had said those same words back to him. But only once.

It was clear from her first look at Leon Donat that he was a sick man. He lay on a bed set against the wall in front of her, his head on the pillow, staring out the small window to his right, from which he would have seen nothing more than heavy gray clouds lumbering across a sky so white it seemed to beg for lightning. He began to turn as the door opened, and Maisie saw the droop of his mouth, an eye half closed. She hurried past Bader to his side.

"Papa, Papa!" She knelt beside the bed and took his hand, then turned to Bader. "Please, Ulli—some privacy."

Bader nodded, closing the door as he left.

Leon Donat lifted his left arm and placed his hand on Maisie's cheek.

"Who are you?" He struggled to form the words, but his ability to speak was not as poor as Maisie had at first dreaded.

She turned toward the only chair in the room, pulling it to her, sat down, and took Donat's hand. "Mr. Donat, do you understand me— can you hear?"

Donat nodded. "It's talking . . ." A thin line of spittle ran from his mouth.

Maisie took out her handkerchief and wiped Donat's lips. "I can understand you, Mr. Donat. Now, has your ability to speak improved since . . . since your stroke?"

Donat nodded.

"Good—it was a small one, I think. But I must get you to a hospital."

"Who are you?" Donat asked again.

"I cannot tell you my name, but in front of everyone here, you must call me Dina—that's your name for Edwina, isn't it?"

"Dina." Donat's eyes filled with tears.

And as Donat uttered his daughter's name, Maisie knew that she could not be the one to tell him that Edwina was failing. For now, she would allow him to think her well in England.

"Mr. Donat, I have been sent from England to bring you home. For that, I had to assume your daughter's name. The British government negotiated with the Germans to secure your freedom—I cannot give you all the details here and now, but there were stipulations. Edwina coming to Munich to bring you home was one of them, but the government decided not to place her in danger, so they sent me. I'm a little more used to these situations, you see."

"I don't understand." Leon began to cough, then added, "But I want so much to go home."

"Mr. Donat—let me call you Papa from now on, so we get used to it, and used to each other." Maisie was speaking close to his ear now, so he could understand what she had to say; she had to keep her voice low so Bader would not hear, if he was standing outside the door. "Papa, can you tell me what happened? Why did you bring money to Ulli Bader?"

"It was a favor for someone I knew." He looked into her eyes; his own were purple-rimmed and bloodshot. "You know this, surely you do." Donat took a deep breath, as if his lungs needed to be filled before he could continue. He coughed, took another breath. "You are aware of these things, if you are working for the government. In any case, I agreed to bring money to Ulli Bader, via Miss Elaine Otterburn. I already knew little Ulli—his father and I had done business together for years. In fact—" He coughed again. "In fact, I knew the boy when he was in short trousers!" His words were slurred, though his thinking was succinct. "His father and mother worried about him, about whether he was wasting his time, as so many of our young seem to be doing these days. They asked me to check on him. I'd suggested I might be able to offer him a job, you know. When I was asked to take the money to Ulli and Elaine, I assumed there had been something between them— goodness knows that Otterburn girl has a reputation. I am glad my Dina is a good woman. I'd only met the Otterburns socially here and there, but it did not seem a strange request, from one parent to the other."

"And then you realized what Ulli was up to." Maisie glanced at the door anxiously. Bader might come back in at any moment.

"Yes, and I applaud him for it. They are brave young people. Elaine, I think, was just on their coattails—I think she wanted something to get her teeth into. I understand she had been unhappy about some-thing that happened in Canada—probably a lost love. With young women, it's always a lost love."

Maisie felt a pressure behind her eyes. She had lost her first love, and her second. *It's always a lost love.*

"You were very brave to help, Papa."

"*Papa.* How I long to hear my Dina say my name." Donat moaned, as if even his daughter's name caused him pain. "That I wasn't caught is a mystery to me, and how they managed to help me away is beyond my imagination. I can remember being in a dark place, Ulli and his friend dragging me away, and then not having enough air, not being able to speak; not a word would come out. My ankle hurt, and I had no control . . ."

"Now we must get you out of here, and home, Mr. Donat."

"Have they been looking for me? I am sure they knew I was there, and . . ." He began to choke on his saliva. Maisie held up his head and wiped his mouth. It was a minute before he could continue. "There are businessmen here who would have loved to see me imprisoned by their government." He tried to laugh, but only a choking sound emitted from his throat. "I have many commercial interests, as I am sure you know, and each one is able to carry on very well without me—but there are men who run everything themselves, their fingers in every pie imaginable, and they are the ones who, I am convinced, thought that if I was investigated, well, something might be found. When I was asked to bring the money to Elaine, none of us knew that. Nor when I was seen with Ulli—and by the way, I wasn't giving him money at the time we were seen. The police were just lucky, I suppose. But they don't seem to be looking for me now."

"Another man was arrested in your stead."

"What has happened to him?"

"I don't know. In my estimation he was suffering from a type of neurasthenia, so he'll be considered mentally deficient, and—"

"And the Nazis don't like that, do they? He will be executed, or subjected to some sort of medical experimentation. I have heard about what goes on in those prisons. Ulli and Anton have told me—they know people."

"They know far too much for their own good, if you ask me," said Maisie. "Now then, I have to make arrangements to get you home."

"How would you have managed to get me out of the prison?"

"Ah, that's a story my superiors will have to tell you. Suffice it to say, Papa, you are a very valuable man, and the British were willing to pay for you to come home. Now it's a bit more tricky. We've paid our dues to release you, but you are supposed to be dead. That's what the Nazis believe, according to Ulli and Anton. And though they are not looking for you—they have other fish to fry—we don't want to slip up when it comes to extracting you from this country."

"How will you get me out of here?"

226

"Can you move?"

"I'm dragging my foot, and my arm hangs like a broken sparrow's wing, but I can get by with help. I've been trying to get myself up and about, if only to walk to the window and back."

"You've done the right thing—you could have been struck down in a much more serious way. Now let me see how you move." Maisie reached for the two walking sticks propped against the bed. "Here. Come on—I know this might be a push."

"It's all right. I understand. You don't need a deadweight, do you?"

Maisie helped Donat bring his legs to the side of the bed, lever himself up, and come to his feet.

"I used to be a nurse, so this is easy for me. Now then—I wish we had crutches, that would give you something more stable to lean into, but let's see how you do."

With one small step after the other, Maisie supporting him with a hand around his waist, Donat managed to walk to the window, dragging one foot and stepping forward with the other.

"I'm too slow. You should leave me behind, let them find me."

"No, that's not part of my brief, Papa. Let's walk back now."

Maisie helped Donat step toward the bed again and made him comfortable. She poured a half glass of water from a carafe next to the bed and supported him as he sipped until the glass was empty. She reached into her bag.

"Here—some aspirin. I want you to take one every day. You twisted your ankle in the escape, but it's your circulation I'm more worried about. I only have a few of these—you never know when they will come in handy. So, one per day."

"How will I get home?"

"We can't risk the train. I'm afraid that, against my better judgment, you will have to fly."

"I don't mind aeroplanes."

"Trouble is, I do. But needs must, and I know who I should be in touch with to plan your departure."

"Who? Who can help us?"

"Once more against my better judgment, Elaine's father can help us."

Donat tried to laugh again. "Now there's a man with a finger in too many pies for comfort."

"I know." Maisie took Leon Donat's hand. "Trust me, Papa. I will have you home within a day or two."

"I wish I knew your real name, dear woman. For now, I will continue to call you Dina. It will remind me of what I have to return to. What I have to live for."

Maisie pressed her lips together and forced a smile. "I'll come back for you, and soon—probably tomorrow. All right?"

Donat nodded, his eyes heavy, his mouth becoming slack. "All right. I will be ready for you each day until you come."

Just as Maisie reached the door, Donat spoke again. "You know, this is a lovely country, Dina. But it is also quite terrifying, when I think of what it might become. My visit here now has made me wonder what it is to be a free man. It's something I have always taken for granted."

"I'll get you home—I promise. You'll be a free man again soon."

Ulli Bader asked to be dropped off as the countryside gave way to the city proper. He instructed the driver to take Maisie wherever she wanted to go, and before they parted, he gave her a telephone number where she could pass a message on to him, and he would return her call within minutes. The person who would assist her was trustworthy. She looked at the number, memorized it, and tore the slip of paper into shreds. As the motor car moved off into traffic, she looked out the windows on each side. There was no sign of Bader. It was as if he had vanished. She asked to be taken to the Schwabing district. She could not ignore her instinct: she needed to return to Elaine Otterburn's old stomping ground.

It was still only early afternoon, allowing plenty of time to walk around—and by now Maisie had a sense of where she was and where she wanted to go. Her first stop would be the pub where she had seen Elaine leaving with Luther Gramm.

She could hear laughter and music even as she came alongside the shop selling women's clothing. She caught the eye of the proprietress, who had stepped outside to look toward the pub. The woman shook her head, as if to communicate her disgust at having such an inconsiderate neighbor. It occurred to Maisie that the hostelry had probably been there before the shop. It wasn't the best place to situate a business—unless, of course, one wanted to sell garments to women whose inebriate lovers had the money and willingness to indulge them.

She watched a few people emerge, laughing, and a few more enter, then took a deep breath and opened the door. Inside, it was dark, and the smell of beer and wine heavy in the air. She closed her eyes to help them adjust to the dim light. She opened them to see the landlord approaching.

"Are you looking for someone?" he asked.

She replied that she was, but only needed a quick glimpse. He endeavored to bring her out of the shadows, but, insisting she was perfectly well placed to find her friends, she began to survey each table, searching for a familiar face. She found three.

In a corner to her left, Elaine Otterburn was seated at a banquette with a Gestapo officer whose back was turned to Maisie. Elaine was laughing, her head tilted, her lipstick-framed teeth catching the light. She reached for her cigarettes on the table in front of her, and the officer took a lighter from his pocket and pressed his thumb against the trigger. Elaine leaned forward, her cigarette between two fingers moving toward the flame. As Maisie looked away, her eyes caught another familiar face. Seated in another corner, Mark Scott was observing the pair. He was not leaning forward as if interested or anxious, instead he leaned back against the banquette, as if he were idly watching people while enjoying his beer. Maisie returned her gaze to Elaine Otterburn, and in that moment the officer leaned across to take a cigarette out of the packet Elaine had set down on the table, and Maisie could see his face in profile. It was Hans Berger, whom she had seen fighting tears in the Hofgarten just the evening before. Of that she had no doubt.

Maisie left the bar with the intention of going at once to the British consulate on Pranner Strasse. A brisk walking pace gave way to a run—she wanted to be away from the pub and arrange for the departure of Leon Donat for England as soon as she could, and she wanted to get Elaine Otterburn out of Germany at the earliest opportunity. It was not lost on Maisie that the latter task might be the more challenging of the two, but she had a plan. Hearing the rumble of a tram behind her, she ran to the stop and joined the queue, stepping up onto the tram and taking a seat. She closed her eyes. *Elaine Otterburn.* Now she was afraid for her. As she watched John Otterburn's daughter, she had felt her heart soften, and compassion rise up for the young woman. She sighed. How would she extract Elaine from a web of her own making?

"That was a big sigh."

Maisie recognized the voice at once. She turned to Mark Scott. "I have little respect for the game you're playing, Mr. Scott, and the way you're playing it."

Scott looked around as if to search for landmarks beyond the window while trying to decide whether he was approaching his stop. Maisie knew he was taking the measure of other passengers. One or perhaps two of them might not be innocent travelers on their way to Marienplatz.

He turned back, keeping his voice low. "Never can be too careful, Fräulein D."

"You should have been more careful when you recruited your local spies, *Herr* Scott. You weren't offering jobs to gnomes to help Santa Claus pack toys and trinkets. When you approached Elaine Otterburn you knew what you had—a disillusioned party girl with a good but broken heart and a desire to do something worthwhile. You knew she had a . . . a need for atonement. You might not have known what had happened in her life, but you knew she was young enough, indulged enough, and vulnerable enough to have some mistakes behind her—and you made hay with them. So she became your mole, your source of information—utterly untrained and unprepared for the job." Maisie turned away, then back to Scott. "You know my feelings on this matter already, but shame on you, Mark Scott. Shame on you."

"She's been very good—more useful than you can imagine."

"Oh, I can imagine, considering the company she's been keeping—so she can report back to you! Now she's on a knife edge, and you know it. And you also know—as do I—who killed her SS officer lover, Luther Gramm. In fact, you may even have set it up to unfold in exactly that way. I wouldn't put it past you."

"Needs must, Fräulein D. You should know that." He raised an eyebrow and whispered, almost as if they were lovers and he was about to declare his passion for her, "You're the one with a weapon in your bag."

Maisie sighed. "You've a job to do on behalf of your government, I know, and it's not an easy one—but for everyone's sake, in future don't use neophytes to mop your floors. It's not fair to someone like Elaine Otterburn, and it's dangerous for everyone concerned."

"Enthusiasm can take a person a long way."

"And it can also kill them." Maisie turned to look at him. "Get on with that difficult job of yours, but try not to put too many innocents in the line of fire in the process."

"My dear Fräulein D, make no mistake. There will be many more innocents taken down before Herr Hitler is done."

Maisie nodded. "I know, Mr. Scott. I've also been keeping my eyes open since I've been in this country. But try not to let Elaine be one of them. She has a son—and I believe that, contrary to what people might think, she loves him very much." Maisie paused. "She is just trying to be worthy of him."

"A son?"

"Didn't your teachers ever tell you to do your homework, Herr Scott? Now then, this is my stop—and I think it's yours too."

Maisie and Scott stood up, shuffling along with other passengers leaving the tram. When they were on the street, she turned to the American and held out her hand. "I think this is good-bye, Mr. Scott. Oh, and by the way—if you want to keep anyone in your six, or whatever you call it, make it Elaine, please. I can look after myself, and she has so much to lose."

Maisie had taken a step away from Mark Scott when he tipped his hat to her and spoke. She came to an abrupt stop when she heard his parting words.

"I take my hat off to you. Not everyone would be so magnanimous, considering what she did to you."

For a moment Maisie thought she would ignore the comment, ignore the fact that Mark Scott knew so much about her. But then she realized she had something to say.

"You know, Mr. Scott, my old mentor, a man named Maurice Blanche, once cautioned me about the fact that I was delving into every book that came within reach. My hunger for education, for learning everything that I could possibly digest, might not always serve me as well as I imagined, he told me. He said I must endeavor to strike a balance, and he gave me a piece of advice I have never forgotten. All the books, all the lectures, all the pages of . . . of *information*, are as nothing against the measure of our experience—and by that he meant the experience we take to heart, that we go back to, trying to work out the why, what, and how of whatever has come about in our lives. That, he said, is where we learn the value of true knowledge, with our life's lessons to draw upon so that we might one day be blessed with wisdom. I may not be there yet, but the better part of me is doing my utmost, and one of the elements of life I am learning the hard way is the wisdom to be found in forgiveness. It's what is setting *me* free. In that regard, Elaine has been a very good lesson. Now then"—Maisie craned her head to check the stop—"I'll be on my way. You'd better be too—you've a lot to report to your superiors, and I have a lot to accomplish in a short time."

"One thing, Fräulein D—did you find your 'father'?"

"No. No, I haven't."

Maisie set off, not quite knowing whether she was walking in the right direction, or if another tram might take her there faster. She was anxious to make haste. That she had a lot to accomplish was an understatement.

As she approached the British consulate, she once again reflected upon Maurice. He had never told her that she should not lie.

CHAPTER 17

"Miss Donat. How are you?" Gilbert Leslie approached Maisie across the reception area of the British consulate. "We have been liaising with the authorities here regarding the search for your father. Come with me, and I'll let you know what they are saying—though, I might add, their efforts to find him have not met with much success."

"Mr. Leslie, I wish to have a secure line to London to place a call, if I may."

Leslie stopped. "Miss Donat, really . . . I—"

"Please, I don't have time for a delay. Would you make arrangements for a call to be placed to the office of Mr. Brian Huntley?"

Leslie looked at Maisie over half-moon glasses. She had never seen him wearing them in the past. The effect was to press his chin down toward his chest, making him seem more like an overbearing headmaster rather than an official in a sensitive position within the British consulate.

"Right you are. Come with me—to the same room we used before." He led her along a corridor and into the room whose walls were adorned, somewhat incongruously, with paintings of the English countryside, and a recent portrait of the king above the fireplace. It felt like a room in the squire's manor house in a small village, a room in which a British visitor might feel at home.

Leslie lifted the receiver on a black telephone on the table at the center of the room and pressed it to his ear. "Ah, yes," he said to an operator. "Secure line, please. Thank you." He replaced the telephone receiver and waited for the second telephone in the room to ring. He took a key from his pocket, placed it in the lock at the side of the telephone, lifted the receiver, and handed it to Maisie.

"Thank you, Mr. Leslie," said Maisie. She waited for him to move, but he remained in place. "I can place the call—and I would like privacy, if you don't mind."

"Oh, yes, quite. Just press that button by the fireplace—the bell will indicate you've finished." Leslie left the room.

As Maisie gave instructions to the operator, she knew that, as far as Gilbert Leslie was concerned, the game was up. He must have guessed by now that she was not Edwina Donat—in fact she suspected he had known for some time, but kept his own counsel. Or he'd had his suspicion confirmed through channels leading to Brian Huntley's office. As she waited for the connection, Maisie felt as if the ground under her feet were becoming less stable with each passing second.

"Brian Huntley."

"It's Edwina Donat here. I have news."

"Be careful, Miss Donat. Let me remind you that 'secure' is a rather loose term with regard to telephony."

"I'll have to do my best and take my chances." Maisie paused, and looked around the room. She knew she was alone, but experience had taught her to double-check. "I have found what I was looking for, and I am ready to return. In fact I have found more than expected. I've an additional package to bring home."

"Urgent?"

"Very."

"I will arrange for passage on the first flight out to Rome tomorrow, and from there to Paris. Are documents required?"

"Yes—but only for the original package. Perhaps our friend Mr. Leslie can expedite issue of the letter of transit required to leave the country and enter another. And travel cannot be by commercial service."

"I'm sorry, but—"

"There has been a *stroke* of bad luck."

Silence.

"All right. Now it's I who'll have to take the chance that this bloody telephone is working as it should." Maisie heard Brian Huntley's very audible sigh. "We've had to increase our oversight in the past few days. Your hosts are cock-a-hoop about their incursion into Austria, and are becoming rather more ambitious. On the one hand, we can take advantage of their ebullience, and on the other, we have to tread carefully, for the snake is ever more confident about his bite. Is a train out of the question? I was under the impression that you would not fly."

"The train offers too many opportunities for us to be intercepted even after it's under way. I want the two passengers to leave Munich no later than mid-morning tomorrow—the earlier the better, for their safety."

"Rather a tall order, Maisie."

"Let Mr. Leslie know what you can do—and you might as well put him out of his misery and allow him to know who I am. I am sure he has guessed. After all, Robbie said he was one of yours, so we're probably passing each other through smoke and mirrors. In the meantime,

I might have another option regarding transportation. If so, I will decline your offer, as I have to grasp the very first opportunity to leave Munich. I'll end the call now."

Maisie pressed the cradle bar to end the call. While the receiver was still in her hand. The telephone began to ring. Maisie released the bar, and heard the operator ask if she would like to place another secure telephone call.

She was surprised, but didn't hesitate. "Yes, thank you." She gave the operator a number and heard a click. The tone changed, and she replaced the receiver. After a moment, and the telephone rang once more.

"Otterburn." The voice was sharp, to the point, that of a man who had neither time nor patience enough to linger.

"Mr. Otterburn. I would like your help."

"Mais—"

"Mr. Otterburn, I am calling from within the British consulate in Munich. I have been told the line is secure, but I would not like to bet my life on it. I cannot dance around with words, though; it takes too much time."

"Right you are. How can I help?"

Maisie knew she had his full attention now. "I am in need of private transportation from Munich to London or Paris. I do not want my passengers to travel via Rome, or through any other country where political sympathies lie with the chancellor. Do you understand?"

"Yes. I do not envisage any difficulty with your request."

"I'm not quite there yet. One of our number is an invalid, and the other—you may be interested to know—is a young woman to whom you are related."

There was a silence on the line. When Otterburn spoke again, his voice was cracking, revealing an emotion Maisie had not expected.

"When?"

"Tomorrow morning. As early as you can manage it."

"It's tight, but I can make the arrangements. Where can I reach you?"

"I'll reach you. I'll place a call from a telephone kiosk, just to be on the safe side, but we will have to be quick with our conversation."

"Leave it to me. I'll expect to hear from you in an hour."

Maisie ended the call, returned the receiver to its cradle, and put her head in her hands.

How would she ever do this? How would she persuade Elaine Otterburn to leave before her predicament became more serious? But first, she had to deal with Leslie. She pressed the button alongside the fireplace.

When Leslie returned to the room, his demeanor had changed. His smile was brief. "I have been on the telephone with Huntley. He has informed me of your position here. I will do all I can to assist you, starting with the documentation. It should be ready by late this afternoon—I will bring it to your hotel."

"Thank you, Mr. Leslie." She stood up and walked to the window, then turned to Leslie. "I appreciate your help, and I must apologize for the necessary secrecy with regard to my presence in Munich. I will be leaving for England as soon as I can, which might well be as early as tomorrow morning. It may be necessary for you to inform Mr. Huntley on my behalf that I have made the required arrangements—one is already in place. In the meantime, I want to make a suggestion—and it's a personal matter. Mr. Leslie, you cannot remain in this country too much longer. I know I'm repeating myself, but you must ask for a transfer to another consular position. Others might not know how your name was changed by—who? Your father or grandfather? Where I came from, there were Jewish families with names that sounded so

English, and I particularly remember a Mr. and Mrs. Leslie—yes, I know, no relation, it's a common enough name. But I remember being told their real name was Levitsky, and along the way it had been changed—to 'fit in,' probably. I would put it to you that if I am correct, you are not as safe as you might believe." She stepped toward the table, took up her bag, and added, "I could arrange for you to leave tomorrow, if you wish."

Leslie pressed the fingers of his right hand to his temple, as if to quell a headache. "I cannot leave my post, Miss Donat. I'm sorry, it's the only name I have for you, though I know you are not who you first claimed to be. I cannot leave my post and will remain here until I am given another consular position through the appropriate channels."

Maisie nodded and held out her hand. "The appropriate channels might not be as fast as you might one day hope. In any case, thank you for your help, Mr. Leslie. I look forward to hearing from you later."

John Otterburn was as good as his word. Maisie placed the call from a kiosk at the railway station. As before, Otterburn answered on the first ring.

"Listen carefully. I am going to give you the name of a small airfield, about a half hour outside Munich. Can you get a driver?"

"Yes," said Maisie. "It's as good as done."

"Good. Right. I've acquired an aeroplane there. I pulled some strings, which isn't as difficult as it might seem, as I'm known to buy aircraft as something of a pastime. The problem is, I've had to take a chance on those strings. I'm not sure exactly where some of the ends might lead—but like you, I've done my best. The important thing is, the aircraft is ours to use. It's a Messerschmitt Taifun, a few years old, and seats four, including the pilot." He paused. "Elaine is very familiar with this craft. The flight will be to Zurich. It should take less than two hours—this is a nifty little ship."

Maisie felt perspiration bead on her forehead. "Elaine?"

"She knows what she's doing. About three years ago, after a German woman named Elly Beinhorn made a flight from Berlin to Constantinople and back in one day, Elaine was convinced she had to have a crack at the same aeroplane. Don't worry, she'll get you out of there. My daughter may have made a fool of herself and her family, but in this matter, I trust she'll do what's asked of her."

"All right."

"Now then, let me give you the information you'll need—and that Elaine will need. All the maps required are already on the aircraft, and she'll know what to do when she gets there, but she won't have time to study the route, so you'll be giving it to her—I'll read everything out to you. The thing to remember is that you have to get in and get out without delay. Do not linger any longer than necessary. The journey will be less than comfortable for the gentleman, but you'll be met by my representative in Zurich, and I've arranged for a nurse to be on the flight home to Croydon. I can let the necessary authorities know when the aircraft carrying the elderly man will be landing."

"I understand."

"The thing that you must remember, and that you must ram home to our aviatrix, is that every airfield in Germany is effectively a Luftwaffe station. Versailles might have placed limitations on the expansion of a German air force, but that didn't stop many young men being recruited as private pilots, ready to form an airborne fighting force when the time came. There are eyes and ears everywhere. So, as I said, get there, board the aeroplane, and get out. Understood?"

"Yes."

"Now then, take down this information—to the very letter. Nothing must be incorrect or you'll end up in Istan-bloody-bul. I want you to read it back to me."

With a piece of paper in hand, covered with details about the airfield and notes for Elaine that made little sense to Maisie, she made one more telephone call, leaving a message. It was not long before Ulli Bader called her back, unable to disguise his surprise when she asked him to arrange for a motor car at an early hour to take her and another person to the smallholding where Leon Donat was in hiding. She informed him that there would be one more stop as soon as Donat was collected, but she would give him the details when she saw him. He stipulated a meeting place and a time the following morning. Maisie knew then that when she left the hotel on the morrow, it would be without her belongings. There must be no indication that she was leaving Munich for good.

Schwabing was as busy as ever as Maisie made her way to the house where Elaine had been living. She hoped Elaine had returned to sleep off her hours in the pub, and had not brought company with her. Maisie watched the door for a few moments, feeling the cool air as it found her neck and wrists. She pulled up her gloves and wrapped her scarf a little tighter. Soon the landlady left the building. She did not turn the key, but set off, leaving it to close and lock in her wake. Seizing her opportunity, Maisie crossed the street, catching the door just as the latch was about to click. Upstairs she rapped on Elaine's door.

"It's open!" Elaine called out in English.

"Hello, Elaine," Maisie said as she entered, closing the door behind her.

Elaine came to her feet. "I thought you were one of the girls. What are you doing here, Maisie? Shouldn't you have left Munich?"

"I had hoped *you'd* have left Munich by now—but you didn't follow my advice."

Elaine shrugged. "I didn't want to leave, and no one came to arrest me, so I took my chances." She scooped up clothing strewn across the chair, threw it onto the bed, and held out her hand. "Take a seat."

"I cannot stay long." Maisie stepped closer to Elaine, so close her request couldn't be ignored or brushed aside. "Elaine, I have a very, very important task for you. It is not one you can refuse, for it is on behalf of your country."

She saw the edge of Elaine's lip began to twitch, as if she wanted to smile, as if she were about to laugh out loud, but at the same time her shock at the gravity in Maisie's tone was apparent. She seemed to stand straighter, staring directly at Maisie. In that second, Maisie saw the look of determination she'd seen before on John Otterburn's face.

"What do you want me to do?"

Maisie explained the mission that lay before them in detail. She described how Elaine would meet Maisie and the motor car, how they would drive to a smallholding and assist a very sick man to the airfield. She gave Elaine information about the aircraft and its destination, handing over the notes she'd made during the call to John Otterburn. She told her that the entire expedition would not be without risk—a high level of risk.

Elaine looked at Maisie and then at the notes, nodding as if someone were giving her verbal instructions. As the seconds passed, Maisie feared she would refuse, that the Otterburn resolve had taken Elaine in the opposite direction, that she would dig in her heels and never leave Munich. But Elaine gave a half smile. "Piece of cake. But I hope my father doesn't think I'm going to be back in his suffocating fold in a couple of days."

"To be frank, I don't care what your father thinks. What you do when you get to Zurich is up to you. You will have done a real service to Britain, and I will ensure you are remunerated for your time and for the chance you're taking. I just want to get Donat to Zurich."

Elaine shrugged. "Switzerland might turn out to be fun. Goodness knows, it was when I was sent to school there."

"One more thing, Elaine—you must not on any account speak to anyone else between now and tomorrow morning. Not Mark Scott, not your officer friends, not even the girls here in the house."

Elaine nodded. "I will follow your instructions without fail, Maisie. But one thing to get straight—*my* country is Canada first, Britain second. I'll do a job for the latter to protect the former—because as sure as God made little apples, where Britain goes, we go too. And if there is one thing I have come to know since I came to Munich— because I've had time to do a lot of thinking—it's that if I wanted to go anywhere, in truth, it would be right back across the Atlantic with my boy."

Maisie looked at Elaine Otterburn, at her bright eyes, her upright stance, the fierce determination in her countenance, as if she were clenching her teeth while she awaited Maisie's reply.

"Help me get Donat out of here, and in turn I will do all I can for you. It's time you were your own woman, Elaine, not a puppet for someone else—your father, Mark Scott, or the likes of Luther Gramm, Hans Berger, and their brother officers."

Elaine blushed. "I'll see you tomorrow, Maisie." Her eyes met Maisie's. "I won't let you down. I promise."

As she left, Maisie hoped that was true. Today she had seen John Otterburn's daughter, given exact instructions and a chance to shine, to rise to the occasion. But, Maisie reminded herself, she had also seen her fall apart—and they were both still suffering the consequences.

Gilbert Leslie came to the hotel to deliver the necessary papers for Leon Donat, should he be asked to present them at the airfield. He lingered only long enough to wish Maisie well, and bon voyage.

"Mr. Leslie, you know it would help very much if you accompanied Mr. Donat all the way back to London. You could help ease the way, you know."

"I thank you once again for your interest, but I think you're quite capable of doing any easing required." He lifted his hat in farewell, but before he could leave, Maisie pressed a piece of paper into his hand.

"This is where I will be at half past nine tomorrow, if you change your mind."

The following morning, the hotel lobby was busier than Maisie had expected. A large and lingering group of travelers from Berlin was leaving the hotel, jostling to form a queue while they waited their turn to check out, and the doorman was helping load luggage into a motor bus. Maisie was able to step out unnoticed. Keeping close to the outside wall of the building, she walked away, following the directions given her by Ulli Bader. Maisie looked up at the sky: it was what James would have called a fine day for taking up a kite. Elaine was already at the meeting place, her long coat almost disguising the thick woolen trousers she had donned in anticipation of her role. She'd wrapped a wide scarf around her head and neck, and brought a leather bag of the type usually carried by doctors on their rounds.

Bader nodded at them both, opened the passenger door, and waited while Maisie and Elaine climbed aboard. The same man was driving as before; Bader took the seat next to him and nodded, and the motor car moved away from the curb and as they began to gather speed, Maisie felt Elaine Otterburn take two deep breaths.

"It'll be all right, Elaine. I know it will. You're a very good aviator. You said it yourself—it'll be a piece of cake."

"At least I turned up this time," said Elaine.

"I never doubted you," said Maisie.

Another white lie, but it was a good one.

Leon Donat was sitting at the kitchen table when Maisie and Ulli Bader entered the farmhouse. He was dressed as if for a gentlemen's luncheon or an important meeting. His suit seemed tired, but it was brushed and pressed, and he wore a clean shirt with a tie and a small handkerchief in the pocket. His shoes had been polished, and over his arm he held a raincoat. His hand rested on the rounded top of an old walking stick. Fatigue marked his bloodshot eyes.

"Are you ready, Mr. Donat?"

Donat nodded. "My strength is mustered." The words seemed to catch upon the drooping lip as he tried to smile, swallowing back saliva. "I can walk, with aid."

Bader nodded at Maisie and pressed a hand to the shoulder of the woman who stood by the sink, wringing a dry cloth. Donat stood up, thanked the woman, and said she would hear from him again. Then, with Maisie and Bader supporting him on either side, he walked to the door, then to the path, and on to the motor car. Elaine was waiting by the front passenger door. She reached out to take Donat's arm.

"Lovely to see you again, Mr. Donat. You're on your way home now."

Mist was rising off the land as the airfield came into view. It was smaller than Maisie had imagined: only a long, low hut, a windsock flying above a narrow runway that looked perilously short. Three aircraft were lined up to one side.

"We will wait only until we see you walk out of the hut toward the aircraft," said Bader.

"I understand," said Maisie. "Once we're on the other side of the hut, we're on our own."

"The name of the game." Elaine had pulled a packet of cigarettes from her bag and proceeded to light one. "Rude of me—anyone care to join me?" No one answered. She extinguished the cigarette between thumb and finger, adding, "Shouldn't really do this anyway, not at an airfield."

One man was on duty as they entered the hut, though they heard laughter from an adjoining room. It was the laughter of boys, thought Maisie, a youthful sound, as if jokes were being told, stories embellished—perhaps with a little help from something stronger than coffee, even at that time in the morning. But what they had been drinking mattered not to her; she only hoped they remained exactly where they were. She approached the desk and handed the man in attendance a sheet of paper with another set of instructions dictated by John Otterburn. The man looked up and nodded, pointing to one aircraft set apart from the others.

"It's ready for you," he said in German. "Your papers?"

Maisie gave him her own and Elaine's passports, and Donat's letters of transit from the consulate.

"My father is ill. I must get him to Zurich for treatment," she explained.

The man blew out his cheeks. He did not seem interested in anything more than the necessary details.

"Who's the pilot?"

"I am."

It was a man's voice. Maisie turned around and paused only for a second before extending a welcome.

"Ah, yes, Mr. Leslie. Very good. Now we can get going." She looked at Elaine and pointed to the door. "Help me with Papa."

In perfect German, Gilbert Leslie presented his papers. The man stood up a little straighter, as if the appearance of a man who appeared to take over had rendered his job more important—better at least than dealing with women. Maisie suspected the process of logging their details and proposed route would proceed with greater speed now.

She looked at the black windup telephone on the wall and at the clock. "We must be in Zurich in time for Papa to eat again. Let's go now."

As she helped Leon Donat limp toward the aeroplane, she heard the motor car that had brought them to the airfield rumbling along the road. She did not ask who had brought Leslie, but assumed he would have taken the precaution of being dropped at a distance, and then walked the rest of the way. And she thought of the woman in her farmhouse kitchen, wringing a dry cloth while the man she'd risked her life to harbor and care for prepared to leave. Now, as he leaned on her, that man was in turn wringing out every last ounce of his will to reach and board the vessel that would bear him home.

Elaine clambered into the pilot's seat, passing her coat to Maisie. As if each person had practiced for a performance, their movements seemed to fit together like a jigsaw puzzle. Leslie helped Donat into the rear passenger seat, then stepped back for Maisie to climb aboard. She leaned forward to tuck Elaine's woolen coat around Donat's shoulders and legs, and folded his mackintosh to use as a pillow.

Now the engines were running; the man who had taken their details had started the propellers, without appearing to notice Elaine's position in the pilot's seat.

"Your turn," said Leslie. "I'll sit up front, if it's all the same to you."

Maisie looked at him, and at Leon Donat, his eyes now closed, waiting for the journey to commence. And she met Elaine Otterburn's eyes as the aviatrix turned to see why there was some delay in her passengers boarding, why she had not heard the door slam shut.

"No," she said. "My work here's not over. Go without me. Go on."

"But Miss . . . Miss *Donat*, I—damn and blast!" Leslie looked beyond Maisie to the road alongside the aerodrome.

Maisie followed his gaze.

"You have to leave, Mr. Leslie. Don't worry about me. Now go!"

Leslie took one last look at Maisie, climbed into the passenger seat, slammed the door, and gave Elaine the thumbs-up. Elaine did not look back, but steered her aircraft toward the runway. As Maisie felt her legs begin to move, carrying her into the shadows at the side of the hut, she heard the Messerschmitt rumble along the stretch of concrete. Then the reverberation changed and soon, with her back against the wall so she could not be seen, she looked up into the sky. Her eyes misted and her cheeks felt hot as she watched the aircraft become ever smaller, making its way toward the horizon and into passing clouds, like a vessel hidden by whitecaps on a rolling sea.

"Godspeed, Elaine Otterburn. Godspeed."

CHAPTER 18

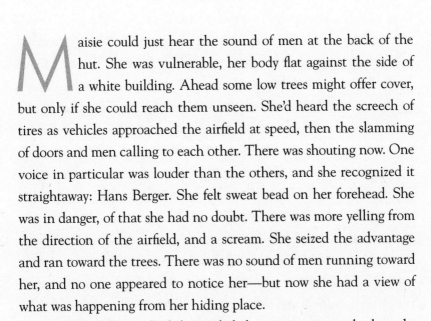

aisie could just hear the sound of men at the back of the hut. She was vulnerable, her body flat against the side of a white building. Ahead some low trees might offer cover, but only if she could reach them unseen. She'd heard the screech of tires as vehicles approached the airfield at speed, then the slamming of doors and men calling to each other. There was shouting now. One voice in particular was louder than the others, and she recognized it straightaway: Hans Berger. She felt sweat bead on her forehead. She was in danger, of that she had no doubt. There was more yelling from the direction of the airfield, and a scream. She seized the advantage and ran toward the trees. There was no sound of men running toward her, and no one appeared to notice her—but now she had a view of what was happening from her hiding place.

It appeared Berger had demanded the young aviators be brought out, so that they could take to the air in pursuit of the aeroplane carrying Elaine Otterburn and her passengers. The man who had checked the papers was holding out a book toward the officer. Berger took it from him, slammed it shut, and smacked it against the side of the man's head. He fell to the ground. Maisie held her hand to her mouth. She thought of Ulli Bader again. Had he and the driver passed the SS vehicles on the road? Or had they taken another route along winding roads that only they knew, across country where they were safe? She prayed that they were now well on their way to Munich.

A shot rang out, and Maisie saw one of the pilots fall to the ground. She could only make out a word here and a word there, but without doubt their crime was that they were barely able to walk, let alone fly an aircraft. Berger stepped in front of the second man, who was being held up by guards on either side of him. He struggled to free himself, yet his efforts only rendered him more helpless. Berger laughed as he thumped his revolver into the side of the man's head, causing him to stumble forward, then screamed at the guards to hold up the man, threatening them with death if the young aviator fell. He laughed and, reaching forward, pinched the man's nostrils—Maisie saw him struggle to breathe through his mouth, choking back blood. And then, with his free hand, the SS officer put his revolver in his pocket so he could hold the man's lips together. At first the struggle became more violent, but Berger held on until the man's eyes rolled back and his frame became limp. Even as his almost lifeless body was supported in place by the two soldiers, Berger continued to clasp the nose and mouth of the dying man until his body shuddered. Then he let go. He nodded to the guards, who dropped the body. He removed his black leather gloves, threw them on top of the dead man, spat on the ground, turned, and walked away, followed by his entourage. She heard doors slam and vehicles drive away at speed.

Maisie watched as the man in charge of the hut came to his feet, staggered, then fell to his knees and vomited. Then he wept.

She knew she could not go to him, could not help him remove the dead. Her own life would be in grave danger if it was known she'd been at the airfield. Her name had been on the manifest, had been logged and documented—but then, it wasn't her name. She was Maisie Dobbs.

If she used her own passport, she could present herself under yet a different name—Margaret, wife of the late Viscount James Compton. Since she began traveling—before marrying James—she'd always kept her passport with her. It was a habit, something to attach her to home, a legal document that gave her a sense of belonging. Though at the outset of her journey to Munich she had been instructed to leave anything connecting her to her real name in England, she had found a place for her passport. But it was hidden in a pocket within her case, which was still in her room at the hotel. And now she wasn't sure how she would get back there or, indeed, the route to the city. In any case, she knew she would have to wait some time before setting out on her own to walk to the road.

It was mid-afternoon, the sun low in a cloudy sky, when Maisie stepped out from her hiding place. In that time she had watched as the Gestapo departed, and as other men came to the airfield and dragged the bodies onto a lorry. The man who had overseen the aircraft's departure left with them, his clothing soiled, his gait unsteady. Two men in blue overalls—they appeared to be mechanics—were left at the hut.

Holding her coat around her, Maisie walked with speed toward the road. There she listened for approaching vehicles and then, keeping close to the verge, began to make her way in what she assumed to be the direction of Munich.

Few motor cars passed her as she walked. It was fortunate that the road was not given to heavy traffic; she could hear a vehicle coming in time to step into the shadow of a tree, or run into a field and hide behind a hedge. On several occasions she thought she might have been seen, when a motor slowed down and then went on its way again.

As dusk began to fall, she accepted a lift from a man with a horse and cart, to whom she wove a story about having yet another argument with her husband, who had—yet again—told her to get out of the motor car and walk. But she assured the man that her spouse would be along soon, and then he would be sorry: this ride on the cart had brought her farther than she might otherwise have come on foot, and she might yet be home before him.

"Er ist ein sehr dummer Mensch, wenn Sie sich kümmern mich sagen nicht," said the man, placing his hand on Maisie's knee. *He's a very stupid man, if you don't mind me saying.*

Maisie picked up the man's hand and placed it on his own knee, reached for the reins, and stopped the horse, smiling at him. "I think so too," she said in German, "but I should start walking again here. I think I can hear his motor car, and it's about time he picked me up."

She stood waving to the man as he tapped the horse's rump with his whip, and went on his way along the road, slowing to allow a motor car to pass. Afraid the driver might have seen her, Maisie stepped back onto the verge, leaning toward the hedge as the headlamps illuminated the driver's route ahead.

She began walking again, and then stopped. It sounded as if the vehicle was turning; she could hear the back-and-forth of gears changing, and the sound of the engine grew louder again. Only a single tree offered any protection.

"Blast!" She uttered the word as if in disgust at her own incompetence, and ran for the tree. "All that training for nothing," she whispered.

Holding her breath as the motor car approached, she heard it slow down as it passed; then the gears changed again as it reversed until it was parallel with the tree. A door whined as it opened. She waited for it to slam shut, but the sound didn't come. Only footsteps toward her hiding place. She reached into her bag, felt the smooth pistol in her hand, and brought it out, readying it to fire.

"I wouldn't kill the knight in shining armor if I were you."

Maisie closed her eyes, slipped the revolver back into her bag, and stepped out from behind the tree.

"You're like a nest of ants, Mr. Scott—seen once, and then you're everywhere."

Mark Scott opened his mouth to speak.

"And don't you dare say anything about the number six," she added.

"Come on," said Scott. "You're in real danger now. We'd better be on our way."

Maisie ran to the passenger side of the motor car without comment, seating herself as Mark Scott closed his door, opened the throttle, and drove into the darkness, on toward the city of Munich.

"I suppose you found out where I might be from one of your informants. Was it Ulli Bader?"

"Not something you want to know, Fräulein D. Let's just say that I learned about your intended departure from sources in Munich, and it occurred to me that you might not make it up into the skies."

"I wasn't afraid," said Maisie.

"I didn't say you were—you would have to be braver to stay, if you want my opinion, though you probably don't. But you had to remain behind for the same reason that Elaine Otterburn will only go as far as—where? My guess is Zurich. She wants to have the last say, and so did you, Fräulein D."

Maisie looked out of the window, by instinct keeping her head low whenever they passed another motor car. "This is not the time to want the last word, Mr. Scott."

"I thought there might be another reason." He lifted one hand from the steering wheel to pat his coat. "Would you look in there? I could do with a smoke."

Maisie reached into the glove compartment, took out a packet of cigarettes, and shook one out toward Scott. She found a box of matches, struck one, and held it toward him. He leaned in to light the cigarette and inhale. She nipped the match's flame with her finger and thumb, throwing the end out of the window.

Scott opened his window, blowing smoke into the wind. "No, I think you wanted to face nasty Hans Berger, the monster, didn't you? I think you wanted to leave him with the realization that you knew very well who he was—a cold-blooded killer. But if he can take the life of his own without compunction, who else can he murder? He's a monster, a man of many faces—an artist, a gentleman, a killer, a torturer, and a man who can shed tears because it's a pretty day in the Hofgarten. Nice combination, don't you think?"

Maisie was silent, gathering her thoughts. Then she spoke as if to the dark night before her.

"Perhaps fear had begun to get the better of me, but in the moment, I know I remained on the ground because I felt I had not finished. So yes, you're right there. In truth, I think I wanted to confront Hans Berger—I wanted to face him. I wanted him to know that I had seen through his shiny veneer into the evil essence inside, and what it represents on a broader scale, here in Germany and beyond its borders. I didn't know I'd pull back from climbing aboard the aircraft until the last moment—but there was something there inside me—as if I wanted to bear witness to Berger's response when I challenged him. Idealistic, I know—but after witnessing his brand of savage evil at the airfield, I would never have crossed him. I'm not brave enough or stupid enough for that kind of showdown." She paused. "A showdown? That's what they call it in the cowboy pictures where you're from, isn't it?" She waited for Scott to say something in reply, but he was silent. "I just watched him kill two men—one of them brutally, stopping air from entering his lungs until he suffocated. The same way he killed Luther Gramm."

"Because of Elaine," said Scott.

"Yes, because of Elaine. But the question is, was it because he wanted to stop the flow of information from Gramm to Elaine and then on to you—if he knew about you, specifically, that is? He couldn't kill Elaine—well, he could, but the murder of the daughter of a wealthy, influential industrialist would be a problem even for the SS at this point. Or did Berger kill Gramm because he was Elaine's lover? Perhaps Berger loved her from afar, and could not bear seeing another man with her. He wouldn't be the first man drawn to her light."

"You know what I think?" said Scott. "I think you could make yourself crazy, working it all out. Berger's a crazy killer, a calm, cool murderer, and he found himself in the right place to get a thing called job satisfaction. That's all we need to know about him."

Maisie pinched the top of her nose. "I always need to know more, Mr. Scott. It's the way I work, just in case I come across a person of the same ilk again. I want to know what makes the boy into a man like that." She took a breath, about to speak, and then stopped.

"What?" said Scott.

"I was thinking about his actions—and those of the guards at Dachau. They remind me of something I was taught by an old friend. He was my teacher—I've told you about him. I've been thinking of him a lot lately." She looked out of the window, into the darkness, seeing only shadows where her reflection met the outline of trees and hedges. "He told me, during a particularly troubling . . . assignment, let's say . . . that everyone has a capacity for evil. And we've all seen it, and done it, even if we think we haven't—there's the slight in conversation that wounds another person, the words we know will cause pain to a loved one but we utter them anyway, and the unkindness that could have been avoided. But then there are people in another league, if you will, people who are capable of so much more, who harbor an evil so deep it scars all our souls. That kind of darkness can lie dormant, as if in a barren desert, but then . . . but then circumstances change to allow their evil to become truly, truly terrible, a boiling storm that encompasses all in its wake." She pressed her hand to her eyes and fought to stop her voice cracking. "And though I knew what I was walking into, it seems that in coming here I fear that I have seen the tip of an iceberg, a mountain of opportunity for evil to envelop the people not only in this country but far beyond her borders." She paused again. "It's one thing to know—in a conversation, let's say—that something is happening. But it's another to see it, to be close to it, and feel helpless to change it."

After a long pause, Scott replied, his voice low, his tone modulated, as if he had chosen honesty over his usual easy wit. "Ma'am, though my ways are different from yours—and believe me, I'm looking at your guys all the way to see how it's done—it's why I'm doing what I'm doing. It's why I fought in the war." He shook his head. "Dirty work, but someone has to do it."

"Mr. Scott—Mark—we've said too much to each other already. You know too much about me, and I believe I know too much about you. But you can help me. I have to leave very soon, and it cannot be by train—that much is clear, for the same reasons I wanted Elaine and Mr. Donat to fly. There are too many opportunities to be intercepted. I must get my case from my room at the hotel. You're pretty good at breaking into hotel rooms. Could you get it for me?"

"Piece of cake," said Scott.

Maisie laughed.

"What?"

"Nothing. Nothing at all."

And as the lights of Munich shone in the distance, she hoped that Elaine Otterburn's journey had been a piece of cake—for by Maisie's reckoning she, Leon Donat, and Gilbert Leslie should be safe in Zurich by now.

Following her arrival at the American embassy—her presence in the building authorized by Mark Scott—Maisie was taken to a small room to await the return of her belongings from the Hotel Vier Jahreszeiten. A woman knocked and entered, giving Maisie a broad smile as she held up the case, raising her eyebrows as if to applaud the accomplishment. She placed the case on a table set against one wall and asked Maisie if she would like to check the contents.

"Thank you so much for this," said Maisie.

"Oh, the thanks should go to our Mr. Scott. He's busy right now, but I've made a reservation for you at the small hotel along the street. It's nothing like the accommodation you've been used to—the French would call it a 'pension'—but there was a room available there, and it's all been booked in the name of Mrs. M. Compton. Is that right?"

Maisie nodded and thanked her again.

The hotel was indeed close to the American consulate, on Lederer Strasse. Registration had been completed with speed by the American woman—who introduced herself as Dorothy Blake—so Maisie was able to retire to her room without undue delay. It was not a large quarter by any means. The bathroom was on the landing, and the furniture comprised a bed, a chest of drawers, a narrow wardrobe, and a washbasin in the corner. The towels were clean but thin and rough, and had seen better days. Above the washbasin was a mirror with brown flecks and fading at the edge. In it Maisie's reflection was muted, as if it were a photograph posed for in a studio and then developed in a way that diminished sharp definition, bringing a softness to the subject.

After she'd opened her case on the floor and unpinned her hat, Maisie lingered in front of the mirror for a few seconds before pulling the wig from her head, scratching her scalp as if to tear every last vestige of her assumed identity from her being. She looked into the mirror again, ran her fingers through her short black hair, and said aloud, "Nice to see you again, Maisie." And she realized that from the moment she had assumed the identity of Edwina Donat, it was as if her body had been removed from her spirit, and now the two were beginning to become joined once more.

She washed her face, running wet fingers through her hair again, then dressed in her nightclothes and climbed into bed, under crisp, clean white cotton sheets, a blanket, and eiderdown. She had pulled back the curtains before getting into bed, and now she stared out into the clear night sky. Tomorrow she would make arrangements for her journey home to England. Once there, she knew exactly what she must do.

The morning brought a cold snap, yet the sunshine was bright and the streets were busy as Maisie walked toward the nearest *Reisebüro*, a sign reading "Deutsche Lufthansa" bold in the window. She made her reservation with ease for that same afternoon and was assured that, upon her arrival in Rome, she'd find a room reserved for her at the Hotel d'Inghilterra, a most appropriate place for an Englishwoman to stay. Maisie returned to her room and made sure that her case was packed and ready for her to leave at noon.

The light was bright enough to warrant wearing dark glasses without attracting undue attention as she walked the streets she had come to know in Munich. She did not tempt fate by returning to stroll past the Nazi headquarters, making her way instead to the Hofgarten. She looked around as she went, wondering how it was that a day out could be enjoyed in such a serene place, when there were those who planned terror just a few streets away. Approaching steps and a low voice interrupted her thoughts.

"Don't tell me you were thinking of leaving without saying good-bye."

Maisie turned. "Mr. Scott." She smiled and slowed, allowing him to walk in step. "I wasn't trying to run out on you—but you're a busy man. I didn't want to interrupt you. I must thank you again for your help and your hospitality. I cannot tell you how much I appreciate it—you came along at just the right time yesterday."

"Turning up again like a bad penny, that's what my ex-wife always said."

"Well, we've had our ups and downs, but I'm very grateful to you. I might still be walking along a country road looking for Munich."

There was a prolonged silence before Scott spoke again.

"Tell me you're really leaving soon, Fräulein D, and this isn't another ruse of yours. You shouldn't remain in Munich."

"You can call me Maisie now. And yes, I really am departing in just three hours, on the Deutsche Lufthansa flight to Rome. I'll stay there for a few days and then return home. Even if it wouldn't be a good idea for copper-haired Edwina Donat to visit a country loyal to Herr Hitler, I thought Mrs. Compton could get away with it for a little sojourn."

"You've done your bit, Maisie."

"Have I?"

Scott nodded. "Leon Donat is now back in—what do you call it?

Blighty? And Miss Otterburn is at this very moment in Paris. Enjoying herself, it has to be said. However, I have it on authority that she will not be staying long."

"I won't ask how you know that."

Scott seemed to brush off the comment. "Need a ride to the airport?"

"At this stage in the proceedings, I won't turn you down."

"Let's grab a bite to eat before you leave, then."

"All right—as long as it's on me, Mr. Scott."

"Are you kidding? I wouldn't have it any other way."

Later, Mark Scott shook Maisie's hand while the motor car idled against the curb at the Munich airport.

"Thank you once again for your help, Mr. Scott."

"I hope we meet again, your ladyship."

"Perhaps we will." She looked up at the sky as two Luftwaffe Messerschmitt aircraft flew overhead. "It's going to get far worse, I know."

"You can count on it."

Maisie nodded. "Take care, Mark."

"Is that all I get for my trouble? A handshake?"

She smiled, stood on tiptoe, and kissed Scott on the cheek.

"Well, that shows promise, Fräulein D. Maybe I'll look you up when I'm in London."

Maisie smiled. "Good-bye, Mr. Scott." She picked up her suitcase and turned to walk into the airport building.

"One more thing, Maisie," Scott called after her.

She looked back toward him. "Yes?"

"Happy landings."

She felt herself stand taller as she continued toward the airport building.

CHAPTER 19

"Well, I must say, it's nice for some—getting a little holiday in before gracing us with your presence, Maisie." MacFarlane was waiting at the bottom of the aircraft steps at Croydon Aerodrome. "They tell me Rome is very pleasant at this time of year, if you've the time and the money, and you seem to have enjoyed a few diversions on the way home."

"If you're going to comment on my travel plans, I hope you've brought a motor car to take me into London and a taxi for yourself."

"Got a destination in mind, your ladyship?"

"Oh, cut it out, MacFarlane!" Maisie smiled. "I'd like to go to Holland Park—Mrs. Partridge's home, if that's all right with you. You know very well where it is."

As the motor car threaded its way from Surrey into London, Robert MacFarlane reported on Leon Donat. "He's going to be in hospital for another week or so, and then to his house in the country, where he'll have a nurse to keep an eye on him, and a couple of men posted for reasons of security. The good news is that he's all right upstairs." MacFarlane pointed to his forehead. "And he's already at his drawing board, even though he's in hospital—had it brought in, he did. I can't say more than that, but the man has proved to be worth his weight in gold. Or at least a good eighteen-year-old malt whiskey."

"I'm glad." She paused and shook her head. "I thought I would never be able to get him out."

"I know, lass—but you did a fine job."

Maisie shrugged. "I made mistakes."

"We all make mistakes, Maisie. We just hope no one dies."

"Ah, and there's the thing. People have died and will die." She paused, shaking her head. "I—I had to make a quick decision, and I believe I caused someone to endure a tortured death in Dachau."

"No, Maisie—only a few have found their way out of that place. I would lay money on the fact that the man would have died anyway. You did what you had to do, and you did your best." He looked out of the window, and they rode on in silence. MacFarlane spoke only when they arrived in Holland Park. "Here we are. That friend of yours will be on the threshold pushing the housekeeper out of the way any minute now."

Maisie laughed. "She probably will."

"Couple of small things, lass. A motor car will be here tomorrow morning to pick you up at ten—debriefing with Huntley and all that sort of thing. You know the form."

She nodded, and as the driver opened the passenger door for her to alight, MacFarlane spoke again.

"And before you toddle off, I think you've forgotten something, lass."

Maisie looked back. "Oh, yes." She reached into her bag and brought out the revolver. "It's clean as a whistle, and I've kept it safe for you." She handed it to MacFarlane.

He inspected the weapon. "You never used it."

"Never had to," said Maisie.

"Or didn't want to," said MacFarlane.

"I scared an American with it."

"I know," said MacFarlane. "News travels fast among friends."

"Maisie! Maisie! Is that you?" a woman called out from the open door of the mansion.

"You'd better get going and put your pal out of her misery. See you tomorrow, Maisie."

Maisie nodded, climbed out of the motor car, allowed the driver to take her case to the top of the steps, and ran up toward Priscilla.

"My, you're glad to be home!" said Priscilla as Maisie wrapped her arms around her friend. "I thought you were going to call me from Paris."

"I went to Rome instead." She turned and waved to MacFarlane as the motor car drew away, then brought her attention back to Priscilla. "Come on, let's have a drink, and I'll tell you all about it."

She knew her stories of Rome would be a fiction, for she had walked the streets in a daze, trying to banish images of men clad in brown uniforms on the streets of Munich, of a dark and terrifying prison, and of circumstances that seemed to pave the way for horror to rise up and envelop a humbled humanity. She was bound by a promise of secrecy to her country, so she would never discuss her work or what had come to pass during her absence. And when she'd looked at Priscilla, smiling, reaching out to embrace her, she knew she would never tell the mother of sons what she knew to be true of the future.

Maisie telephoned early the following morning to refuse the offer of a motor car to take her to Huntley's office in Whitehall, preferring to travel on the Underground, and then by bus. She wanted to immerse herself in the feeling of being in her own country again, in a city she loved and knew like the back of her hand. She hadn't been away long, in the grand scheme of things, but she felt as if her absence had dragged on for months. She experienced a strange disconnect in the fabric of time as she approached her destination. Looking back, it seemed as if she had been in Munich a long time ago.

Once in Brian Huntley's office, she again chose the seat with a view of the Cenotaph. Huntley and MacFarlane were present for the debriefing, which would last as long as it took to answer a series of questions, to describe everything she had seen during the visit to Dachau, Nazi headquarters, and other places the assignment took her. Photographs were passed back and forth, individuals identified where she could offer a name, until at last Huntley leaned back in his chair.

"I think Robbie has told you we're very happy with Mr. Donat's progress, both in terms of his health and the work he is willing to undertake for us." Huntley cleared his throat and reached for a glass of water before continuing. "There are, of course, problems with manual dexterity and fatigue—he is, after all, not a young man, and has been through a traumatic time—but we have a draughtsman from the Royal Engineers earmarked to work with him, which will be an enormous help. The situation is extremely promising." He looked directly at Maisie. "Everything you had to do to ensure the safe return of Mr. Donat to Britain was worth it—everything. Even in the early stages of debriefing, you and Mr. Donat have been able to provide us with a wealth of knowledge regarding what is happening in Munich—which of course reflects events in the rest of Germany."

"Thank you," said Maisie. "Am I free to leave?"

"What will you do now, Maisie?" asked Robbie MacFarlane.

"I have several things on my list. Now we're coming into summer, I want to spend time with my father. And I want to see more of

Chelstone, and my home there. To be honest, since my husband's death, I have avoided my in-laws to some extent, and I must put that right. Then we'll see."

Huntley and MacFarlane exchanged glances.

"No, gentlemen," said Maisie. "I can tell you now that I will not be accepting any assignments in the near future, or even the distant future, though I do have what you could call plans of a professional nature."

"We might at some juncture ask you to reconsider," said Huntley.

Maisie smiled as she stood up and reached out to shake hands with each man in turn.

"Thank you for your service, Maisie," said Huntley. "Maurice would have been proud of you."

"I forgot to ask," said Maisie. "Do you have news of Mr. Leslie? I should take all responsibility for his return to London—I felt he should accompany Mr. Donat on the aeroplane."

Huntley smiled. "Yes, so he said. Mr. Leslie will remain in London for a month, and then he is taking up a position in Washington. We feel his experience will serve him well in time—and of course the interests of His Majesty's government."

Maisie smiled. "Good. I'm glad."

"I'll see you out, lass," said MacFarlane.

The door closed behind MacFarlane and Maisie as they stepped into the corridor. He led the way along the maze of hallways and down stairs that led to the street.

"Doing anything interesting today? You should go out with your friend and treat yourself—you deserve it, lass."

"Funny you should say that—treating myself is exactly what's on my list."

MacFarlane laughed. "And what's the treat, if I may ask?"

"A new motor car." Maisie pulled a brochure from her bag and passed it to MacFarlane. "My friend thought it would suit me well."

"Oh, take that away. You'll have me green with envy."

Maisie pulled back the brochure and waved as she stepped out onto the pavement.

"Don't be a stranger, Maisie."

"Oh, I intend to be just that. Bye, Robbie!" She waved and walked back along Whitehall, looking back once to see Robbie MacFarlane lift his hand to wave before returning to the offices of Brian Huntley's section within the Secret Service.

It was as she walked along that she saw a woman she recognized coming toward her. She knew better than to acknowledge Francesca Thomas, but as they drew close, the woman seemed to step in her direction. She did not stop, but as she passed, Maisie saw her almost imperceptible nod as she whispered the words "Good work," and continued on her way.

EPILOGUE

Maisie immersed herself in finding a new London flat, and spending time at Chelstone Manor. At first she found it troubling to stay for even one night at the Dower House—and even more difficult to be in the company of her in-laws, who were still mourning the loss of their only son. And when they learned of James' death, they had been forced to relive the grief endured when their daughter died in childhood.

It was Brenda, Maisie's stepmother, who galvanized her, making it clear that there was something she must do.

"My suggestion, if you don't mind my saying so . . ." said Brenda, pouring another cup of tea while they were seated at the kitchen table in the Dower House. "My suggestion is that it's high time you did your bit to help Lord Julian and Lady Rowan out of the pit of despair they're in. Look at them—they go about their lives in a terrible gray cloud, and who can blame them? We've all lost, Maisie—but we can all help each other, when it comes down to it." She put her hand up as if to stem any comment. "I know this isn't easy for anyone—nothing worth doing is ever easy, and it's certainly not easy for you—but I worked for Mr. Blanche for a good number of years, and some of his understanding of life, God bless him, rubbed off on me. Don't just go and visit them, Maisie. Every time you do that, it's like a painful duty, and you do nothing to help each other. No, you've got do something to take them out of themselves."

Maisie placed her hand on Brenda's. "You're right, Brenda—I'll come up with an idea. But there are other things I want to do too, and I must get on with them."

Maisie's stepmother nodded. "Good—you can't just wait, drifting along until something turns up. It's nice to see you having a plan or two."

By July, Maisie was halfway through executing those plans, starting with the purchase of a new motor car, the one advertised in the brochure she had handed to MacFarlane—an Alvis 12/70 drophead coupe. It was, she knew, an indulgence, but she had fallen under the influence of Priscilla, who gave her the final nudge, almost tearing the checkbook from her handbag and writing the check herself as they stood in the showroom.

"It's not as if you'll be able to drive a motor like that when you're in your dotage, Maisie. Might as well enjoy it while you can—and at least you'll be able to fit me and the boys in there!"

As they were leaving the showroom where the transaction had taken place, the manager took pains to tell Maisie that although there was a new model coming out in just a few months, she would be assured of the very best in automobile engineering. He added, in a low voice, "We're very proud, you know. I probably shouldn't say anything, but our engineers are working on designs for the army even as we speak— armored cars, that sort of thing, and we're also designing aero engines. That should tell you something about the quality of your new motor!"

Now the shining Alvis was parked outside a flat comprising two bedrooms, a drawing room with French doors leading to a walled garden, a dining room, study, kitchen, and maid's scullery. Maisie had not purchased the flat, but had instructed her solicitor, Mr. Klein, to lease it with an option to buy after one year. She wanted to see how it felt to be in a flat just one hundred yards from the mansion where Priscilla and Douglas Partridge lived with their three sons. It might be a delightful choice, with the boys visiting to see Tante Maisie, and more time with Priscilla—but the latter could also prove to be somewhat overbearing. Maisie smiled when she pictured her friend tripping along the street toward her door, carrying a bottle of gin and two glasses.

One of Maisie's first visitors was Sandra, who had telephoned her at Priscilla's house, asking if she could spare a moment or two to talk about something quite important. Although Maisie kept an open mind, she suspected she knew what Sandra might reveal in the conversation.

As they sat on a sofa situated to face the open doors and the garden in summer bloom, Sandra revealed her news.

"Lawrence has asked me to be his wife—and I've accepted him."

"That's wonderful to hear—I am so happy for you, Sandra." She took Sandra's hands in her own. "It was time. You loved your Eric and you have mourned him, and you've come through it all a new person—I take my hat off to you, really I do."

Sandra bit her lip. "I used to worry, you know—that I was changing so much, we wouldn't recognize each other when my time came and I passed over. They say that, don't they—that you meet again on the other side, you and the love of your life."

Maisie shook her head. "No one knows, Sandra, and best not to think about it. But you love Lawrence, and he loves you, so you must trust your instinct."

"There is one fly in the ointment, though."

"Is there?" Maisie reached for the teapot and poured for them both.

"Well, the company has grown now, and we have more people—not a huge number, but six all told."

"Oh, I see. And as a married woman—to the owner, no less—they would have something to say about you being in the business. It could make things difficult."

"Yes, that's about the measure of it. And being married, I can't get another job—and I'm like you, not the sitting-at-home type. Never have been. I've always worked, even before I left school at twelve. Now I've educated myself, and I don't want to languish in a house all day. Lawrence said I should talk to you, and I was going to anyway. He's suggested I could work at home for the company, part-time—but I don't know, it doesn't sound right."

Maisie set down her cup. "Are you busy on Thursday?"

Sandra frowned. "Um, no—well, yes, but I mean, I don't have to be."

Maisie nodded. "Good. I have a plan. I want you to meet me at this address." She took a pad of paper from the table next to the sofa, and scribbled an address, handing the sheet to her former secretary.

Sandra's eyes widened. "I'll be there, miss."

"It's Maisie—please, I've had enough of all this 'miss.' "

"You'll never get Billy to change—he'll never call you anything but 'miss.' "

"How is Billy? I haven't spoken to him lately."

Sandra shrugged. "Doreen is doing very well, the boys are growing, and little Margaret Rose is a gem of a child—you should see her, all blond curls and red lips. Everyone in the family dotes on her, you know." She sighed. "But since . . . well, since things changed, after Edward Compton came in to take charge under Lord Julian, who came out of retirement, it hasn't been easy for anyone, apparently."

"Yes, I have heard." Maisie noticed how Sandra could not speak James' name. Edward Compton was a second cousin who had been earmarked to take James' place in the event of his no longer being at the helm of the Compton Corporation—it was a line of accession planned during the war, in case James died while serving in the Royal Flying Corps. No one imagined his death would come much later. The tragedy had also affected her former assistant, Billy Beale. When she left for India, closing her inquiry agency, Maisie had arranged for James to employ Billy to oversee security at the company's City headquarters. He was grateful for the steady work, but did not care for Edward Compton.

"Billy doesn't sound very happy to me," said Sandra.

"No, I can imagine the change must be affecting everyone."

Hugo Watson paced up and down the pavement in front of a whitewashed former mansion. The fact that he was to meet a woman who had been more than displeased with him when he was with his previous employer was worrisome indeed, especially for an agent working on commission.

"Mr. Watson, what a surprise. Moved from residential to commercial properties, have you?" Maisie approached him, looking up at the familiar building.

"I think it suits me more than residential," said Watson.

"As long as you don't say 'Up we go' as if you're putting a child to bed when we ascend the stairs, I think we'll do well. Ah, here's my friend now."

Sandra smiled and waved as she walked across the square toward Maisie. "I can't wait to see it," she said as she approached.

"Shall we?" said Watson, holding out a hand to the now open door.

Maisie nodded, turned to Sandra, and raised her eyebrows. "Here we go."

They made their way up one flight of stairs, whereupon Watson unlocked the door to the first-floor premises.

"Now, you will note that the office has changed quite a lot since you rented a few years ago. The new tenant tore back the plaster where doors were originally fitted, and opened it up again."

"Oh, goodness me," said Sandra, stepping into the room, looking between the tall windows that faced the square and the space where a wall had been last time she was in the office. "I never knew there had been doors there."

Maisie stepped from what was once her office into the place where their neighbor had been, now part of a larger room, with white-painted folding doors drawn back like a concertina. "When it was a house, this would have been the dining room, I think—and this the drawing room." She shrugged. "Not sure—but it's much bigger and lighter now, and see, there's a window at the back too, though the view is only into the yard." She began to walk around the room, then to the window to look out across Fitzroy Square.

How many times had she taken up this position in the past? How many times had she watched while a new client approached the door, or left after a meeting? She had waited so many times by that window, hoping for the insight that might lead to the successful closure of a case. She turned to Sandra.

"What do you think?"

"They've made a good job of it, haven't they? I like that new gas fire, the paint is as fresh as a new pin, and now it's bigger, it won't be so cramped. Mind you, there will be only the two of us, and I'll only be part-time—until you need me for more hours."

Maisie turned back to the window again and smiled. She beckoned to Sandra to join her as she pointed to a man walking in their direction, a slight catch to his step marking him as a soldier of the Great War. "Actually, there will be three of us, Sandra."

The front door slammed and footsteps could be heard on the stairs before Billy opened the door and stepped into the room, his smile broad and his hair as unruly as it had ever been. "Sorry I'm a bit late, miss. Hallo, Sandra!" He stopped speaking and whistled as he looked around the room. "Blimey, miss, it don't look like the same place, does it? Changed as much as we have, I wouldn't wonder."

Maisie looked at Watson. "I'll take it, Mr. Watson. Please send the leasing documents to Mr. Klein, my solicitor—I believe you have the details."

She nodded to her two former employees, who would soon be working with her once again. But as she moved toward the door, Billy held out a brown-paper-wrapped package to her.

"Thought you might like this. I did a little bit of engraving, down in my shed."

Maisie glanced at Billy, then Sandra, who both seemed to be on tenterhooks. She unwrapped the paper to reveal a brass plaque.

M. Dobbs

Psychologist & Investigator

"I wondered if I should've put 'Margaret,' seeing as it's your proper name, but then Sandra thought it would be best as just 'M'—but I can start all over again, if you don't like it."

"Oh, thank you, Billy, I think it will do very well—very well indeed." Maisie wrapped the plaque in the brown paper once more. "Right, then—anyone for a cuppa around the corner? We've some plans to make."

I t was in September that Maisie received word that Edwina Donat had succumbed to the consumption she had fought for so long. Although Maisie had visited Leon Donat once after returning from Munich, she had not stayed long, as he was both tired and at the same time preoccupied with what was being asked of him. Now she decided to wait until the end of the month, when she would make the journey to his home outside the village of Shere in Surrey, to pay her respects and hopefully stay a little longer than before. This was, after all, the man she had once called "Papa."

The drive to Shere allowed Maisie to put her new motor car through its paces, negotiating twisting country lanes and longer stretches where the road opened up and she could ease out the throttle. Donat's house, which had been built at the turn of the century, was set in manicured grounds, with a lawn mowed in stripes that made it seem as if it were being readied for a game of cricket. She parked the Alvis on a pad of gravel adjacent to the house, and was surprised to see Leon Donat at the side door, leaning on two canes, waiting for her to arrive.

"Mr. Donat—" She walked toward him, placing a hand on his arm as she reached his side. "I am so very sorry to hear of your loss."

"Thank you, my dear. It's thoughtful of you to pay a visit." He leaned forward and pressed his cheek to hers. "Please come in—my housekeeper has laid out lunch in the dining room. Did you have a good journey?"

Maisie replied that it was a lovely day for driving, warm with the promise of an Indian summer. She followed Donat into the dining room, aware of his fragility, still. After the housekeeper had helped him into a chair, Maisie took her seat and poured water for them both. The housekeeper returned with a platter of steamed fish and serving bowls with small white potatoes, peas, and runner beans.

"I have a young man staying here now. He was sent to help me with drawings, but he's quite good company, so he's living in the room over the garage. It was built by the last owner for his chauffeur, and it's come in handy, as Andrew is very good with engines and keeps my motor running quite nicely too. He drives me anywhere I need to go." Donat stopped speaking to press a hand to his chest and catch his breath. "In fact, I occasionally have another visitor, and they get on very well. I could even be accused of matchmaking." He looked at Maisie as she took up the silver water jug to fill his glass. "Elaine comes every other week or so—she brings her boy. That's indeed nice at my age, to have a young person around me. She was quite the surprise, Miss Otterburn."

"Really?" said Maisie. "Perhaps she's finding her feet."

"Perhaps she is—and though I cannot say I hold with this sort of thing, I think it will be better all around when her divorce is made final and she receives her decree absolute. She's used some money she earned to rent a flat in London, but she's told me she'll be going to Canada just as soon as she's free to do so, and can take the boy with her. Lovely little man, he is—such a smile. I would rather they stayed, to tell you the truth. I miss Dina so very much, and it's nice to think . . ." He seemed to look into the distance as Maisie served the fish and vegetables. "I wish Edwina had known motherhood—such a shame."

"Her fiancé perished in the war, didn't he?"

"And she was never the same after that. She didn't lock herself away, but for her there was only the one true love."

Maisie nodded and waited for the right moment to speak of Munich once more.

"Mr. Donat, do you mind if I ask you something? I know you were taking money to Elaine in Munich, but I think some details are missing. Just to put it to rest in my mind, perhaps you can tell me more."

He lifted his hand from the table with some difficulty and placed it on her own. "Yes, I think I owe you an explanation or two, don't I?"

"It would help me. I like to sew up things in my mind—in my work, I used to call it my 'final accounting.' It was something I was taught a long time ago, that it's a way of picking up all the pieces we can when something important has happened. It's rather like making sure we know where every penny has gone after we've been shopping. It's not always possible, but I do my best." She took a sip of water. "Why did you agree to bring the money to Elaine? I mean, I can see how she might have met Ulli Bader and Anton Schmidt—there was the connection of knowing England, and people overseas like connections—but you are not thought to be best friends with John Otterburn."

"Oh, I'm all right with him—he's just a fiercely competitive man, and of course we moved in the same circles. When I won a contract that he thought he had in the bag, people said it was like the hare and the tortoise—and I know I look like an old tortoise now!"

"But there's something else, isn't there?"

Donat nodded. "Yes, there is. And perhaps you are only the third person who knows this." His eyes filled with tears. "Lorraine Otterburn and I . . . well . . . we had an affair, for a time. Not a long time, but it was a heady moment for us both. I loved my wife dearly, but—who can say? Summer madness twenty-six years ago, and of course, Lorraine is a very dear woman."

"And—"

"Elaine does not know, but as you saw, she is drawn to me—like a homing pigeon, now that she has found me. She's a lot like John, no doubt about it, but I think she's discovering what it's like to be another kind of person. And now we are joined by what happened in Munich—I agreed to do something without a shred of doubt that it was the right thing to do, and she brought me home when you asked it of her." He laughed. "My goodness, but she is a fearless woman—you should have been in the aircraft with her. I was so very ill, but I knew I was in safe hands." He took a bite of fish and a few sips of water. "As I understand it, she made a dreadful error where you are concerned, my dear."

"In the past, Mr. Donat. It's in the past." Maisie wanted to move the conversation onto another aspect of the journey to Munich. "You were involved in the *Voice of Freedom*, weren't you? And I think it might have been more than that."

"Very observant of you, Maisie. Yes, I was."

"Forging papers for people who wanted to leave Germany."

He pressed his lips together and then spoke again. "I don't know that I helped, but I funded what Ulli and Anton were trying to do. They had the press, they had the connections, so I made it possible to get the special quality papers and other materials they needed, and of course to buy favors from people in the right places. It wasn't only Lorraine's money that came in to help them, but mine. I hope they are still doing it, and I hope they are successful. They are both brave young men. Braver than I might have been in their shoes."

They continued to eat in silence for a while, and Maisie realized that Donat might become overtired. As he finished lunch, placing his knife and fork together to signal he'd had enough, the housekeeper knocked on the door and stepped into the room.

"You asked to be reminded about the broadcast, Mr. Donat."

"Oh, yes, of course. Would you turn on the wireless? I want to listen to the news." He turned to Maisie. "Do you mind very much, my dear? They're broadcasting Chamberlain's speech. He arrived home from Munich with an important announcement, and I want to hear what he has to say."

"Not at all. I think we all want to know what's happened." Maisie leaned forward to listen.

"Sit down, Mrs. Randall—you too," said Donat.

Maisie kept watch on Leon Donat, and as the housekeeper took a seat, the radio broadcast began, the speaker crackling as Neville Chamberlain's voice echoed into the dining room.

We, the German Führer and Chancellor, and the British Prime Minister, have had a further meeting today and are agreed in recognizing that the question of Anglo-German relations is of the first importance for our two countries and for Europe. We regard the agreement signed last night and the Anglo-German Naval Agreement as symbolic of the desire of our two peoples never to go to war with one another again.

As the broadcast continued, Maisie watched Donat close his eyes and become still. Maisie reached out to touch his hand, and he grasped hers in return.

The housekeeper stood up and turned off the wireless as the announcer moved on to other news. "They say it's peace for our time, now that man Hitler over there has signed this agreement. After 1918,

I can't imagine that any of them has the gall to go to war again. We paid a high enough price the last time."

Donat looked up. "Quite right, Mrs. Randall. I think Maisie and I will take our coffee in the conservatory."

Maisie helped Donat into the conservatory, making sure he was seated in comfort on a wicker chair and had enough cushions to support his back. She took a seat next to him as they waited for Mrs. Randall to bring coffee.

"What do you think, Mr. Donat?"

Donat shook his head. "What do I think? I think you know exactly what I think—we were both in Munich. We saw the Brownshirts. We saw the Gestapo, and we both know what goes on in Dachau—and Dachau is only one prison of its kind; there are others, and more being built. So what do I think? I think our prime minister is either a fool or a liar. And it might be better for him if he were a fool—though the outcome will be the same."

Maisie watched as Donat's eyes seemed to become heavy again. She stood up, placed her hand on his shoulder, and in a low voice, told her host that she should be on her way.

At a slow pace, with Maisie supporting him, Donat accompanied Maisie to the door. She insisted he remain at the threshold. It was as she reached the Alvis that Leon Donat mustered his strength to call out to her.

"Maisie—we have our freedom, both of us. We are lucky, very lucky. Make sure you use it well." He waved. "Come again, won't you?"

Maisie returned the wave as she stepped into the motor car. As she began to drive toward the road, she saw a young man come to Donat's side to help him indoors. She had no doubt that, following a brief nap, he would be back at his drawing board. A valuable boffin at work for his country.

S oon after Maisie's return from Munich, she had received an invitation to lunch from John Otterburn, and two subsequent requests to
meet. She had declined, each reply courteous, but lacking the warmth
she would have extended to a friend. Two days after Neville Chamberlain's broadcast, she received another letter from Otterburn.

Dear Maisie,

*I cannot say I was surprised by your refusal to meet. Perhaps that
was too much to ask of you, in the circumstances. I appreciate your note
of thanks, but I must confess my reason for assistance in procuring the
aircraft in Munich was purely selfish. I wanted my daughter home, and you
gave me the perfect opportunity. The gratitude should be all mine, because
you kept your word.*

*This letter is by way of a confession, and the contents reflect what I
would have spoken to you about, had we met in person. I would therefore
appreciate it if you would be so kind as to destroy this letter after reading.*

*I fear I contributed to the arrest of Leon Donat in Munich. I allowed it
to be known that he was in the city and, more to the point, that he was vulnerable. My wife and I enjoy a happy marriage, but I am not an easy man,
nor was I attentive to her for many years. Indeed, our grandson has helped
bring us together again. Leon bettered me in business on several occasions,
and for a while in the past he bettered me in my wife's affections. I discovered she was providing him with funds to pass on to Elaine, and though
I never confronted her, I realized that Leon and my wife had something I
could not have—contact with Elaine. Lorraine had turned to another man
before me, and had kept details of my daughter's communications from
me. My pride took the upper hand—I had the ear of men in Germany
who wanted to see Leon Donat fall, so I sowed a seed of information, and
allowed it to flourish.*

That is my confession. Any apologies I make will never absolve me of

my actions. My punishment is that Leon Donat is and always will be the
better man—he would never, I know, have stooped so low.

    Yours, with regret,

    John

Maisie read the letter once, then took it to the fireplace, where she placed it in the grate and held a lighted match to the paper, taking a brass poker to ensure every scrap of John Otterburn's handwriting burned.

Maisie looked at those gathered around the table in the dining room at the Dower House, her home on the Chelstone estate. It was mid-October, and the monthly Sunday lunch had become a firm entry on the calendar of all present. From the first invitation, she had instructed each and every person invited, "There will be no standing on ceremony, children will be present and we're there to enjoy ourselves. There might well be games." To their credit, Lord Julian and Lady Rowan walked up from the manor house for that first luncheon, and proved to be good sports when it came to sitting down in a dining room where two tables had to be pushed together to accommodate everyone who came. All told, seventeen people sat down to lunch, twenty if Leon Donat was well enough to make the journey with his housekeeper and Andrew.

At first Maisie had worried that her idea might fail, but she went on—it was time to go about her days in a different way. So much had conspired to change her in recent years, but losing James, and then her work in Spain and Munich, had altered her perspective, and not only of the world. Time had brought her back to herself. Yet she had felt as if her way of seeing life had taken on a growth of its own, and it had begun in a hospital close to the Tajo River, when she held a small newborn babe named Esperanza—Hope—in her arms. And then there was the vision that would come back to her time and again, of two little girls playing together in Munich—how they held hands in friendship, and let go when they feared they might be seen. Those things told Maisie it was time to hold on to those she loved, to bring them together, closer to her, no matter the outcome—and to take her chances as to whether they, in turn, would accept her efforts, for she was asking each to step out of his or her own world and into that of another.

With Leon Donat she had listened to the prime minister's promise of "peace for our time" and now she remembered the cautionary words from the man she had journeyed to Munich to bring home, as he raised his glass to her. She could hear others in their company chatting and laughing around the table, and saw her father deep in conversation with Douglas Partridge. Little Margaret Rose Beale clambered onto Lady Rowan's lap and patted a dog—Maisie wasn't sure whose dog it was—who begged for food from a plate. There had been toasts to celebrate the reopening of Maisie's business, discussions about motor cars and schools, about the rambunctiousness of boys, whose heart Margaret Rose would break in a few years, and the merits of a new horse in the pasture. Maisie could hear Priscilla's voice ricocheting back and forth between Doreen and Sandra, Billy and Lord Julian, so that soon everyone was leaning forward to join in the joke. Maisie lifted her glass toward Leon Donat, not least to let him know she had heeded his message.

Maisie, we have our freedom, both of us. We are lucky, very lucky. Make sure you use it well.

AUTHOR'S NOTE

JOURNEY TO MUNICH was inspired by a story told by my mother of a man she worked for in 1944, when she was seventeen years old. He had taken her into his confidence—perhaps because she reminded him of a daughter who had died—and told her that before the war he had been set free from a German concentration camp into the hands of the British government after they had paid for his release. The German authorities did not know that he was an inventor who had come to the notice of the British intelligence services when they were informed that he had ideas of "some interest" to them—certain circles of government were preparing for war, and therefore had the need for development of specialist transportation. As soon as the plans were drawn up and handed over to the authorities, this man was given funding for a completely new business, one that would take him into a peaceful retirement. *Journey to Munich* is not his story, but it only takes one small nugget of an idea to create a whole novel. My mother's story was the nugget.

ABOUT THE AUTHOR

JACQUELINE WINSPEAR is the author of the *New York Times* bestsellers *A Dangerous Place, Leaving Everything Most Loved, Elegy for Eddie, A Lesson in Secrets, The Mapping of Love and Death*, and *Among the Mad*, as well as five other national bestselling Maisie Dobbs novels. Her standalone novel *The Care and Management of Lies* was also a *New York Times* and national bestseller, and a finalist for the Dayton Literary Peace Prize. She has won numerous awards, including the Agatha, Alex, and Macavity awards for the first book in the Maisie Dobbs series, which received seven award nominations, including a nomination for the Edgar Award for Best Novel. *Maisie Dobbs* was also named a *New York Times* Notable Book. Originally from the United Kingdom, Jacqueline now lives in California.